THE LOST PRINCESS
AND OTHER TALES

* * *

Collected Tales of George MacDonald, Vol. I

Other books by GEORGE MACDONALD
available from CLUNY MEDIA

THE PRINCESS AND THE CURDIE

THE PRINCESS AND THE GOBLIN

LILITH: A ROMANCE

PHANTASTES: A FAERIE ROMANCE

THE COLLECTED TALES OF GEORGE MACDONALD
    VOLUME I: THE LOST PRINCESS AND OTHER TALES
    VOLUME II: THE SHADOWS AND OTHER TALES
    VOLUME III: THE GIFTS OF THE CHILD CHRIST AND OTHER TALES

THE LOST PRINCESS
AND OTHER TALES

GEORGE MACDONALD

* * *

Collected Tales of George MacDonald, Vol. I

CLUNY
Providence, Rhode Island

CLUNY MEDIA EDITION, 2021

For information regarding this title
or any other Cluny Media publication,
please write to info@clunymedia.com, or to
Cluny Media, P.O. Box 1664, Providence, RI 02901

✻ VISIT US ONLINE AT WWW.CLUNYMEDIA.COM ✻

The stories in this collection first appeared in the following:
"The Lost Princess, Or The Wise Woman": serialized under the title "A Double Story" in *Good Things* (1874); also published as "Princess Rosamond" and "The Lost Princess" (1895).
"The Castle: A Parable": reprinted from *Adela Cathcart* (1864).
"The Broken Swords": reprinted from *Monthly Christian Spectator* (1854).
"The Wow O'Rivven": first appeared as "The Bell" in *Good Words* (1864); reprinted in *Adela Cathcart* (1864).
"Birth, Dreaming, Death" reprinted from *Adela Cathcart* (1864).
"The Light Princess" reprinted from *Adela Cathcart* (1864).

Cluny Media edition copyright © 2021 Cluny Media LLC

All rights reserved.

ISBN: 978-1685950033

Cover design by Clarke & Clarke
Cover image: Edward Burne-Jones, *Hero*,
date unknown, oil on canvas
Courtesy of Wikimedia Commons

CONTENTS

Collected Tales of George MacDonald, Vol. I

* * *

THE LOST PRINCESS, OR THE WISE WOMAN:
A DOUBLE STORY   1

THE CASTLE: A PARABLE   101

THE BROKEN SWORDS   117

THE WOW O'RIVVEN   143

BIRTH, DREAMING, DEATH   161

THE LIGHT PRINCESS   175

THE LOST PRINCESS, OR THE WISE WOMAN: A DOUBLE STORY

* * *

I.

THERE was a certain country where things used to go rather oddly. For instance, you could never tell whether it was going to rain or hail, or whether or not the milk was going to turn sour. It was impossible to say whether the next baby would be a boy, or a girl, or even, after he was a week old, whether he would wake sweet-tempered or cross.

In strict accordance with the peculiar nature of this country of uncertainties, it came to pass one day, that in the midst of a shower of rain that might well be called golden, seeing the sun, shining as it fell, turned all its drops into molten topazes, and every drop was good for a grain of golden corn, or a yellow cowslip, or a buttercup, or a dandelion at least—while this splendid rain was falling, I say, with a musical patter upon the great leaves of the horse-chestnuts, which hung like Vandyke collars about the necks of the creamy, red-spotted blossoms, and on the leaves of the sycamores, looking as if they had blood in their veins, and on a multitude of flowers, of which some stood up and boldly held out their cups to catch their share, while others cowered down, laughing, under the soft patting blows of the heavy warm drops—while this lovely rain was washing all the air clean from the motes, and the bad odors, and the poison-seeds that had escaped from their prisons during the long drought—while it fell, splashing and sparkling, with a hum, and a rush, and a soft clashing—but stop! I am stealing, I find, and not that only, but with clumsy hands spoiling what I steal:

> "O Rain! with your dull twofold sound,
> The clash hard by, and the murmur all round—"

—there! take it, Mr. Coleridge—while, as I was saying, the lovely little rivers whose fountains are the clouds, and which cut their own channels through the air, and make sweet noises rubbing against their banks as they hurry down and down, until at length they are pulled up on a sudden, with a musical plash, in the very heart of an odorous flower, that first gasps and then sighs up a blissful scent, or on the bald head of a stone that never says, Thank you—while the very sheep felt it blessing them, though it could never reach their skins through the depth of their long wool, and the veriest hedgehog—I mean the one with the longest spikes—came and spiked himself out to impale as many of the drops as he could—while the rain was thus falling, and the leaves, and the flowers, and the sheep, and the cattle, and the hedgehog, were all busily receiving the golden rain, something happened. It was not a great battle, nor an earthquake, nor a coronation, but something more important than all those put together. *A baby girl was born*; and her father was a king; and her mother was a queen; and her uncles and aunts were princes and princesses; and her first-cousins were dukes and duchesses; and not one of her second-cousins was less than a marquis or marchioness, or of their third-cousins less than an earl or countess; and below a countess they did not care to count. So the little girl was Somebody; and yet for all that strange to say, the first thing she did was to cry. I told you it was a strange country.

As she grew up, everybody about her did his best to convince her that she was Somebody; and the girl herself was so easily persuaded of it that she quite forgot that anybody had even told her so, and took it for a fundamental, innate, primary, first-born, self-evident, necessary, and incontrovertible idea and principle that *she was Somebody*. And far be it from me to deny it I will even go so far as to assert that in this odd country there was a huge number of Somebodies. Indeed, it was one of its oddities that every boy and girl in it was rather too ready to think he or she was Somebody; and the worst of it was that the princess never thought of there being more than one Somebody—and that was herself.

Far away to the north in the same country, on the side of a bleak hill, where a horse chestnut or a sycamore was never seen, where were no meadows rich with buttercups, only steep, rough, breezy slopes, covered with dry prickly furze and its flowers of red gold, or moister, softer broom with its flowers of yellow gold, and great sweeps of purple heather, mixed with bilberries, and crowberries, and cranberries—no, I am all wrong: there was nothing out yet but a few furze-blossoms; the rest were all waiting behind their doors till they were called; and no full, slow-gliding river with meadow-sweet along its oozy banks, only a little brook here and there, that dashed past without a moment to say, "How do you do?"—there (would you believe it?) while the same cloud that was dropping down golden rain all about the queen's new baby was dashing huge fierce handfuls of hail upon the hills, with such force that they flew spinning off the rocks and stones, went burrowing in the sheep's wool, stung the cheeks and chin of the shepherd with their sharp spiteful little blows, and made his dog wink and whine as they bounded off his hard wise head, and long sagacious nose; only, when they dropped plump down the chimney, and fell hissing in the fire, they caught it then, for the clever little fire soon sent them up the chimney again, a good deal swollen, and harmless enough for a while, there (what do you think?) among the hailstones, and the heather, and the cold mountain air, another little girl was born, whom the shepherd her father, and shepherdess her mother, and a good many of her kindred too, thought Somebody. She had not an uncle or an aunt that was less than a shepherd or dairymaid, not a cousin that was less than a farm-laborer, not a second-cousin that was less than a grocer, and they did not count farther. And yet (would you believe it?) she too cried the very first thing. It *was* an odd country! And, what is still more surprising, the shepherd and shepherdess and the dairymaids and the laborers were not a bit wiser than the king and the queen and the dukes and the marquises and the earls; for they too, one and all, so constantly taught the little woman that she was Somebody, that she also forgot that there were a great many more Somebodies besides herself in the world.

It was, indeed, a peculiar country, very different from ours—so different, that my reader must not be too much surprised when I add the amazing fact that most of its inhabitants, instead of enjoying the things they had, were always wanting the things they had not, often even the things it was least likely they ever could have. The grown men and women being like this, there is no reason to be further astonished that the Princess Rosamond—the name her parents gave her because it means *Rose of the World*—should grow up like them, wanting everything she could and everything she couldn't have. The things she could have were a great many too many, for her foolish parents always gave her what they could; but still there remained a few things they couldn't give her, for they were only a common king and queen. They could and did give her a lighted candle when she cried for it, and managed by much care that she should not burn her fingers or set her frock on fire; but when she cried for the moon, that they could not give her. They did the worst thing possible, instead, however; for they pretended to do what they could not. They got her a thin disc of brilliantly polished silver, as near the size of the moon as they could agree upon; and, for a time she was delighted. But unfortunately, one evening she made the discovery that her moon was a little peculiar, inasmuch as she could not shine in the dark. Her nurse happened to snuff out the candles as she was playing with it and instantly came a shriek of rage, for her moon had vanished. Presently, through the opening of the curtains, she caught sight of the real moon, far away in the sky, and shining quite calmly, as if she had been there all the time; and her rage increased to such a degree that if it had not passed off in a fit, I do not know what might have come of it.

As she grew up it was still the same, with this difference, that not only must she have everything, but she got tired of everything almost as soon as she had it There was an accumulation of things in her nursery and schoolroom and bedroom that was perfectly appalling. Her mother's wardrobes were almost useless to her, so packed were they with things of which she never took any notice. When she was five years old, they gave her a splendid gold repeater, so close set with diamonds and rubies, that the back was just one crust of gems. In one of her little tempers, as they called her hideously ugly rages, she dashed it against the back of the chimney, after which it never gave a single tick; and some of the diamonds went to the ash-pit. As she grew older still, she became fond of animals, not in a way that brought them much pleasure, or herself much satisfaction. When angry, she would beat them, and try to pull them to pieces, and as soon as she became a little used to them, would neglect them altogether. Then, if they could, they would run away, and she was furious. Some white mice, which she had ceased feeding altogether, did so; and soon the palace was swarming with white mice. Their red eyes might be seen glowing, and their white skins gleaming, in every dark corner; but when it came to the king's finding a nest of them in his second-best crown, he was angry and ordered them to be drowned. The princess heard of it, however, and raised such a clamor, that there they were left until they should run away of themselves; and the poor king had to wear his best crown every day till then. Nothing that was the princess's property, whether she cared for it or not, was to be meddled with.

Of course, as she grew, she grew worse; for she never tried to grow better. She became more and more peevish and fretful every day—dissatisfied not only with what she had, but with all that was around her, and constantly wishing things in general to be different. She found fault with everything and everybody, and all that happened, and grew more and more disagreeable to everyone who had to do with her. At last when she had nearly killed her nurse, and had all but succeeded in hanging herself, and was miserable from morning to night her parents thought it time to do something.

A long way from the palace, in a heart of a deep wood of pine trees, lived a wise woman. In some countries she would have been called a witch; but that would have been a mistake, for she never did anything wicked, and had more power than any witch could have. As her fame was spread through all the country, the king heard of her, and thinking she might perhaps be able to suggest something, sent for her. In the dead of the night, lest the princess should know it, the king's messenger brought into the palace a tall woman, muffled from head to foot in a cloak of black cloth. In the presence of both their Majesties, the king, to do her honor, requested her to sit; but she declined, and stood waiting to hear what they had to say. Nor had she to wait long, for almost instantly they began to tell her the dreadful trouble they were in with their only child; first the king talking, then the queen interposing with some yet more dreadful fact, and at times both letting out a torrent of words together, so anxious were they to show the wise woman that their perplexity was real, and their daughter a very terrible one. For a long while there appeared no sign of approaching pause. But the wise woman stood patiently folded in her black cloak, and listened without word or motion. At length silence fell; for they had talked themselves tired, and could not think of anything more to add to the list of their child's enormities.

After a minute, the wise woman unfolded her arms; and her cloak dropping open in front, disclosed a garment made of a strange stuff, which an old poet who knew her well has thus described:

> *"All lilly white, withoutten spot or pride,*
> *That seemd like silke and silver woven neare.*
> *But neither silke nor silver therin did appeare."*

"How very badly you have treated her!" said the wise woman. "Poor child!"

"Treated her badly?" gasped the king.

"She is a very wicked child," said the queen, and both glared with indignation.

"Yes, indeed!" returned the wise woman. "She is very naughty indeed, and that she must be made to feel; but it is half your fault too."

"What!" stammered the king. "Haven't we given her every mortal thing she wanted?"

"Surely," said the wise woman; "what else could have all but killed her? You should have given her a few things of the other sort. But you are far too dull to understand me."

"You are very polite," remarked the king, with royal sarcasm on his thin, straight lips.

The wise woman made no answer beyond a deep sigh; and the king and queen sat silent also in their anger, glaring at the wise woman. The silence lasted again for a minute, and then the wise woman folded her cloak around her, and her shining garment vanished like the moon when a great cloud comes over her. Yet another minute passed and the silence endured, for the smouldering wrath of the king and queen choked the channels of their speech. Then the wise woman turned her back on them, and so stood. At this, the rage of the king broke forth; and he cried to the queen, stammering in his fierceness, "How should such an old hag as that teach Rosamond good manners? She knows nothing of them herself! Look how she stands! Actually with her back to us."

At the word the wise woman walked from the room. The great folding doors fell to behind her; and the same moment the king and queen were quarrelling like apes as to which of them was to blame for her departure. Before their altercation was over, for it lasted till the early morning, in rushed Rosamond, clutching in her hand a poor little white rabbit, of which she was very fond, and from which, only because it would not come to her when she called it, she was pulling handfuls of fur in the attempt to tear the squealing, pink-eared, red-eyed thing to pieces.

"Rosa, Rosamond!" cried the queen; whereupon Rosamond threw the rabbit in her mother's face. The king started up in a fury, and ran to seize her. She darted shrieking from the room. The king rushed after her; but, to his amazement, she was nowhere to be seen: the huge hall was empty—No: just outside the door, close to the threshold, with her back to it, sat the figure of the wise woman, muffled in her dark cloak, with her head bowed over her knees. As the king stood looking at her, she rose slowly, crossed the hall, and walked away down the marble staircase. The king called to her; but she never turned her head, or gave the least sign that she heard him. So quietly did she pass down the wide marble stair, that the king was all but persuaded he had seen only a shadow gliding across the

THE LOST PRINCESS, OR THE WISE WOMAN

white steps.

For the princess, she was nowhere to be found. The queen went into hysterics; and the rabbit ran away. The king sent out messengers in every direction, but in vain.

In a short time the palace was quiet—as quiet as it used to be before the princess was born. The king and queen cried a little now and then, for the hearts of parents were in that country strangely fashioned; and yet I am afraid the first movement of those very hearts would have been a jump of terror if the ears above them had heard the voice of Rosamond in one of the corridors. As for the rest of the household, they could not have made up a single tear amongst them. They thought, whatever it might be for the princess, it was, for everyone else, the best thing that could have happened; and as to what had become of her, if their heads were puzzled, their hearts took no interest in the question. The lord-chancellor alone had an idea about it, but he was far too wise to utter it.

II.

THE fact, as is plain, was that the princess had disappeared in the folds of the wise woman's cloak. When she rushed from the room, the wise woman caught her to her bosom and flung the black garment around her. The princess struggled wildly, for she was in fierce terror, and screamed as loud as choking fright would permit her; but her father, standing in the door, and looking down upon the wise woman, saw never a movement of the cloak, so tight was she held by her captor. He was indeed aware of a most angry crying, which reminded him of his daughter; but it sounded to him so far away, that he took it for the passion of some child in the street, outside the palace gates. Hence, unchallenged, the wise woman carried the princess down the marble stairs, out the palace door, down a great flight of steps outside, across a paved court, through the brazen gates, along half-roused streets where people were opening their shops, through the huge gates of the city, and out into the wide road, vanishing northwards; the princess struggling and screaming all the time, and the wise woman holding her tight. When at length she was too tired to struggle or scream anymore, the wise woman unfolded her cloak, and set her down; and the princess saw the light and opened her swollen eyelids. There was nothing in sight that she had ever seen before. City and palace had disappeared. They were upon a wide road going straight on, with a ditch on each side of it that behind them widened into the great moat surrounding the city. She cast up a terrified look into the wise woman's face, that gazed down upon her gravely and kindly. Now the princess did not in the least understand kindness. She always took it for a sign either of partiality or fear. So when the wise woman looked kindly upon her, she rushed at her, butting with her head like a ram: but the folds of the cloak had closed around the wise woman; and, when the princess ran against it, she found it hard as the cloak of a bronze statue, and fell back upon the road with a great bruise on her head. The wise woman lifted her again, and put her once more under the cloak, where she fell asleep, and where she awoke again only to find that she was still being carried on and on.

When at length the wise woman again stopped and set her down, she saw around her a bright moonlit night, on a wide heath, solitary and houseless. Here she felt more frightened than before; nor was her terror assuaged when, looking up, she saw a stern immovable countenance, with cold eyes fixedly regarding her. All she knew of the world being derived from nursery-tales, she concluded that the wise woman was an ogress, carrying her home to eat her.

I have already said that the princess was, at this time of her life, such a low-minded creature, that severity had greater influence over her than kindness. She understood terror better far than tenderness. When the wise woman looked at her thus, she fell on her knees, and held up her hands to her, crying, "Oh, don't eat me! Don't eat me!"

Now this being the best *she* could do, it was a sign she was a low creature. Think of it—to kick at kindness, and kneel from terror. But the sternness on the face of the wise woman came from the same heart and the same feeling as the kindness that had shone from it before. The only thing that could save the princess from her hatefulness, was that she should be made to mind somebody else than her own miserable Somebody.

Without saying a word, the wise woman reached down her hand, took one of Rosamond's, and, lifting her to her feet, led her along through the moonlight. Every now and then a gush of obstinacy would well up in the heart of the princess, and she would give a great ill-tempered tug, and pull her hand away; but then the wise woman would gaze down upon her with such a look, that she instantly sought again the hand she had rejected, in pure terror lest she should be eaten upon the spot. And so they would walk on again; and when the wind blew the folds of the cloak against the princess, she found them soft as her mother's camel-hair shawl.

After a little while the wise woman began to sing to her, and the princess could not help listening; for the soft wind amongst the low dry bushes of the heath, the rustle of their own steps, and the trailing of the wise woman's cloak, were the only sounds beside.

And this is the song she sang:

Out in the cold,
With a thin-worn fold
Of withered gold
Around her rolled,
Hangs in the air the weary moon.

She is old, old, old,
And her bones all cold,
And her tales all told,
And her things all sold,
And she has no breath to croon.

Like a castaway clout,
She is quite shut out!
She might call and shout,
But no one about
Would ever call back, "Who's there?"
There is never a hut,
Not a door to shut,
Not a footpath or rut,
Long road or short cut,
Leading to anywhere!

She is all alone
Like a dog-picked bone,
The poor old crone!
She fain would groan,
But she cannot find the breath.
She once had a fire.
But she built it no higher,
And only sat nigher
Till she saw it expire,
And now she is cold as death.

She never will smile
All the lonesome while
Oh the mile after mile,

And never a stile!
And never a tree or a stone!
She has not a tear:
Afar and anear
It is all so drear,
But she does not care,
Her heart is as dry as a bone.

None to come near her!
No one to cheer her!
No one to jeer her!
Not a thing to lift and hold!
She is always awake,
But her heart will not break:
She can only quake,
Shiver, and shake:
The old woman is very cold.

As strange as the song, was the crooning wailing tune that the wise woman sung. At the first note almost, you would have thought she wanted to frighten the princess; and so indeed she did. For when people will be naughty, they have to be frightened, and they are not expected to like it. The princess grew angry, pulled her hand away, and cried: "*You* are the ugly old woman. I hate you!"

Therewith she stood still, expecting the wise woman to stop also, perhaps coax her to go on: if she did, she was determined not to move a step. But the wise woman never even looked about she kept walking on steadily, the same space as before. Little Obstinate thought for certain she would turn; for she regarded herself as much too precious to be left behind. But on and on the wise woman went until she had vanished away in the dim moonlight. Then all at once the princess perceived that she was left alone with the moon, looking down on her from the height of her loneliness. She was horribly frightened, and began to run after the wise woman, calling aloud. But the song she had just heard came back to the sound of her own running feet—

> *All, all alone,*
> *Like a dog-picked bone!*

and again—

> *She might call and shout,*
> *And no one about*
> *Would ever call back, "Who's there?"*

and she screamed as she ran. How she wished she knew the old woman's name, that she might call it after her through the moonlight!

But the wise woman had, in truth, heard the first sound of her running feet, and stopped and turned, waiting. What with running and crying, however, and a fall or two as she ran, the princess never saw her until she fell right into her arms—and the same moment into a fresh rage; for as soon as any trouble was over the princess was always ready to begin another. The wise woman therefore pushed her away, and walked on; while the princess ran scolding and storming after her. She had to run till, from very fatigue, her rudeness ceased. Her heart gave way; she burst into tears, and ran on, silently weeping.

A minute more and the wise woman stooped, and lifting her in her arms, folded her cloak around her. Instantly she fell asleep, and slept as soft and as soundly as if she had been in her own bed. She slept till the moon went down; she slept till the sun rose up; she slept till he climbed the topmost sky; she slept till he went down again, and poor old moon came peaking and peering out once more: and all that time the wise woman went walking on and on very fast. And now they had reached a spot where a few fir trees came to meet them through the moonlight.

At the same time the princess awaked, and popping her head out between the folds of the wise woman's cloak—a very ugly little owlet she looked—saw that they were entering the wood. Now there is something awful about every wood, especially in the moonlight; and perhaps a fir-wood is more awful than other woods. For one thing, it lets a little more light through, rendering the darkness a little more visible, as it were; and then the trees go stretching away up towards the moon, and look as if they cared nothing about the creatures below them—not like the broad trees with soft wide leaves that, in the darkness even, look sheltering. So the princess is not to be blamed that she was very much frightened. She is hardly to be blamed either that, assured the wise woman was an ogress carrying her to her castle to eat her up, she began again to kick and scream violently, as those of my readers who are of the same sort as herself will consider the right and natural thing to do. The wrong in her was this—that she had led such a bad life, that she did not know a good woman when she saw her; took her for one like herself, even after she had slept in her arms.

Immediately the wise woman set her down, and, walking on, within a few paces vanished among the trees. Then the cries of the princess rent the air, but the fir trees never heeded her; not one of their hard little needles gave a single shiver for all the noise she made. But there were creatures in the forest who were soon quite as much interested in her cries as the fir trees were indifferent to them. They began to hearken and howl and snuff about, and run hither and thither, and grin with their white teeth, and light up the green lamps in their eyes. In a minute or two a whole army of wolves and hyenas were rushing from all quarters through the pillar-like stems of the fir trees, to the place where she stood calling them, without knowing it. The noise she made herself, however, prevented her from hearing either their howls or the soft pattering of their many trampling feet as they bounded over the fallen fir needles and cones.

One huge old wolf had outsped the rest—not that he could run faster, but that from experience he could more exactly judge whence the cries came, and as he shot through the wood, she caught sight at last of his lamping eyes coming swiftly nearer and nearer. Terror silenced her. She stood with her mouth open, as if she were going to eat the wolf, but she had no breath to scream with, and her tongue curled up in her mouth like a withered and frozen leaf. She could do nothing but stare at the coming monster. And now he was taking a few shorter bounds, measuring the distance for the one final leap that should bring him upon her, when out stepped the wise woman from behind the very tree by which she had set the princess down, caught the wolf by the throat halfway in his last spring, shook him once, and threw him from her dead. Then she turned towards the princess, who flung herself into her arms, and was instantly lapped in the folds of her cloak.

But now the huge army of wolves and hyenas had rushed like a sea around them, whose waves leaped with hoarse roar and hollow yell up against the wise woman. But she, like a strong stately vessel, moved unhurt through the midst of them. Even as they leaped against her cloak, they dropped and slunk away back through the crowd. Others ever succeeded, and ever in their turn fell, and drew back confounded. For some time she walked on attended and assailed on all sides by the howling pack. Suddenly they turned and swept away, vanishing in the depths of the forest She neither slackened nor hastened her step, but went walking on as before.

In a little while she unfolded her cloak, and let the princess look out. The firs had ceased; and they were on a lofty height of moorland, stony and bare and dry, with tufts of heather and a few small plants here and there. About the heath, on every side, lay the forest looking in the moonlight like a cloud; and above the forest, like the shaven crown of a monk, rose the bare moor over which they were walking. Presently, a little way in front of them, the princess espied a white-washed cottage, gleaming in the moon. As they came nearer, she saw that the roof was covered with thatch, over which the moss had grown green. It was a very simple, humble place, not in the least terrible to look at, and yet, as soon as she saw it, her fear again awoke, and always, as soon as her fear awoke, the trust of the princess fell into a dead sleep. Foolish and useless as she might by this time have known it, she once more began kicking and screaming, whereupon, yet once more, the wise woman set her down on the heath, a few yards from the back of the cottage, and saying only, "No one ever gets into my house who does not knock at the door, and ask to come in," disappeared round the corner of the cottage, leaving the princess alone with the moon—two white faces in the cone of the night.

III.

THE moon stared at the princess, and the princess stared at the moon; but the moon had the best of it and the princess began to cry. And now the question was between the moon and the cottage. The princess thought she knew the worst of the moon, and she knew nothing at all about the cottage, therefore she would stay with the moon. Strange, was it not, that she should have been so long with the wise woman, and yet know *nothing* about that cottage? As for the moon, she did not by any means know the worst of her, or even, that, if she were to fall asleep where she could find her, the old witch would certainly do her best to twist her face.

But she had scarcely sat a moment longer before she was assailed by all sorts of fresh fears. First of all, the soft wind blowing gently through the dry stalks of the heather and its thousands of little bells raised a sweet rustling, which the princess took for the hissing of serpents, for you know she had been naughty for so long that she could not in a great many things tell the good from the bad. Then nobody could deny that there, all round about the heath, like a ring of darkness, lay the gloomy fir-wood, and the princess knew what it was full of, and every now and then she thought she heard the howling of its wolves and hyenas. And who could tell but some of them might break from their covert and sweep like a shadow across the heath? Indeed, it was not once nor twice that for a moment she was fully persuaded she saw a great beast coming leaping and bounding through the moonlight to have her all to himself. She did not know that not a single evil creature dared set foot on that heath, or that, if one should do so, it would that instant wither up and cease. If an army of them had rushed to invade it, it would have melted away on the edge of it, and ceased like a dying wave. She even imagined that the moon was slowly coming nearer and nearer down the sky to take her and freeze her to death in her arms. The wise woman, too, she felt sure, although her cottage looked asleep, was watching her at some little window. In this, however, she would have been quite right, if she had only imagined enough—namely, that the wise woman was watching *over* her from the little window. But after all, somehow, the thought of the wise woman was less frightful than that of any of her other terrors, and at length she began to wonder whether it might not turn out that she was no ogress, but only a rude, ill-bred, tyrannical, yet on the whole not altogether ill-meaning person. Hardly had the possibility arisen in her mind, before she was on her feet if the woman was anything short of an ogress, her cottage must be better than that horrible loneliness, with nothing in all the world but a stare; and even an ogress had at least the shape and look of a human being.

She darted round the end of the cottage to find the front. But to her surprise, she came only to another back, for no door was to be seen. She tried the farther end, but still no door. She must have passed it as she ran—but no—neither in gable nor in side was any to be found.

A cottage without a door! She rushed at it in a rage and kicked at the wall with her feet. But the wall was hard as iron, and hurt her sadly through her gay silken slippers. She threw herself on the heath, which came up to the walls of the cottage on every side, and roared and screamed with rage. Suddenly, however, she remembered how her screaming had brought the horde of wolves and hyenas about her in the forest and, ceasing at once, lay still, gazing yet again at the moon. And then came the thought of her parents in the palace at home. In her mind's eye she saw her mother sitting at her embroidery with the tears dropping upon it and her father staring into the fire as if he were looking for her in its glowing caverns. It is true that if they had both been in tears by her side because of her naughtiness, she would not have cared a straw; but now her own forlorn condition somehow helped her to understand their grief at having lost her, and not only a great longing to be back in her comfortable home, but a feeble flutter of genuine love for her parents awoke in her heart as well, and she burst into real tears—soft mournful tears—very different from those of rage and disappointment to which she was so much used. And another very remarkable thing was that the moment she began to love her father and mother, she began to wish to see the wise woman again. The idea of her being an ogress vanished utterly, and she thought of her only as one to take her in from the moon, and the loneliness, and the terrors of the forest-haunted heath, and hide her in a cottage with not even a door for the horrid wolves to howl against.

But the old woman—as the princess called her, not knowing that her real name was the Wise Woman—had told her that she must knock at the door: how was she to do that when there was no door? But again she bethought herself—that if she could not do all she was told, she could, at least, do a part of it if she could not knock at the door, she could at least knock—say on the wall, for there was nothing else to knock upon—and perhaps the old woman would hear her, and lift her in by some window. Thereupon, she rose at once to her feet, and picking up a stone, began to knock on the wall with it. A loud noise was the result, and she found she was knocking on the very door itself. For a moment she feared the old woman would be offended, but the next, there came a voice, saying, "Who is there?"

The princess answered, "Please, old woman, I did not mean to knock so loud."

To this there came no reply.

Then the princess knocked again, this time with her knuckles, and the voice came again, saying, "Who is there?"

And the princess answered, "Rosamond."

Then a second time there was silence. But the princess soon ventured to knock a third time.

"What do you want?" said the voice.

"Oh, please, let me in!" said the princess. "The moon will keep staring at me; and I hear the wolves in the wood."

Then the door opened, and the princess entered. She looked all around, but saw nothing of the wise woman.

It was a single bare little room, with a white deal table, and a few old wooden chairs, a fire of fir-wood on the hearth, the smoke of which smelt sweet, and a patch of thick-growing heath in one corner. Poor as it was, compared to the grand place Rosamond had left, she felt no little satisfaction as she shut the door, and looked around her. And what with the sufferings and terrors she had left outside, the new kind of tears she had shed, the love she had begun to feel for her parents, and the trust she had begun to place in the wise woman, it seemed to her as if her soul had grown larger of a sudden, and she had left the days of her childishness and naughtiness far behind her. People are so ready to think themselves changed when it is only their mood that is changed! Those who are good-tempered because it is a fine day, will be ill-tempered when it rains: their selves are just the same both days; only in the one case, the fine weather has got into them, in the other the rainy. Rosamond, as she sat warming herself by the glow of the peat-fire, turning over in her mind all that had passed, and feeling how pleasant the change in her feelings was, began by degrees to think how very good she had grown, and how *very* good she was to have grown good, and how extremely good she must always have been that she was able to grow so very good as she now felt she had grown; and she became so absorbed in her self-admiration as never to notice either that the fire was dying, or that a heap of fire-cones lay in a corner near it. Suddenly, a great wind came roaring down the chimney, and scattered the ashes about the floor; a tremendous rain followed, and fell hissing on the embers; the moon was swallowed up, and there was darkness all about her. Then a flash of lightning, followed by a peal of thunder, so terrified the princess, that she cried aloud for the old woman, but there came no answer to her cry.

Then in her terror the princess grew angry, and saying to herself, "She must be somewhere in the place, else who was there to open the door to me?" began to shout and yell, and call the wise woman all the bad names she had been in the habit of throwing at her nurses. But there came not a single sound in reply.

Strange to say, the princess never thought of telling herself now how naughty she was, though that would surely have been reasonable. On the contrary, she thought she had a perfect right to be angry, for was she not most desperately ill used—and a princess too? But the wind howled on, and the rain kept pouring down the chimney, and every now and then the lightning burst out, and the thunder rushed after it, as if the great lumbering sound could ever think to catch up with the swift light!

At length the princess had again grown so angry, frightened, and miserable, all together, that she jumped up and hurried about the cottage with outstretched arms, trying to find the wise woman. But being in a bad temper always makes people stupid, and presently she struck her forehead such a blow against something—she thought herself it felt like the old woman's cloak—that she fell back—not on the floor, though, but on the patch of heather, which felt as soft and pleasant as any bed in the palace. There, worn out with weeping and rage, she soon fell fast asleep.

She dreamed that she was the old cold woman up in the sky, with no home and no friends, and no nothing at all, not even a picket; wandering, wandering forever, over a desert of blue sand, never to get to anywhere, and never to lie down or die. It was no use stopping to look about her, for what had she to do but forever look about her as she went on and on and on—never seeing any thing, and never expecting to see any thing! The only shadow of a hope she had was that she might by slow degrees grow thinner and thinner, until at last she wore away to nothing at all; only alas! She could not detect the least sign that she had yet begun to grow thinner. The hopelessness grew at length so unendurable that she woke with a start. Seeing the face of the wise woman bending over her, she threw her arms around her neck and held up her mouth to be kissed. And the kiss of the wise woman was like the rose-gardens of Damascus.

IV.

THE wise woman lifted her tenderly, and washed and dressed her far more carefully than even her nurse. Then she set her down by the fire, and prepared her breakfast. The princess was very hungry, and the bread and milk as good as it could be, so that she thought she had never in her life eaten anything nicer. Nevertheless, as soon as she began to have enough, she said to herself: "Ha! I see how it is! The old woman wants to fatten me! That is why she gives me such nice creamy milk. She doesn't kill me now because she's going to kill me then! She *is* an ogress, after all!"

Thereupon she laid down her spoon, and would not eat another mouthful—only followed the basin with longing looks, as the wise woman carried it away.

When she stopped eating, her hostess knew exactly what she was thinking; but it was one thing to understand the princess, and quite another to make the princess understand her: that would require time. For the present she took no notice, but went about the affairs of the house, sweeping the floor, brushing down the cobwebs, cleaning the hearth, dusting the table and chairs, and watering the bed to keep it fresh and alive—for she never had more than one guest at a time, and never would allow that guest to go to sleep upon anything that had no life in it. All the time she was thus busied, she spoke not a word to the princess, which, with the princess, went to confirm her notion of her purposes. But whatever she might have said would have been only perverted by the princess into yet stronger proof of her evil designs, for a fancy in her own head would outweigh any multitude of facts in another's. She kept staring at the fire, and never looked round to see what the wise woman might be doing.

By and by she came close up to the back of her chair, and said, "Rosamond!"

But the princess had fallen into one of her sulky moods, and shut herself up with her own ugly Somebody; so she never looked round or even answered the wise woman.

"Rosamond," she repeated, "I am going out. If you are a good girl, that is, if you do as I tell you, I will carry you back to your father and mother the moment I return."

The princess did not take the least notice.

"Look at me, Rosamond," said the wise woman.

But Rosamond never moved—never even shrugged her shoulders—perhaps because they were already up to her ears, and could go no farther.

"I want to help you to do what I tell you," said the wise woman. "Look at me."

Still Rosamond was motionless and silent, saying only to herself,

"I know what she's after! She wants to show me her horrid teeth. But I won't look. I'm not going to be frightened out of my senses to please her."

"You had better look, Rosamond. Have you forgotten how you kissed me this morning?"

But Rosamond now regarded that little throb of affection as a momentary weakness into which the deceitful ogress had betrayed her, and almost despised herself for it. She was one of those who the more they are coaxed are the more disagreeable. For such, the wise woman had an awful punishment but she remembered that the princess had been very ill brought up, and therefore wished to try her with all gentleness first.

She stood silent for a moment to see what effect her words might have. But Rosamond only said to herself: "She wants to fatten and eat me."

And it was such a little while since she had looked into the wise woman's loving eyes, thrown her arms round her neck, and kissed her!

"Well," said the wise woman gently, after pausing as long as it seemed possible she might bethink herself, "I must tell you then without; only whoever listens with her back turned, listens but half, and gets but half the help."

"She wants to fatten me," said the princess.

"You must keep the cottage tidy while I am out. When I come back, I must see the fire bright, the hearth swept, and the kettle boiling; no dust on the table or chairs, the windows clear, the floor clean, and the heather in blossom—which last comes of sprinkling it with water three times a day. When you are hungry, put your hand into that hole in the wall, and you will find a meal."

"She wants to fatten me," said the princess.

"But on no account leave the house till I come back," continued the wise woman, "or you will grievously repent it. Remember what you have already gone through to reach it. Dangers lie all around this cottage of mine, but inside, it is the safest place—in fact the only quite safe place in all the country."

"She means to eat me," said the princess, "and therefore wants to frighten me from running away."

She heard the voice no more. Then, suddenly startled at the thought of being alone, she looked hastily over her shoulder. The cottage was indeed empty of all visible life. It was soundless, too: there was not even a ticking clock or a flapping flame. The fire burned still and smouldering-wise; but it was all the company she had, and she turned again to stare into it.

Soon she began to grow weary of having nothing to do. Then she remembered that the old woman, as she called her, had told her to keep the house tidy.

"The miserable little pig-sty!" she said. "Where's the use of keeping such a hovel clean!"

But in truth she would have been glad of the employment, only just because she had been told to do it, she was unwilling; for there *are* people—however unlikely it may seem—who object to doing a thing for no other reason than that it is required of them.

"I am a princess," she said, "and it is very improper to ask me to do such a thing."

She might have judged it quite as suitable for a princess to sweep away the dust as to sit the centre of a world of dirt. But just because she ought, she wouldn't. Perhaps she feared that if she gave in to doing her duty once, she might have to do it always—which was true enough—for that was the very thing for which she had been specially born.

Unable, however, to feel quite comfortable in the resolve to neglect it, she said to herself, "I'm sure there's time enough for such a nasty job as that!" and sat on, watching the fire as it burned away, the glowing red casting off white flakes, and sinking lower and lower on the hearth.

By and by, merely for want of something to do, she would see what the old woman had left for her in the hole of the wall. But when she put in her hand she found nothing there, except the dust which she ought by this time to have wiped away. Never reflecting that the wise woman had told her she would find food there *when she was hungry*, she flew into one of her furies, calling her a cheat, and a thief, and a liar, and an ugly old witch, and an ogress, and I do not know how many wicked names besides. She raged until she was quite exhausted, and then fell fast asleep on her chair. When she awoke, the fire was out.

By this time she was hungry; but without looking in the hole, she began again to storm at the wise woman, in which labor she would no doubt have once more exhausted herself, had not something white caught her eye: it was the corner of a napkin hanging from the hole in the wall. She bounded to it, and there was a dinner for her of something strangely good—one of her favorite dishes, only better than she had ever tasted it before. This might surely have at least changed her mood towards the wise woman; but she only grumbled to herself that it was as it ought to be, ate up the food, and lay down on the bed, never thinking of fire, or dust, or water for the heather.

The wind began to moan about the cottage, and grew louder and louder, till a great gust came down the chimney, and again scattered the white ashes all over the place. But the princess was by this time fast asleep, and never woke till the wind had sunk to silence. One of the consequences, however, of sleeping when one ought to be awake is waking when one ought to be asleep; and the princess awoke in the black midnight, and found enough to keep her awake. For although the wind had fallen, there was a far more terrible howling than that of the wildest wind all about the cottage. Nor was the howling all; the air was full of strange cries; and everywhere she heard the noise of claws scratching against the house, which seemed all doors and windows, so crowded were the sounds, and from so many directions. All the night long she lay half swooning, yet listening to the hideous noises. But with the first glimmer of morning they ceased.

Then she said to herself, "How fortunate it was that I woke! They would have eaten me up if I had been asleep." The miserable little wretch actually talked as if she had kept them out! If she had done her work in the day, she would have slept through the terrors of the darkness, and awaked fearless; whereas now, she had in the storehouse of her heart a whole harvest of agonies, reaped from the dun fields of the night!

They were neither wolves or hyenas which had caused her such dismay, but creatures of the air, more frightful still, which, as soon as the smoke of the burning fir-wood ceased to spread itself abroad, and the sun was a sufficient distance down the sky, and the lone cold woman was out, came flying and howling about the cottage, trying to get in at every door and window. Down the chimney they would have got, but that at the heart of the fire there always lay a certain fir-cone, which looked like solid gold red-hot, and which, although it might easily get covered up with ashes, so as to be quite invisible, was continually in a glow fit to kindle all the fir-cones in the world; this it was which had kept the horrible birds—some say they have a claw at the tip of every wing-feather—from tearing the poor naughty princess to pieces, and gobbling her up.

When she rose and looked about her, she was dismayed to see what a state the cottage was in. The fire was out, and the windows were all dim with the wings and claws of the dirty birds, while the bed from which she had just risen was brown and withered, and half its purple bells had fallen. But she consoled herself that she could set all to rights in a few minutes—only she must breakfast first. And, sure enough, there was a basin of the delicious bread and milk ready for her in the hole of the wall!

After she had eaten it, she felt comfortable, and sat for a long time building castles in the air—till she was actually hungry again, without having done an atom of work. She ate again, and was idle again, and ate again. Then it grew dark, and she went trembling to bed, for now she remembered the horrors of the last night. This time she never slept at all, but spent the long hours in grievous terror, for the noises were worse than before. She vowed she would not pass another night in such a hateful, haunted old shed for all the ugly women, witches, and ogresses in the wide world. In the morning, however, she fell asleep, and slept late.

Breakfast was of course her first thought, after which she could not avoid that of work. It made her very miserable, but she feared the consequences of being found with it undone. A few minutes before noon, she actually got up, took her pinafore for a duster, and proceeded to dust the table. But the wood-ashes flew about so that it seemed useless to attempt getting rid of them, and she sat down again to think what was to be done. But there is very little indeed to be done when we will not do that which we have to do.

Her first thought now was to run away at once while the sun was high, and get through the forest before night came on. She fancied she could easily go back the way she had come, and get home to her father's palace. But not the most experienced traveller in the world can ever go back the way the wise woman has brought him.

She got up and went to the door. It was locked! What could the old woman have meant by telling her not to leave the cottage? She was indignant.

The wise woman had meant to make it difficult but not impossible. Before the princess, however, could find the way out, she heard a hand at the door, and darted in terror behind it. The wise woman opened it and, leaving it open, walked straight to the hearth. Rosamond immediately slid out, ran a little way, and then laid herself down in the long heather.

V.

THE wise woman walked straight up to the hearth, looked at the fire, looked at the bed, glanced round the room, and went up to the table. When she saw the one streak in the thick dust which the princess had left there, a smile, half sad, half pleased, like the sun peeping through a cloud on a rainy day in spring, gleamed over her face. She went at once to the door, and called in a loud voice:

"Rosamond, come to me."

All the wolves and hyenas, fast asleep in the wood, heard her voice, and shivered in their dreams. No wonder then that the princess trembled, and found herself compelled, she could not understand how, to obey the summons. She rose, like the guilty thing she felt, forsook of herself the hiding-place she had chosen, and walked slowly back to the cottage she had left full of the signs of her shame. When she entered, she saw the wise woman on her knees, building up the fire with fir-cones. Already the flame was climbing through the heap in all directions, crackling gently, and sending a sweet aromatic odor through the dusty cottage.

"That is my part of the work," she said, rising. "Now you do yours. But first let me remind you that if you had not put it off, you would have found it not only far easier, but by and by quite pleasant work, much more pleasant than you can imagine now; nor would you have found the time go wearily: you would neither have slept in the day and let the fire out, nor waked at night and heard the howling of the beast-birds. More than all, you would have been glad to see me when I came back; and would have leaped into my arms instead of standing there, looking so ugly and foolish."

As she spoke, suddenly she held up before the princess a tiny mirror, so clear that nobody looking into it could tell what it was made of, or even see it at all—only the thing reflected in it. Rosamond saw a child with dirty fat cheeks, greedy mouth, cowardly eyes—which, not daring to look forward, seemed trying to hide behind an impertinent nose—stooping shoulders, tangled hair, tattered clothes, and smears and stains everywhere. That was what she had made herself. And to tell the truth, she was shocked at the sight, and immediately began, in her dirty heart, to lay the blame on the wise woman, because she had taken her away from her nurses and her fine clothes; while all the time she knew well enough that, close by the heather-bed, was the loveliest little well, just big enough to wash in, the water of which was always springing fresh from the ground and running away through the wall. Beside it lay the whitest of linen towels, with a comb made of mother-of-pearl, and a brush of fir-needles, any one of which she had been far too lazy to use. She dashed the glass out of the wise woman's hand, and there it lay, broken into a thousand pieces!

Without a word, the wise woman stooped, and gathered the fragments—did not leave searching until she had gathered the last atom, and she laid them all carefully, one by one, in the fire, now blazing high on the hearth. Then she stood up and looked at the princess, who had been watching her sulkily.

"Rosamond," she said, with a countenance awful in its sternness, "until you have cleansed this room—"

"She calls it a room!" sneered the princess to herself.

"You shall have no morsel to eat. You may drink of the well, but nothing else you shall have. When the work I set you is done, you will find food in the same place as before. I am going from home again; and again I warn you not to leave the house."

"She calls it a house! It's a good thing she's going out of it anyhow!" said the princess, turning her back for mere rudeness, for she was one who, even if she liked a thing before, would dislike it the moment any person in authority over her desired her to do it.

When she looked again, the wise woman had vanished.

Thereupon the princess ran at once to the door, and tried to open it; but open it would not. She searched on all sides, but could discover no way of getting out. The windows would not open—at least she could not open them; and the only outlet seemed the chimney, which she was afraid to try because of the fire, which looked angry, she thought, and shot out green flames when she went near it. So she sat down to consider. One may well wonder what room for consideration there was—with all her work lying undone behind her. She sat thus, however, considering, as she called it until hunger began to sting her, when she jumped up and put her hand as usual in the hole of the wall: there was nothing there. She fell straight into one of her stupid rages; but neither her hunger nor the hole in the wall heeded her rage. Then, in a burst of self-pity, she fell a-weeping, but neither the hunger nor the hole cared for her tears. The darkness began to come on, and her hunger grew and grew, and the terror of the wild noises of the last night invaded her. Then she began to feel cold, and saw that the fire was dying. She darted to the heap of cones, and fed it. It blazed up cheerily, and she was comforted a little. Then she thought with herself it would surely be better to give in so far, and do a little work, than die of hunger. So catching up a duster, she began upon the table. The dust flew about and nearly choked her. She ran to the well to drink, and was refreshed and encouraged. Perceiving now that it was a tedious plan to wipe the dust from the table on to the floor, whence it would have all to be swept up again, she got a wooden platter, wiped the dust into that, carried it to the fire, and threw it in. But all the time she was getting more and more hungry and, although she tried the hole again and again, it was only to become more and more certain that work she must if she would eat.

At length all the furniture was dusted, and she began to sweep the floor, which, happily, she thought of sprinkling with water, as from the window she had seen them do to the marble court of the palace. That swept, she rushed again to the hole—but still no food! She was on the verge of another rage, when the thought came that she might have forgotten something. To her dismay she found that table and chairs and everything was again covered with dust—not so badly as before, however. Again she set to work, driven by hunger, and drawn by the hope of eating, and yet again, after a second careful wiping, sought the hole. But no! Nothing was there for her! What could it mean?

Her asking this question was a sign of progress: it showed that she expected the wise woman to keep her word. Then she bethought her that she had forgotten the household utensils, and the dishes and plates, some of which wanted to be washed as well as dusted.

Faint with hunger, she set to work yet again. One thing made her think of another, until at length she had cleaned everything she could think of. Now surely she must find some food in the hole!

When this time also there was nothing, she began once more to abuse the wise woman as false and treacherous—but ah! There was the bed unwatered! That was soon amended—Still no supper! Ah! There was the hearth unswept, and the fire wanted making up— Still no supper! What else could there be? She was at her wits' end, and in very weariness, not laziness this time, sat down and gazed into the fire. There, as she gazed, she spied something brilliant, shining even, in the midst of the fire: it was the little mirror all whole again; but little she knew that the dust which she had thrown into the fire had helped to heal it. She drew it out carefully, and, looking into it saw, not indeed the ugly creature she had seen there before, but still a very dirty little animal; whereupon she hurried to the well, took off her clothes, plunged into it and washed herself clean. Then she brushed and combed her hair, made her clothes as tidy as might be, and ran to the hole in the wall: there was a huge basin of bread and milk!

Never had she eaten anything with half the relish! Alas! however, when she had finished, she did not wash the basin, but left it as it was, revealing how entirely all the rest had been done only from hunger. Then she threw herself on the heather, and was fast asleep in a moment. Never an evil bird came near her all that night, nor had she so much as one troubled dream.

In the morning as she lay awake before getting up, she spied what seemed a door behind the tall eight-day clock that stood silent in the corner.

"Ah!" she thought, "that must be the way out!" and got up instantly. The first thing she did, however, was to go to the hole in the wall. Nothing was there.

"Well, I am hardly used!" she cried aloud. "All that cleaning for the cross old woman yesterday, and this for my trouble—nothing for breakfast! Not even a crust of bread! Does Mistress Ogress fancy a princess will bear that?"

The poor foolish creature seemed to think that the work of one day ought to serve for the next day too! But that is nowhere the way in the whole universe. How could there be a universe in that case? And even she never dreamed of applying the same rule to her breakfast.

"How good I was all yesterday!" she said, "and how hungry and ill used I am today!"

But she would *not* be a slave, and do over again today what she had done only last night! *She* didn't care about her breakfast! She might have it no doubt if she dusted all the wretched place again, but she was not going to do that—at least without seeing first what lay behind the clock!

Off she darted, and putting her hand behind the clock found the latch of a door. It lifted, and the door opened a little way. By squeezing hard, she managed to get behind the clock, and so through the door. But how she stared, when instead of the open heath, she found herself on the marble floor of a large and stately room, lighted only from above. Its walls were strengthened by pilasters, and in every space between was a large picture, from cornice to floor. She did not know what to make of it. Surely she had run all round the cottage, and certainly had seen nothing of this size near it! She forgot that she had also run round what she took for a hay-mow, a peat-stack, and several other things which looked of no consequence in the moonlight.

"So, then," she cried, "the old woman *is* a cheat! I believe she's an ogress, after all, and lives in a palace—though she pretends it's only a cottage, to keep people from suspecting that she eats good little children like me!"

Had the princess been tolerably tractable, she would, by this time, have known a good deal about the wise woman's beautiful house, whereas she had never till now got farther than the porch. Neither was she at all in its innermost places now.

But, king's daughter as she was, she was not a little daunted when, stepping forward from the recess of the door, she saw what a great lordly hall it was. She dared hardly look to the other end, it seemed so far off: so she began to gaze at the things near her, and the pictures first of all, for she had a great liking for pictures. One in particular attracted her attention. She came back to it several times, and at length stood absorbed in it.

A blue summer sky, with white fleecy clouds floating beneath it, hung over a hill green to the very top, and alive with streams darting down its sides toward the valley below. On the face of the hill strayed a flock of sheep feeding, attended by a shepherd and two dogs. A little way apart, a girl stood with bare feet in a brook, building across it a bridge of rough stones. The wind was blowing her hair back from her rosy face. A lamb was feeding close beside her; and a sheepdog was trying to reach her hand to lick it.

"Oh, how I wish I were that little girl!" said the princess aloud. "I wonder how it is that some people are made to be so much happier than others! If I were that little girl, no one would ever call me naughty."

She gazed and gazed at the picture. It is the real country, with a real hill, and a real little girl upon it. "I shall soon see whether this isn't another of the old witch's cheats!"

She went close up to the picture, lifted her foot, and stepped over the frame.

"I am free, I am free!" she exclaimed; and she felt the wind upon her cheek.

The sound of a closing door struck on her ear. She turned—and there was a blank wall, without door or window, behind her. The hill with the sheep was before her, and she set out at once to reach it.

Now, if I am asked how this could be, I can only answer, that it was a result of the interaction of things outside and things inside, of the wise woman's skill, and the silly child's folly. If this does not satisfy my questioner, I can only add, that the wise woman was able to do far more wonderful things than this.

VI.

MEANTIME the wise woman was busy as she always was; and her business now was with the child of the shepherd and shepherdess, away in the north. Her name was Agnes.

Her father and mother were poor, and could not give her many things. Rosamond would have utterly despised the rude, simple playthings she had. Yet in one respect they were of more value far than hers: the king bought Rosamond's with his money; Agnes's father made hers with his hands.

And while Agnes had but few things—not seeing many things about her, and not even knowing that there were many things anywhere, she did not wish for many things, and was therefore neither covetous nor avaricious.

She played with the toys her father made her, and thought them the most wonderful things in the world—windmills, and little crooks, and water-wheels, and sometimes lambs made all of wood, and dolls made out of the leg-bones of sheep, which her mother dressed for her; and of such playthings she was never tired. Sometimes, however, she preferred playing with stones, which were plentiful, and flowers, which were few, or the brooks that ran down the hill, of which, although they were many, she could only play with one at a time, and that, indeed, troubled her a little—or live lambs that were not all wool, or the sheepdogs, which were very friendly with her, and the best of playfellows, as she thought, for she had no human ones to compare them with. Neither was she greedy after nice things, but content, as well she might be, with the homely food provided for her. Nor was she by nature particularly self-willed or disobedient; she generally did what her father and mother wished, and believed what they told her. But by degrees they had spoiled her; and this was the way: they were so proud of her that they always repeated everything she said, and told everything she did, even when she was present; and so full of admiration of their child were they, that they wondered and laughed at and praised things in her which in another child would never have struck them as the least remarkable, and some things even which would in another have disgusted them altogether. Impertinent and rude things done by *their* child they thought *so* clever! Laughing at them as something quite marvellous; her commonplace speeches were said over again as if they had been the finest poetry; and the pretty ways which every moderately good child has were extolled as if the result of her excellent taste, and the choice of her judgment and will. They would even say sometimes that she ought not to hear her own praises for fear it should make her vain, and then whisper them behind their hands, but so loud that she could not fail to hear every word. The consequence was that she soon came to believe—so soon, that she could not recall the time when she did not believe, as the most absolute fact in the universe, that she was *Somebody*; that is, she became most immoderately conceited.

Now as the least atom of conceit is a thing to be ashamed of, you may fancy what she was like with such a quantity of it inside her! At first it did not show itself outside in any very active form; but the wise woman had been to the cottage, and had seen her sitting alone, with such a smile of self-satisfaction upon her face as would have been quite startling to her, if she had ever been startled at any thing; for through that smile she could see lying at the root of it the worm that made it. For some smiles are like the ruddiness of certain apples, which is owing to a centipede, or other creeping thing, coiled up at the heart of them. Only her worm had a face and shape the very image of her own; and she looked so simpering, and mawkish, and self-conscious, and silly, that she made the wise woman feel rather sick.

Not that the child was a fool. Had she been, the wise woman would have only pitied and loved her, instead of feeling sick when she looked at her. She had very fair abilities, and were she once but made humble, would be capable not only of doing a good deal in time, but of beginning at once to grow to no end. But, if she were not made humble, her growing would be to a mass of distorted shapes all huddled together; so that, although the body she now showed might grow up straight and well-shaped and comely to behold, the new body that was growing inside of it, and would come out of it when she died, would be ugly, and crooked this way and that, like an aged hawthorn that has lived hundreds of years exposed upon all sides to salt sea-winds.

As time went on, this disease of self-conceit went on too, gradually devouring the good that was in her. For there is no fault that does not bring its brothers and sisters and cousins to live with it. By degrees, from thinking herself so clever, she came to fancy that whatever seemed to her, must of course be the correct judgment and whatever she wished, the right thing; and grew so obstinate, that at length her parents feared to thwart her in any thing, knowing well that she would never give in. But there are victories far worse than defeats; and to overcome an angel too gentle to put out all his strength, and ride away in triumph on the back of a devil, is one of the poorest.

So long as she was left to take her own way and do as she would, she gave her parents little trouble. She would play about by herself in the little garden with its few hardy flowers, or amongst the heather where the bees were busy; or she would wander away amongst the hills, and be nobody knew where, sometimes from morning to night; nor did her parents venture to find fault with her.

She never went into rages like the princess, and would have thought Rosamond—oh, so ugly and vile—if she had seen her in one of her passions. But she was no better, for all that, and was quite as ugly in the eyes of the wise woman, who could not only see but read her face. What is there to choose between a face distorted to hideousness by anger, and one distorted to silliness by self-complacency? True, there is more hope of helping the angry child out of her form of selfishness than the conceited child out of hers; but on the other hand, the conceited child was not so terrible or dangerous as the wrathful one. The conceited one, however, was sometimes very angry, and then her anger was more spiteful than the other's; and, again, the wrathful one was often very conceited too. So that, on the whole, of two very unpleasant creatures, I would say that the king's daughter would have been the worse, had not the shepherd's been quite as bad.

But, as I have said, the wise woman had her eye upon her: she saw that something special must be done, else she would be one of those who kneel to their own shadows till feet grow on their knees;

then go down on their hands till their hands grow into feet; then lay their faces on the ground till they grow into snouts; when at last they are a hideous sort of lizards, each of which believes himself the best, wisest, and loveliest being in the world, yea, the very centre of the universe. And so they run about forever looking for their own shadows, that they may worship them, and miserable because they cannot find them, being themselves too near the ground to have any shadows; and what becomes of them at last there is but one who knows.

The wise woman, therefore, one day walked up to the door of the shepherd's cottage, dressed like a poor woman, and asked for a drink of water. The shepherd's wife looked at her, liked her, and brought her a cup of milk. The wise woman took it, for she made it a rule to accept every kindness that was offered her.

Agnes was not by nature a greedy girl, as I have said; but self-conceit will go far to generate every other vice under the sun. Vanity, which is a form of self-conceit, has repeatedly shown itself as the deepest feeling in the heart of a horrible murderess.

That morning, at breakfast, her mother had stinted her in milk—just a little—that she might have enough to make some milk-porridge for their dinner. Agnes did not mind it at the time, but when she saw the milk now given to a beggar, as she called the wise woman—though, surely, one might ask a draught of water, and accept a draught of milk, without being a beggar in any such sense as Agnes's contemptuous use of the word implied—a cloud came upon her forehead, and a double vertical wrinkle settled over her nose. The wise woman saw it, for all her business was with Agnes though she little knew it, and, rising, went and offered the cup to the child, where she sat with her knitting in a corner. Agnes looked at it, did not want it, was inclined to refuse it from a beggar, but thinking it would show her consequence to assert her rights, took it and drank it up. For whoever is possessed by a devil, judges with the mind of that devil; and hence Agnes was guilty of such a meanness as many who are themselves capable of something just as bad will consider incredible.

The wise woman waited till she had finished it—then, looking into the empty cup, said:

"You might have given me back as much as you had no claim upon!"

Agnes turned away and made no answer—far less from shame than indignation.

The wise woman looked at the mother.

"You should not have offered it to her if you did not mean her to have it," said the mother, siding with the devil in her child against the wise woman and her child too. Some foolish people think they take another's part when they take the part he takes.

The wise woman said nothing, but fixed her eyes upon her, and soon the mother hid her face in her apron weeping. Then she turned again to Agnes, who had never looked round but sat with her back to both, and suddenly lapped her in the folds of her cloak. When the mother again lifted her eyes, she had vanished.

Never supposing she had carried away her child, but uncomfortable because of what she had said to the poor woman, the mother went to the door, and called after her as she toiled slowly up the hill. But she never turned her head; and the mother went back into her cottage.

The wise woman walked close past the shepherd and his dogs, and through the midst of his block of sheep. The shepherd wondered where she could be going—right up the hill. There was something strange about her too, he thought; and he followed her with his eyes as she went up and up.

It was near sunset, and as the sun went down, a gray cloud

settled on the top of the mountain, which his last rays turned into a rosy gold. Straight into this cloud the shepherd saw the woman hold her pace, and in it she vanished. He little imagined that his child was under her cloak.

He went home as usual in the evening, but Agnes had not come in. They were accustomed to such an absence now and then, and were not at first frightened; but when it grew dark and she did not appear, the husband set out with his dogs in one direction, and the wife in another, to seek their child. Morning came and they had not found her. Then the whole countryside arose to search for the missing Agnes; but day after day and night after night passed, and nothing was discovered of or concerning her, until at length all gave up the search in despair except the mother, although she was nearly convinced now that the poor woman had carried her off.

One day she had wandered some distance from her cottage, thinking she might come upon the remains of her daughter at the foot of some cliff, when she came suddenly, instead, upon a disconsolate-looking creature sitting on a stone by the side of a stream. Her hair hung in tangles from her head; her clothes were tattered, and through the rents her skin showed in many places; her cheeks were white, and worn thin with hunger; the hollows were dark under her eyes, and they stood out scared and wild. When she caught sight of the shepherdess, she jumped to her feet, and would have run away, but fell down in a faint.

At first sight the mother had taken her for her own child, but now she saw, with a pang of disappointment, that she was mistaken. Full of compassion, nevertheless, she said to herself:

"If she is not my Agnes, she is as much in need of help as if she were. If I cannot be good to my own, I will be as good as I can to some other woman's; and though I should scorn to be consoled for the loss of one by the presence of another, I yet may find some gladness in rescuing one child from the death which has taken the other."

Perhaps her words were not just like these, but her thoughts were. She took up the child, and carried her home. And this is how Rosamond came to occupy the place of the little girl whom she had envied in the picture.

VII.

NOTWITHSTANDING the differences between the two girls, which were, indeed, so many that most people would have said they were not in the least alike, they were the same in this, that each cared more for her own fancies and desires than for anything else in the world. But I will tell you another difference: the princess was like several children in one—such was the variety of her moods; and in one mood she had no recollection or care about anything whatever belonging to a previous mood—not even if it had left her but a moment before, and had been so violent as to make her ready to put her hand in the fire to get what she wanted. Plainly she was the mere puppet of her moods, and more than that, any cunning nurse who knew her well enough could call or send away those moods almost as she pleased, like a showman pulling strings behind a show. Agnes, on the contrary, seldom changed her mood, but kept that of calm assured self-satisfaction. Father nor mother had ever by wise punishment helped her to gain a victory over herself, and do what she did not like or choose; and their folly in reasoning with one unreasonable had fixed her in her conceit. She would actually nod her head to herself in complacent pride that she had stood out against them. This, however, was not so difficult as to justify even the pride of having conquered, seeing she loved them so little, and paid so little attention to the arguments and persuasions they used.

Neither, when she found herself wrapped in the dark folds of the wise woman's cloak, did she behave in the least like the princess, for she was not afraid. "She'll soon set me down," she said, too self-important to suppose that any one would dare do her an injury.

Whether it be a good thing or a bad not to be afraid depends on what the fearlessness is founded upon. Some have no fear, because they have no knowledge of the danger: there is nothing fine in that. Some are too stupid to be afraid: there is nothing fine in that. Some who are not easily frightened would yet turn their backs and run, the moment they were frightened: such never had more courage than fear. But the man who will do his work in spite of his fear is a man of true courage. The fearlessness of Agnes was only ignorance: she did not know what it was to be hurt; she had never read a single story of giant or ogress, or wolf; and her mother had never carried out one of her threats of punishment. If the wise woman had but pinched her, she would have shown herself an abject little coward, trembling with fear at *every* change of motion so long as she carried her.

Nothing such, however, was in the wise woman's plan for the curing of her. On and on she carried her without a word. She knew that if she set her down she would never run after her like the princess, at least not before the evil thing was already upon her. On and on she went, never halting, never letting the light look in, or Agnes look out. She walked very fast and got home to her cottage very soon after the princess had gone from it.

But she did not set Agnes down either in the cottage or in the great hall. She had other places, none of them alike. The place she had chosen for Agnes was a strange one—such a one as is to be found nowhere else in the wide world.

It was a great hollow sphere, made of a substance similar to that of the mirror which Rosamond had broken, but differently compounded. That substance no one could see by itself. It had neither door, nor window, nor any opening to break its perfect roundness.

The wise woman carried Agnes into a dark room, there undressed her, took from her hand her knitting-needles, and put her, naked as she was born, into the hollow sphere.

What sort of a place it was she could not tell. She could see nothing but a faint cold bluish light all about her. She could not feel that anything supported her, and yet she did not sink. She stood for a while, perfectly calm, then sat down. Nothing bad could happen to *her*—she was so important! And, indeed, it was but this: she had cared only for Somebody, and now she was going to have only Somebody. Her own choice was going to be carried a good deal farther for her than she would have knowingly carried it for herself.

After sitting a while, she wished she had something to do, but nothing came. A little longer, and it grew wearisome. She would see whether she could not walk out of the strange luminous dusk that surrounded her.

Walk she found she could, well enough, but walk out she could not. On and on she went keeping as much in a straight line as she might, but after walking until she was thoroughly tired, she found herself no nearer out of her prison than before. She had, not indeed, advanced a single step; for, in whatever direction she tried to go, the sphere turned round and round, answering her feet accordingly. Like a squirrel in his cage she but kept placing another spot of the cunningly suspended sphere under her feet, and she would have been still only at its lowest point after walking for ages.

At length she cried aloud; but there was no answer. It grew dreary and drearier—in her, that is: outside there was no change. Nothing was overhead, nothing under foot, nothing on either hand, but the same pale, faint, bluish glimmer. She wept at last, then grew very angry, and then sullen; but nobody heeded whether she cried or laughed. It was all the same to the cold unmoving twilight that rounded her. On and on went the dreary hours—or did they go at all?—"no change, no pause, no hope"—on and on till she *felt* she was forgotten, and then she grew strangely still and fell asleep.

The moment she was asleep, the wise woman came, lifted her out, and laid her in her bosom; fed her with a wonderful milk, which she received without knowing it; nursed her all the night long, and, just ere she woke, laid her back in the blue sphere again.

When first she came to herself, she thought the horrors of the preceding day had been all a dream of the night. But they soon asserted themselves as facts for here they were!—Nothing to see but a cold blue light, and nothing to do but see it. Oh, how slowly the hours went by! She lost all notion of time. If she had been told that she had been there twenty years, she would have believed it—or twenty minutes—it would have been all the same: except for weariness, time was for her no more.

Another night came, and another still, during both of which the wise woman nursed and fed her. But she knew nothing of that, and the same one dreary day seemed ever brooding over her.

All at once, on the third day, she was aware that a naked child was seated beside her. But there was something about the child that made her shudder. She never looked at Agnes, but sat with her chin sunk on her chest, and her eyes staring at her own toes. She was the color of pale earth, with a pinched nose, and a mere slit in her face for a mouth.

"How ugly she is!" thought Agnes. "What business has she beside me!"

But it was so lonely that she would have been glad to play with a serpent, and put out her hand to touch her. She touched nothing. The child, also, put out her hand—but in the direction away from

Agnes. And that was well, for if she had touched Agnes it would have killed her. Then Agnes said, "Who are you?" And the little girl said, "Who are you?" "I am Agnes," said Agnes; and the little girl said, "I am Agnes." Then Agnes thought she was mocking her, and said, "You are ugly"; and the little girl said, "You are ugly."

Then Agnes lost her temper, and put out her hands to seize the little girl; but lo! The little girl was gone, and she found herself tugging at her own hair. She let go; and there was the little girl again! Agnes was furious now, and flew at her to bite her. But she found her teeth in her own arm, and the little girl was gone—only to return again; and each time she came back she was tenfold uglier than before. And now Agnes hated her with her whole heart.

The moment she hated her, it flashed upon her with a sickening disgust that the child was not another, but her Self, her Somebody, and that she was now shut up with her forever and ever—no more for one moment ever to be alone. In her agony of despair, sleep descended, and she slept.

When she woke, there was the little girl, heedless, ugly, miserable, staring at her own toes. All at once, the creature began to smile, but with such an odious, self-satisfied expression, that Agnes felt ashamed of seeing her. Then she began to pat her own cheeks, to stroke her own body, and examine her finger-ends, nodding her head with satisfaction. Agnes felt that there could not be such another hateful, ape-like creature, and at the same time was perfectly aware she was only doing outside of her what she herself had been doing, as long as she could remember, inside of her.

She turned sick at herself, and would gladly have been put out of existence, but for three days the odious companionship went on. By the third day, Agnes was not merely sick but ashamed of the life she had hitherto led, was despicable in her own eyes, and astonished that she had never seen the truth concerning herself before.

The next morning she woke in the arms of the wise woman; the horror had vanished from her sight and two heavenly eyes were gazing upon her. She wept and clung to her, and the more she clung, the more tenderly did the great strong arms close around her.

When she had lain thus for a while, the wise woman carried her into her cottage, and washed her in the little well; then dressed her in clean garments, and gave her bread and milk. When she had eaten it, she called her to her, and said very solemnly, "Agnes, you must not imagine you are cured. That you are ashamed of yourself now is no sign that the cause for such shame has ceased. In new circumstances, especially after you have done well for a while, you will be in danger of thinking just as much of yourself as before. So beware of yourself. I am going from home, and leave you in charge of the house. Do just as I tell you till my return."

She then gave her the same directions she had formerly given Rosamond—with this difference, that she told her to go into the picture-hall when she pleased, showing her the entrance, against which the clock no longer stood—and went away, closing the door behind her.

VIII.

AS soon as she was left alone, Agnes set to work tidying and dusting the cottage, made up the fire, watered the bed, and cleaned the inside of the windows: the wise woman herself always kept the outside of them clean. When she had done, she found her dinner—of the same sort she was used to at home, but better—in the hole of the wall. When she had eaten it, she went to look at the pictures.

By this time her old disposition had begun to rouse again. She had been doing her duty, and had in consequence begun again to think herself Somebody. However strange it may well seem, to do one's duty will make any one conceited who only does it sometimes. Those who do it always would as soon think of being conceited of eating their dinner as of doing their duty. What honest boy would pride himself on not picking pockets? A thief who was trying to reform would. To be conceited of doing one's duty is then a sign of how little one does it, and how little one sees what a contemptible thing it is not to do it. Could any but a low creature be conceited of not being contemptible? Until our duty becomes to us common as breathing, we are poor creatures.

So Agnes began to stroke herself once more, forgetting her late self-stroking companion, and never reflecting that she was not doing what she had then abhorred. And in this mood she went into the picture-gallery.

The first picture she saw represented a square in a great city, one side of which was occupied by a splendid marble palace, with great flights of broad steps leading up to the door. Between it and the square was a marble-paved court, with gates of brass, at which stood sentries in gorgeous uniforms, and to which was affixed the following proclamation in letters of gold, large enough for Agnes to read—

> "*By the will of the king, from this time until further notice, every stray child found in the realm shall be brought without a moment's delay to the palace. Whoever shall be found having done otherwise shall straightway lose his head by the hand of the public executioner.*"

Agnes's heart beat loud, and her face flushed.

"Can there by such a city in the world?" she said to herself. "If I only knew where it was, I should set out for it at once. *There* would be the place for a clever girl like me!"

Her eyes fell on the picture which had so enticed Rosamond. It was the very country where her father fed his flocks. Just round the shoulder of the hill was the cottage where her parents lived, where she was born and whence she had been carried by the beggar-woman.

"Ah!" she said, "they didn't know me there. They little thought what I could be, if I had the chance. If I were but in this good, kind, loving, generous king's palace, I should soon be such a great lady as they never saw! Then they would understand what a good little girl I had always been! And I shouldn't forget my poor parents like some I have read of. *I* should never be selfish and proud like girls in story-books!"

As she said this, she turned her back with disdain upon the picture of her home, and setting herself before the picture of the palace, stared at it with wide ambitious eyes, and a heart whose every beat was a throb of arrogant self-esteem.

The shepherd-child was now worse than ever the poor princess had been. For the wise woman had given her a terrible lesson, one of which the princess was not capable, and she had known what it meant; yet here she was as bad as ever, therefore worse than before. The ugly creature whose presence had made her so miserable had indeed crept out of sight and mind too—but where was she? Nestling in her very heart, where most of all she had her company and least of all could see her. The wise woman had called her out, that Agnes might see what sort of creature she was herself; but now she was snug in her soul's bed again, and she did not even suspect she was there.

After gazing a while at the palace picture, during which her ambitious pride rose and rose, she turned yet again in condescending mood, and honored the home picture with one stare more.

"What a poor, miserable spot it is compared with this lordly palace!" she said.

But presently she spied something in it she had not seen before, and drew nearer. It was the form of a little girl, building a bridge of stones over one of the hill-brooks.

"Ah, there I am myself" she said. "That is just how I used to do—No," she resumed, "it is not me. That snub-nosed little fright could never be meant for me! It was the frock that made me think so. But it *is* a picture of the place. I declare, I can see the smoke of the cottage rising from behind the hill! What a dull, dirty, insignificant spot it is! And what a life to lead there!"

She turned once more to the city picture. And now a strange thing took place. In proportion as the other, to the eyes of her mind, receded into the background, this, to her present bodily eyes, appeared to come forward and assume reality. At last, after it had been in this way growing upon her for some time, she gave a cry of conviction, and said aloud, "I do believe it is real! That frame is only a trick of the woman to make me fancy it a picture lest I should go and make my fortune. She is a witch, the ugly old creature! It would serve her right to tell the king and have her punished for not taking me to the palace—one of his poor lost children he is so fond of! I should like to see her ugly old head cut off. Anyhow I will try my luck without asking her leave. How she has ill used me!"

But at that moment, she heard the voice of the wise woman calling, "Agnes!" and, smoothing her face, she tried to look as good as she could, and walked back into the cottage. There stood the wise woman, looking all round the place, and examining her work. She fixed her eyes upon Agnes in a way that confused her, and made her cast hers down, for she felt as if she were reading her thoughts. The wise woman, however, asked no questions, but began to talk about her work, approving of some of it, which filled her with arrogance, and showing how some of it might have been done better, which filled her with resentment. But the wise woman seemed to take no care of what she might be thinking, and went straight on with her lesson. By the time it was over, the power of reading thoughts would not have been necessary to a knowledge of what was in the mind of Agnes, for it had all come to the surface—that is up into her face, which is the surface of the mind. Ere it had time to sink down again, the wise woman caught up the little mirror, and held it before her: Agnes saw her Somebody—the very embodiment of miserable conceit and ugly ill-temper. She gave such a scream of horror that the wise woman pitied her, and laying aside the mirror, took her upon her knees, and talked to her most kindly and solemnly; in particular about the necessity of destroying the ugly things that come out of the heart—so ugly that they make the very face over them ugly also.

And what was Agnes doing all the time the wise woman was talking to her? Would you believe it? Instead of thinking how to kill the ugly things in her heart, she was with all her might resolving to be more careful of her face, that is, to keep down the things in her heart so that they should not show in her face, she was resolving to be a hypocrite as well as a self-worshipper. Her heart was wormy, and the worms were eating very fast at it now.

Then the wise woman laid her gently down upon the heather-bed, and she fell asleep, and had an awful dream about her Somebody.

When she woke in the morning, instead of getting up to do the work of the house, she lay thinking—to evil purpose. In place of taking her dream as a warning, and thinking over what the wise woman had said the night before, she communed with herself in this fashion:

"If I stay here longer, I shall be miserable. It is nothing better than slavery. The old witch shows me horrible things in the day to set me dreaming horrible things in the night. If I don't run away, that frightful blue prison and the disgusting girl will come back, and

I shall go out of my mind. How I do wish I could find the way to the good king's palace! I shall go and look at the picture again—if it be a picture—as soon as I've got my clothes on. The work can wait. It's not my work. It's the old witch's; and she ought to do it herself."

She jumped out of bed, and hurried on her clothes. There was no wise woman to be seen; and she hastened into the hall. There was the picture, with the marble palace, and the proclamation shining in letters of gold upon its gates of brass. She stood before it and gazed and gazed; and all the time it kept growing upon her in some strange way, until at last she was fully persuaded that it was no picture, but a real city, square, and marble palace, seen through a framed opening in the wall. She ran up to the frame, stepped over it, felt the wind blow upon her cheek, heard the sound of a closing door behind her, and was free. *Free* was she, with that creature inside her?

The same moment a terrible storm of thunder and lightning, wind and rain, came on. The uproar was appalling. Agnes threw herself upon the ground, hid her face in her hands, and there lay until it was over. As soon as she felt the sun shining on her, she rose. There was the city far away on the horizon. Without once turning to take a farewell look of the place she was leaving, she set off, as fast as her feet would carry her, in the direction of the city. So eager was she, that again and again she fell, but only to get up, and run on faster than before.

IX.

THE shepherdess carried Rosamond home, gave her a warm bath in the tub in which she washed her linen, made her some bread and milk, and after she had eaten it, put her to bed in Agnes's crib, where she slept all the rest of that day and all the following night.

When at last she opened her eyes, it was to see around her a far poorer cottage than the one she had left—very bare and uncomfortable indeed, she might well have thought; but she had come through such troubles of late, in the way of hunger and weariness and cold and fear, that she was not altogether in her ordinary mood of fault-finding, and so was able to lie enjoying the thought that at length she was safe, and going to be fed and kept warm. The idea of doing anything in return for shelter and food and clothes, did not, however, even cross her mind.

But the shepherdess was one of that plentiful number who can be wiser concerning other women's children than concerning their own. Such will often give you very tolerable hints as to how you ought to manage your children, and will find fault neatly enough with the system you are trying to carry out; but all their wisdom goes off in talking, and there is none left for doing what they have themselves said. There is one road talk never finds, and that is the way into the talker's own hands and feet. And such never seem to know themselves—not even when they are reading about themselves in print. Still, not being specially blinded in any direction but their own, they can sometimes even act with a little sense towards children who are not theirs. They are affected with a sort of blindness like that which renders some people incapable of seeing, except sideways.

She came up to the bed, looked at the princess, and saw that she was better. But she did not like her much. There was no mark of a princess about her, and never had been since she began to run alone. True, hunger had brought down her fat cheeks, but it had not turned down her impudent nose, or driven the sullenness and greed from her mouth. Nothing but the wise woman could do that—and not even she, without the aid of the princess herself. So the shepherdess thought what a poor substitute she had got for her own lovely Agnes—who was in fact equally repulsive, only in a way to which she had got used; for the selfishness in her love had blinded her to the thin pinched nose and the mean self-satisfied mouth. It was well for the princess, though, sad as it is to say, that the shepherdess did not take to her, for then she would most likely have only done her harm instead of good.

"Now, my girl," she said, "you must get up, and do something. We can't keep idle folk here."

"I'm not a folk," said Rosamond; "I'm a princess."

"A pretty princess—with a nose like that! And all in rags too! If you tell such stories, I shall soon let you know what I think of you."

Rosamond then understood that the mere calling herself a princess, without having anything to show for it, was of no use. She obeyed and rose, for she was hungry; but she had to sweep the floor ere she had anything to eat.

The shepherd came in to breakfast, and was kinder than his wife. He took her up in his arms and would have kissed her; but she took it as an insult from a man whose hands smelt of tar, and kicked and screamed with rage. The poor man, finding he had made a mistake, set her down at once. But to look at the two, one might well have judged it condescension rather than rudeness in such a man to kiss such a child. He was tall, and almost stately, with a thoughtful forehead, bright eyes, eagle nose, and gentle mouth; while the princess was such as I have described her.

Not content with being set down and let alone, she continued to storm and scold at the shepherd, crying she was a princess, and would like to know what right he had to touch her! But he only looked down upon her from the height of his tall person with a benignant smile, regarding her as a spoiled little ape whose mother had flattered her by calling her a princess.

"Turn her out of doors, the ungrateful hussy!" cried his wife. "With your bread and your milk inside her ugly body, this is what she gives you for it! Troth, I'm paid for carrying home such an ill-bred tramp in my arms! My own poor angel Agnes! As if that ill-tempered toad were one hair like her!"

These words drove the princess beside herself; for those who are most given to abuse can least endure it. With fists and feet and teeth, as was her wont, she rushed at the shepherdess, whose hand was already raised to deal her a sound box on the ear, when a better appointed minister of vengeance suddenly showed himself. Bounding in at the cottage door came one of the sheepdogs, who was called Prince, and whom I shall not refer to with a *which*, because he was a very superior animal indeed, even for a sheepdog, which is the most intelligent of dogs: he flew at the princess, knocked her down, and commenced shaking her so violently as to tear her miserable clothes to pieces. Used, however, to mouthing little lambs, he took care not to hurt her much, though for her good he left her a blue nip or two by way of letting her imagine what biting might be. His master, knowing he would not injure her, thought it better not to call him off, and in half a minute he left her of his own accord, and, casting a glance of indignant rebuke behind him as he went, walked slowly to the hearth, where he laid himself down with his tail toward her. She rose, terrified almost to death, and would have crept again into Agnes's crib for refuge; but the shepherdess cried—

"Come, come, princess! I'll have no skulking to bed in the good daylight. Go and clean your master's Sunday boots there."

"I will not!" screamed the princess, and ran from the house.

"Prince!" cried the shepherdess, and up jumped the dog, and looked in her face, wagging his bushy tail.

"Fetch her back," she said, pointing to the door.

With two or three bounds Prince caught the princess, again threw her down, and taking her by her clothes dragged her back into the cottage, and dropped her at his mistress' feet, where she lay like a bundle of rags.

"Get up," said the shepherdess.

Rosamond got up as pale as death.

"Go and clean the boots."

"I don't know how."

"Go and try. There are the brushes, and yonder is the blacking-pot."

Instructing her how to black boots, it came into the thought of the shepherdess what a fine thing it would be if she could teach this miserable little wretch, so forsaken and ill-bred, to be a good, well-behaved, respectable child. She was hardly the woman to do it, but everything well meant is a help, and she had the wisdom to beg her husband to place Prince under her orders for a while, and not take him to the hill as usual, that he might help her in getting the princess into order.

When the husband was gone, and his boots, with the aid of her own finishing touches, at last quite respectably brushed, the shepherdess told the princess that she might go and play for a while, only she must not go out of sight of the cottage door.

The princess went right gladly, with the firm intention, however, of getting out of sight by slow degrees, and then at once taking to her heels. But no sooner was she over the threshold than the shepherdess said to the dog, "Watch her"; and out shot Prince.

The moment she saw him, Rosamond threw herself on her face, trembling from head to foot. But the dog had no quarrel with her, and of the violence against which he always felt bound to protest in dog fashion, there was no sign in the prostrate shape before him; so he poked his nose under her, turned her over, and began licking her face and hands. When she saw that he meant to be friendly, her love for animals, which had had no indulgence for a long time now, came wide awake, and in a little while they were romping and rushing about, the best friends in the world.

Having thus seen one enemy, as she thought changed to a friend, she began to resume her former plan, and crept cunningly farther and farther. At length she came to a little hollow, and instantly rolled down into it. Finding then that she was out of sight of the cottage, she ran off at full speed.

But she had not gone more than a dozen paces, when she heard a growling rush behind her, and the next instant was on the ground, with the dog standing over her, showing his teeth, and flaming at her with his eyes. She threw her arms round his neck, and immediately he licked her face, and let her get up. But the moment she would have moved a step farther from the cottage, there he was in front of her, growling, and showing his teeth. She saw it was of no use, and went back with him.

Thus was the princess provided with a dog for a private tutor—just the right sort for her.

Presently the shepherdess appeared at the door and called her. She would have disregarded the summons, but Prince did his best to let her know that, until she could obey herself, she must obey him. So she went into the cottage, and there the shepherdess ordered her to peel the potatoes for dinner. She sulked and refused. Here Prince could do nothing to help his mistress, but she had not to go far to find another ally.

"Very well, Miss Princess!" she said. "We shall soon see how you like to go without when dinnertime comes."

Now the princess had very little foresight, and the idea of future hunger would have moved her little; but happily, from her game of romps with Prince, she had begun to be hungry already, and so the threat had force. She took the knife and began to peel the potatoes.

By slow degrees the princess improved a little. A few more outbreaks of passion, and a few more savage attacks from Prince, and she had learned to try to restrain herself when she felt the passion coming on; while a few dinnerless afternoons entirely opened her eyes to the necessity of working in order to eat. Prince was her first, and Hunger her second dog-counsellor.

But a still better thing was that she soon grew very fond of Prince. Towards the gaining of her affections, he had three advantages: first, his nature was inferior to hers; next, he was a beast; and last, she was afraid of him; for so spoiled was she that she could more easily love what was below than what was above her, and a beast, than one of her own kind, and indeed could hardly have ever come to love anything much that she had not first learned to fear, and the white teeth and flaming eyes of the angry Prince were more terrible to her than anything had yet been, except those of the wolf, which she had now forgotten. Then again, he was such a delightful playfellow, that so long as she neither lost her temper, nor went against orders, she might do almost anything she pleased with him. In fact, such was his influence upon her, that she who had scoffed at the wisest woman in the whole world, and derided the wishes of her own father and mother, came at length to regard this dog as a superior being, and to look up to him as well as love him. And this was best of all.

The improvement upon her, in the course of a month, was plain. She had quite ceased to go into passions, and had actually begun to take a little interest in her work and try to do it well.

Still, the change was mostly an outside one. I do not mean that she was pretending. Indeed she had never been given to pretence of any sort. But the change was not in *her*, only in her mood. A second change of circumstances would have soon brought a second change of behavior; and, so long as that was possible, she continued the same sort of person she had always been. But if she had not gained much, a trifle had been gained for her: a little quietness and order of mind, and hence a somewhat greater possibility of the first idea of right arising in it, whereupon she would begin to see what a wretched creature she was, and must continue until she herself was right.

Meantime the wise woman had been watching her when she least fancied it and taking note of the change that was passing upon her. Out of the large eyes of a gentle sheep she had been watching her—a sheep that puzzled the shepherd; for every now and then she would appear in his flock, and he would catch sight of her two or three times in a day, sometimes for days together, yet he never saw her when he looked for her, and never when he counted the flock into the fold at night. He knew she was not one of his; but where could she come from, and where could she go to? For there was no other flock within many miles, and he never could get near enough to her to see whether or not she was marked. Nor was Prince of the least use to him for the unravelling of the mystery; for although, as often as he told him to fetch the strange sheep, he went bounding to her at once, it was only to lie down at her feet.

At length, however, the wise woman had made up her mind, and after that the strange sheep no longer troubled the shepherd.

As Rosamond improved, the shepherdess grew kinder. She gave her all Agnes's clothes, and began to treat her much more like a daughter. Hence she had a great deal of liberty after the little work required of her was over, and would often spend hours at a time with the shepherd, watching the sheep and the dogs, and learning a little from seeing how Prince, and the others as well, managed their charge—how they never touched the sheep that did as they were told and turned when they were bid, but jumped on a disobedient flock, and ran along their backs, biting, and barking, and half choking themselves with mouthfuls of their wool.

Then also she would play with the brooks and learn their songs, and build bridges over them. And sometimes she would be seized with such delight of heart that she would spread out her arms to the wind, and go rushing up the hill till her breath left her, when she would tumble down in the heather, and lie there till it came back again.

A noticeable change had by this time passed also on her countenance. Her coarse shapeless mouth had begun to show a glimmer of lines and curves about it, and the fat had not returned with the roses to her cheeks, so that her eyes looked larger than before; while, more noteworthy still, the bridge of her nose had grown higher, so that it was less of the impudent, insignificant thing inherited from a certain great-great-great-grandmother, who had little else to leave her. For a long time, it had fitted her very well, for it was just like her; but now there was ground for alteration, and already the granny who gave it her would not have recognized it. It was growing a little like Prince's; and Prince's was a long, perceptive, sagacious nose—one that was seldom mistaken.

One day about noon, while the sheep were mostly lying down, and the shepherd, having left them to the care of the dogs, was himself stretched under the shade of a rock a little way apart, and the princess sat knitting, with Prince at her feet, lying in wait for a snap at a great fly, for even he had his follies—Rosamond saw a poor woman come toiling up the hill, but took little notice of her until she was passing, a few yards off, when she heard her utter the dog's name in a low voice.

Immediately on the summons. Prince started up and followed her—with hanging head, but gently-wagging tail. At first the princess thought he was merely taking observations, and consulting with his nose whether she was respectable or not, but she soon saw that he was following her in meek submission. Then she sprung to her feet and cried, "Prince, Prince!" But Prince only turned his head and gave her an odd look, as if he were trying to smile, and could not. Then the princess grew angry, and ran after him, shouting, "Prince, come here directly." Again Prince turned his head, but this time to growl and show his teeth.

The princess flew into one of her forgotten rages, and picking up a stone, flung it at the woman. Prince turned and darted at her, with fury in his eyes, and his white teeth gleaming. At the awful sight the princess turned also, and would have fled, but he was upon her in a moment, and threw her to the ground, and there she lay.

It was evening when she came to herself. A cool twilight wind, that somehow seemed to come all the way from the stars, was blowing upon her. The poor woman and Prince, the shepherd and his sheep were all gone, and she was left alone with the wind upon the heather.

She felt sad, weak, and, perhaps, for the first time in her life, a little ashamed. The violence of which she had been guilty had vanished from her spirit, and now lay in her memory with the calm morning behind it, while in front the quiet dusky night was now closing in the loud shame betwixt a double peace. Between the two her passion looked ugly. It pained her to remember. She felt it was hateful, and *hers*.

But, alas, Prince was gone! That horrid woman had taken him away! The fury rose again in her heart, and raged—until it came to her mind how her dear Prince would have flown at her throat if he had seen her in such a passion. The memory calmed her, and she rose and went home. There, perhaps, she would find Prince, for surely he could never have been such a silly dog as to go away altogether with a strange woman!

She opened the door and went in. Dogs were asleep all about the cottage, it seemed to her, but nowhere was Prince. She crept away to her little bed, and cried herself asleep.

In the morning the shepherd and shepherdess were indeed glad to find she had come home, for they thought she had run away.

"Where is Prince?" she cried, the moment she waked.

"His mistress has taken him," answered the shepherd.

"Was that woman his mistress?"

"I fancy so. He followed her as if he had known her all his life. I am very sorry to lose him, though."

The poor woman had gone close past the rock where the shepherd lay. He saw her coming, and thought of the strange sheep which had been feeding beside him when he lay down. "Who can she be?" he said to himself; but when he noted how Prince followed her, without even looking up at him as he passed, he remembered how Prince had come to him. And this was how: as he lay in bed one fierce winter morning, just about to rise, he heard the voice of a woman call to him through the storm, "Shepherd, I have brought you a dog. Be good to him. I will come again and fetch him away." He dressed as quickly as he could, and went to the door. It was half snowed up, but on the top of the white mound before it stood Prince. And now he had gone as mysteriously as he had come, and he felt sad.

Rosamond was very sorry too, and hence when she saw the looks of the shepherd and shepherdess, she was able to understand them. And she tried for a while to behave better to them because of their sorrow. So the loss of the dog brought them all nearer to each other.

X.

AFTER the thunderstorm, Agnes did not meet with a single obstruction or misadventure. Everybody was strangely polite, gave her whatever she desired, and answered her questions, but asked none in return, and looked all the time as if her departure would be a relief. They were afraid, in fact, from her appearance, lest she should tell them that she was lost, when they would be bound, on pain of public execution, to take her to the palace.

But no sooner had she entered the city than she saw it would hardly do to present herself as a lost child at the palace gates; for how were they to know that she was not an imposter, especially since she really was one, having run away from the wise woman? So she wandered about looking at everything until she was tired, and bewildered by the noise and confusion all around her. The wearier she got, the more was she pushed in every direction. Having been used to a whole hill to wander upon, she was very awkward in the crowded streets, and often on the point of being run over by the horses, which seemed to her to be going every way like a frightened flock. She spoke to several persons, but no one stopped to answer her; and at length, her courage giving way, she felt lost indeed, and began to cry. A soldier saw her, and asked what was the matter.

"I've nowhere to go to," she sobbed.

"Where's your mother?" asked the soldier.

"I don't know," answered Agnes. "I was carried off by an old woman, who then went away and left me. I don't know where she is, or where I am myself."

"Come," said the soldier, "this is a case for his majesty."

So saying, he took her by the hand, led her to the palace, and begged an audience of the king and queen. The porter glanced at Agnes, immediately admitted them, and showed them into a great splendid room, where the king and queen sat every day to review lost children, in the hope of one day thus finding their Rosamond. But they were by this time beginning to get tired of it. The moment they cast their eyes upon Agnes, the queen threw back her head, threw up her hands, and cried, "What a miserable, conceited, white-faced ape!" And the king turned upon the soldier in wrath, and cried, forgetting his own decree, "What do you mean by bringing such a dirty, vulgar-looking, pert creature into my palace? The dullest soldier in my army could never for a moment imagine a child like *that*, one hair's-breadth like the lovely angel we lost!"

"I humbly beg your majesty's pardon," said the soldier, "but what was I to do? There stands your majesty's proclamation in gold letters on the brazen gates of the palace."

"I shall have it taken down," said the king. "Remove the child."

"Please, your majesty, what am I to do with her?"

"Take her home with you."

"I have six already, sire, and do not want her."

"Then drop her where you picked her up."

"If I do, sire, someone else will find her and bring her back to your majesties."

"That will never do," said the king. "I cannot bear to look at her."

"For all her ugliness," said the queen, "she is plainly lost, and so is our Rosamond."

"It may be only a pretence, to get into the palace," said the king.

"Take her to the head scullion, soldier," said the queen, "and tell her to make her useful. If she should find out she has been pretending to be lost, she must let me know."

The soldier was so anxious to get rid of her, that he caught her up in his arms, hurried her from the room, found his way to the scullery, and gave her, trembling with fear, in charge to the head maid, with the queen's message.

As it was evident that the queen had no favor for her, the servants did as they pleased with her, and often treated her harshly. Not one amongst them liked her, nor was it any wonder, seeing that, with every step she took from the wise woman's house, she had grown more contemptible, for she had grown more conceited. Every civil answer given her, she attributed to the impression she made, not to the desire to get rid of her; and every kindness, to approbation of her looks and speech, instead of friendliness to a lonely child. Hence by this time she was twice as odious as before; for whoever has had such severe treatment as the wise woman gave her, and is not the better for it, always grows worse than before. They drove her about, boxed her ears on the smallest provocation, laid every thing to her charge, called her all manner of contemptuous names, jeered and scoffed at her awkwardnesses, and made her life so miserable that she was in a fair way to forget every thing she had learned, and know nothing but how to clean saucepans and kettles.

They would not have been so hard upon her, however, but for her irritating behavior. She dared not refuse to do as she was told, but she obeyed now with a pursed-up mouth, and now with a contemptuous smile. The only think that sustained her was her constant contriving how to get out of the painful position in which she found herself. There is but one true way, however, of getting out of any position we may be in, and that is, to do the work of it so well that we grow fit for a better: I need not say this was not the plan upon which Agnes was cunning enough to fix.

She had soon learned from the talk around her the reason of the proclamation which had brought her hither.

"Was the lost princess so very beautiful?" she said one day to the youngest of her fellow servants.

"Beautiful!" screamed the maid; "she was just the ugliest little toad you ever set eyes upon."

"What was she like?" asked Agnes.

"She was about your size, and quite as ugly, only not in the same way; for she had red cheeks, and a cocked little nose, and the biggest, ugliest mouth you ever saw."

Agnes fell a-thinking.

"Is there a picture of her anywhere in the palace?" she asked.

"How should I know? You can ask a housemaid."

Agnes soon learned that there was one, and contrived to get a peep of it. Then she was certain of what she had suspected from the description of her, namely, that she was the same she had seen in the picture at the wise woman's house. The conclusion followed, that the lost princess must be staying with her father and mother, for assuredly in the picture she wore one of her frocks.

She went to the head scullion, and with a humble manner, but proud heart, begged her to procure for her the favor of a word with the queen.

"A likely thing indeed!" was the answer, accompanied by a resounding box on the ear.

She tried the head cook next, but with no better success, and so was driven to her meditations again, the result of which was that she began to drop hints that she knew something about the princess. This came at length to the queen's ears, and she sent for her.

Absorbed in her own selfish ambitions, Agnes never thought of the risk to which she was about to expose her parents, but told the queen that in her wanderings she had caught sight of just such a lovely creature as she described the princess, only dressed like a peasant—saying, that, if the king would permit her to go and look for her, she had little doubt of bringing her back safe and sound within a few weeks.

But although she spoke the truth, she had such a look of cunning on her pinched face, that the queen could not possibly trust her, but believed that she made the proposal merely to get away, and have money given her for her journey. Still there was a chance, and she would not say anything until she had consulted the king.

Then they had Agnes up before the lord chancellor, who, after much questioning of her, arrived at last, he thought, at some notion of the part of the country described by her—that was, if she spoke the truth, which, from her looks and behavior, he also considered entirely doubtful. Thereupon she was ordered back to the kitchen, and a band of soldiers, under a clever lawyer, sent out to search every foot of the supposed region. They were commanded not to return until they brought with them, bound hand and foot, such a shepherd pair as that of which they received a full description.

And now Agnes was worse off than before. For to her other miseries was added the fear of what would befall her when it was discovered that the persons of whom they were in quest, and whom she was certain they must find, were her own father and mother.

By this time the king and queen were so tired of seeing lost children, genuine or pretended—for they cared for no child any longer than there seemed a chance of its turning out their child—that with this new hope, which, however poor and vague at first, soon began to grow upon such imaginations as they had, they commanded the proclamation to be taken down from the palace gates, and directed the various sentries to admit no child whatever, lost or found, be the reason or pretence what it might, until further orders.

"I'm sick of children!" said the king to his secretary, as he finished dictating the direction.

XI.

AFTER Prince was gone, the princess, by degrees, fell back into some of her bad old ways, from which only the presence of the dog, not her own betterment, had kept her. She never grew nearly so selfish again, but she began to let her angry old self lift up its head once more, until by and by she grew so bad that the shepherdess declared she should not stop in the house a day longer, for she was quite unendurable.

"It is all very well for you, husband," she said, "for you haven't her all day about you, and only see the best of her. But if you have her in work instead of play hours, you would like her no better than I do. And then it's not her ugly passions only, but when she's in one of her tantrums, it's impossible to get any work out of her. At such times she's just as obstinate as—as—as"—

She was going to say "as Agnes," but the feelings of a mother overcame her, and she could not utter the words.

"In fact," she said instead, "she makes my life miserable."

The shepherd felt he had no right to tell his wife she must submit to have her life made miserable, and therefore, although he was really much attached to Rosamond, he would not interfere; and the shepherdess told her she must look out for another place.

The princess was, however, this much better than before, even in respect of her passions, that they were not quite so bad, and after one was over, she was really ashamed of it. But not once, ever since the departure of Prince, had she tried to check the rush of the evil temper when it came upon her. She hated it when she was out of it, and that was something; but while she was in it, she went full swing with it wherever the prince of the power of it pleased to carry her. Nor was this all: although she might by this time have known well enough that as soon as she was out of it she was certain to be ashamed of it, she would yet justify it to herself with twenty different arguments that looked very poor indeed afterwards, if then she had even remembered them.

She was not sorry to leave the shepherd's cottage, for she felt certain of soon finding her way back to her father and mother; and she would, indeed, have set out long before, but that her foot had somehow got hurt when Prince gave her his last admonition, and she had never since been able for long walks, which she sometimes blamed as the cause of her temper growing worse. But if people are good-tempered only when they are comfortable, what thanks have they? Her foot was now much better; and as soon as the shepherdess had thus spoken, she resolved to set out at once, and work or beg her way home. At the moment she was quite unmindful of what she owed the good people, and, indeed, was as yet incapable of understanding a tenth part of her obligation to them. So she bade them goodbye without a tear, and limped her way down the hill, leaving the shepherdess weeping, and the shepherd looking very grave.

When she reached the valley she followed the course of the stream, knowing only that it would lead her away from the hill where the sheep fed, into richer lands where were farms and cattle. Rounding one of the roots of the hill she saw before her a poor woman walking slowly along the road with a burden of heather upon her back, and presently passed her, but had gone only a few paces farther when she heard her calling after her in a kind old voice: "Your shoe-tie is loose, my child."

But Rosamond was growing tired, for her foot had become painful, and so she was cross, and neither returned answer, nor paid heed to the warning. For when we are cross, all our other faults grow busy, and poke up their ugly heads like maggots, and the princess's old dislike to doing anything that came to her with the least air of advice about it returned in full force.

"My child," said the woman again, "if you don't fasten your shoe-tie, it will make you fall."

"Mind your own business," said Rosamond, without even turning her head, and had not gone more than three steps when she fell flat on her face on the path. She tried to get up, but the effort forced from her a scream, for she had sprained the ankle of the foot that was already lame.

The old woman was by her side instantly.

"Where are your hurt, child?" she asked, throwing down her

burden and kneeling beside her.

"Go away," screamed Rosamond. "You made me fall, you bad woman!"

The woman made no reply, but began to feel her joints, and soon discovered the sprain. Then, in spite of Rosamond's abuse, and the violent pushes and even kicks she gave her, she took the hurt ankle in her hands, and stroked and pressed it, gently kneading it, as it were, with her thumbs, as if coaxing every particle of muscles into its right place. Nor had she done so long before Rosamond lay still. At length she ceased, and said:

"Now, my child, you may get up."

"I can't get up, and I'm not your child," cried Rosamond. "Go away."

Without another word the woman left her, took up her burden, and continued her journey.

In a little while Rosamond tried to get up, and not only succeeded, but found she could walk, and, indeed, presently discovered that her ankle and foot also were now perfectly well.

"I wasn't much hurt after all," she said to herself, nor sent a single grateful thought after the poor woman, whom she speedily passed once more upon the road without even a greeting.

Late in the afternoon she came to a spot where the path divided into two, and was taking the one she liked the looks of better, when she started at the sound of the poor woman's voice, whom she thought she had left far behind, again calling her. She looked round, and there she was, toiling under her load of heather as before.

"You are taking the wrong turn, child," she cried.

"How can you tell that?" said Rosamond. "You know nothing about where I want to go."

"I know that road will take you where you don't want to go," said the woman.

"I shall know when I get there, then," returned Rosamond, "and no thanks to you."

She set off running. The woman took the other path, and was soon out of sight.

By and by, Rosamond found herself in the midst of a peat-moss—a flat lonely, dismal, black country. She thought however, that the road would soon lead her across to the other side of it among the farms, and went on without anxiety. But the stream, which had hitherto been her guide, had now vanished; and when it began to grow dark, Rosamond found that she could no longer distinguish the track. She turned, therefore, but only to find that the same darkness covered it behind as well as before. Still she made the attempt to go back by keeping as direct a line as she could, for the path was straight as an arrow. But she could not see enough even to start her in a line, and she had not gone far before she found herself hemmed in, apparently on every side, by ditches and pools of black, dismal, slimy water. And now it was so dark that she could see nothing more than the gleam of a bit of clear sky now and then in the water. Again and again she stepped knee-deep in black mud, and once tumbled down in the shallow edge of a terrible pool; after which she gave up the attempt to escape the meshes of the watery net, stood still, and began to cry bitterly, despairingly. She saw now that her unreasonable anger had made her foolish as well as rude, and felt that she was justly punished for her wickedness to the poor woman who had been so friendly to her. What would Prince think of her, if he knew? She cast herself on the ground, hungry, and cold, and weary.

Presently, she thought she saw long creatures come heaving out of the black pools. A toad jumped upon her, and she shrieked, and sprang to her feet, and would have run away headlong, when she spied in the distance a faint glimmer. She thought it was a Will-o'-the-wisp. What could he be after? Was he looking for her? She dared not run, lest he should see and pounce upon her. The light came nearer, and grew brighter and larger. Plainly, the little fiend was looking for her—he would torment her. After many twistings and turnings among the pools, it came straight towards her, and she would have shrieked, but that terror made her dumb.

It came nearer and nearer, and lo! It was borne by a dark figure, with a burden on its back: it was the poor woman, and no demon, that was looking for her! She gave a scream of joy, fell down weeping at her feet, and clasped her knees. Then the poor woman threw away her burden, laid down her lantern, took the princess up in her arms, folded her cloak around her, and having taken up her lantern again, carried her slowly and carefully through the midst of the black pools, winding hither and thither. All night long she carried her thus, slowly and wearily, until at length the darkness grew a little thinner, an uncertain hint of light came from the east, and the poor woman, stopping on the brow of a little hill, opened her cloak, and set the princess down.

"I can carry you no farther," she said. "Sit there on the grass till the light comes. I will stand here by you."

Rosamond had been asleep. Now she rubbed her eyes and looked, but it was too dark to see anything more than that there was a sky over her head. Slowly the light grew, until she could see the form of the poor woman standing in front of her; and as it went on growing, she began to think she had seen her somewhere before, till all at once she thought of the wise woman, and saw it must be she. Then she was so ashamed that she bent down her head, and could look at her no longer. But the poor woman spoke, and the voice was that of the wise woman, and every word went deep into the heart of the princess.

"Rosamond," she said, "all this time, ever since I carried you from your father's palace, I have been doing what I could to make you a lovely creature: ask yourself how far I have succeeded."

All her past story, since she found herself first under the wise woman's cloak, arose, and glided past the inner eyes of the princess, and she saw, and in a measure understood it all. But she sat with her eyes on the ground, and made no sign.

Then said the wise woman:

"Below there is the forest which surrounds my house. I am going home. If you please to come there to me, I will help you, in a way I could not do now, to be good and lovely. I will wait you there all day, but if you start at once, you may be there long before noon. I shall have your breakfast waiting for you. One thing more: the beasts have not yet all gone home to their holes; but I give you my word, not one will touch you so long as you keep coming nearer to my house."

She ceased. Rosamond sat waiting to hear something more; but nothing came. She looked up; she was alone.

Alone once more! Always being left alone, because she would not yield to what was right! Oh, how safe she had felt under the wise woman's cloak! She had indeed been good to her, and she had in return behaved like one of the hyenas of the awful wood! What a wonderful house it was she lived in! And again all her own story came up into her brain from her repentant heart.

"Why didn't she take me with her?" she said. "I would have gone gladly." And she wept. But her own conscience told her that in the very middle of her shame and desire to be good, she had returned no answer to the words of the wise woman; she had sat like a tree-stump, and done nothing. She tried to say there was nothing to be done; but she knew at once that she could have told the wise woman she had been very wicked, and asked her to take her with her. Now there was nothing to be done.

"Nothing to be done!" said her conscience. "Cannot you rise, and walk down the hill, and through the wood?"

"But the wild beasts!"

"There it is! You don't believe the wise woman yet! Did she not tell you the beasts would not touch you?"

"But they are so horrid!"

"Yes, they are; but it would be far better to be eaten up alive by them than live on—such a worthless creature as you are. Why, you're not fit to be thought about by any but bad, ugly creatures."

This was how her Self talked to her.

XII.

ALL at once she jumped to her feet, and ran at full speed down the hill and into the wood. She heard howlings and yellings on all sides of her, but she ran straight on, as near as she could judge. Her spirits rose as she ran. Suddenly she saw before her, in the dusk of the thick wood, a group of some dozen wolves and hyenas, standing all together right in her way, with their green eyes fixed upon her staring. She faltered one step, then bethought her of what the wise woman had promised, and keeping straight on, dashed right into the middle of them. They fled howling, as if she had struck them with fire. She was no more afraid after that, and ere the sun was up she was out of the wood and upon the heath, which no bad thing could step upon and live. With the first peep of the sun above the horizon, she saw the little cottage before her, and ran as fast as she could run towards it. When she came near it, she saw that the door was open, and ran straight into the outstretched arms of the wise woman.

The wise woman kissed her and stroked her hair, set her down by the fire, and gave her a bowl of bread and milk.

When she had eaten it she drew her before her where she sat, and spoke to her thus:

"Rosamond, if you would be a blessed creature instead of a mere wretch, you must submit to be tried."

"Is that something terrible?" asked the princess, turning white.

"No, my child; but it is something very difficult to come well out of. Nobody who has not been tried knows how difficult it is; but whoever has come well out of it, and those who do not overcome never do come out of it, always looks back with horror, not on what she has come through, but on the very idea of the possibility of having failed, and being still the same miserable creature as before."

"You will tell me what it is before it begins?" said the princess.

"I will not tell you exactly. But I will tell you some things to help you. One great danger is that perhaps you will think you are in it before it has really begun, and say to yourself, 'Oh! this is really nothing to me. It may be a trial to some, but for me I am sure it is not worth mentioning.' And then, before you know, it will be upon you, and you will fail utterly and shamefully."

"I will be very, very careful," said the princess. "Only don't let me be frightened."

"You shall not be frightened, except it be your own doing. You are already a brave girl, and there is no occasion to try you more that way. I saw how you rushed into the middle of the ugly creatures; and as they ran from you, so will all kinds of evil things, as long as you keep them outside of you, and do not open the cottage of your heart to let them in. I will tell you something more about what you will have to go through.

"Nobody can be a real princess—do not imagine you have yet been anything more than a mock one—until she is a princess over herself, that is, until, when she finds herself unwilling to do the thing that is right, she makes herself do it. So long as any mood she is in makes her do the thing she will be sorry for when that mood is over, she is a slave, and no princess. A princess is able to do what is right even should she unhappily be in a mood that would make another unable to do it. For instance, if you should be cross and angry, you are not a whit the less bound to be just, yes, kind even—a thing most difficult in such a mood—though ease itself in a good mood, loving and sweet. Whoever does what she is bound to do, be she the dirtiest little girl in the street, is a princess, worshipful, honorable. Nay, more; her might goes farther than she could send it, for if she act so, the evil mood will wither and die, and leave her loving and clean. Do you understand me, dear Rosamond?"

As she spoke, the wise woman laid her hand on her head and looked—oh, so lovingly!—into her eyes.

"I am not sure," said the princess, humbly.

"Perhaps you will understand me better if I say it just comes to this, that you must *not do* what is wrong, however much you are inclined to do it and you must *do* what is right, however much you are disinclined to do it."

"I understand that," said the princess.

"I am going, then, to put you in one of the mood-chambers of which I have many in the house. Its mood will come upon you, and you will have to deal with it."

She rose and took her by the hand. The princess trembled a little, but never thought of resisting.

The wise woman led her into the great hall with the pictures, and through a door at the farther end, opening upon another large hall, which was circular, and had doors close to each other all round it. Of these she opened one, pushed the princess gently in, and closed it behind her.

The princess found herself in her old nursery. Her little white rabbit came to meet her in a lumping canter as if his back were going to tumble over his head. Her nurse, in her rocking chair by the chimney corner, sat just as she had used. The fire burned brightly, and on the table were many of her wonderful toys, on which, however, she now looked with some contempt. Her nurse did not seem at all surprised to see her, anymore than if the princess had but just gone from the room and returned again.

"Oh! How different I am from what I used to be!" thought the princess to herself, looking from her toys to her nurse. "The wise woman has done me so much good already! I will go and see mamma at once, and tell her I am very glad to be at home again, and very sorry I was so naughty."

She went towards the door.

"Your queen-mamma, princess, cannot see you now," said her nurse.

"I have yet to learn that it is my part to take orders from a servant," said the princess with temper and dignity.

"I beg your pardon, princess," returned her nurse, politely; "but it is my duty to tell you that your queen-mamma is at this moment engaged. She is alone with her most intimate friend, the Princess of the Frozen Regions."

"I shall see for myself," returned the princess, bridling, and walked to the door.

Now little bunny, leap-frogging near the door, happened that moment to get about her feet, just as she was going to open it, so that she tripped and fell against it, striking her forehead a good blow. She caught up the rabbit in a rage, and, crying, "It is all your fault you ugly old wretch!" threw it with violence in her nurse's face.

Her nurse caught the rabbit, and held it to her face, as if seeking to sooth its fright. But the rabbit looked very limp and odd, and, to her amazement Rosamond presently saw that the thing was no rabbit but a pocket-handkerchief. The next moment she removed it from her face, and Rosamond beheld—not her nurse, but the wise woman—standing on her own hearth, while she herself stood by the door leading from the cottage into the hall.

"First trial a failure," said the wise woman quietly.

Overcome with shame, Rosamond ran to her, fell down on her knees, and hid her face in her dress.

"Need I say any thing?" said the wise woman, stroking her hair.

"No, no," cried the princess. "I am horrid."

"You know now the kind of thing you have to meet: are you ready to try again?"

"May I try again?" cried the princess, jumping up. "I'm ready. I do not think I shall fail this time."

"The trial will be harder."

Rosamond drew in her breath, and set her teeth. The wise woman looked at her pitifully, but took her by the hand, led her to the round hall, opened the same door, and closed it after her.

The princess expected to find herself again in the nursery, but in the wise woman's house no one ever has the same trial twice. She was in a beautiful garden, full of blossoming trees and the loveliest roses and lilies. A lake was in the middle of it, with a tiny boat. So delightful was it that Rosamond forgot all about how or why she had come there, and lost herself in the joy of the flowers and the trees and the water. Presently came the shout of a child, merry and glad, and from a clump of tulip trees rushed a lovely little boy, with his arms stretched out to her. She was charmed at the sight, ran to meet him, caught him up in her arms, kissed him, and could hardly let him go again. But the moment she set him down he ran from her towards the lake, looking back as he ran, and crying "Come, come."

She followed. He made straight for the boat, clambered into it, and held out his hand to help her in. Then he caught up the little boat-hook, and pushed away from the shore: there was a great white flower floating a few yards off, and that was the little fellow's goal. But, alas! No sooner had Rosamond caught sight of it, huge and glowing as a harvest moon, than she felt a great desire to have it herself. The boy, however, was in the bow of the boat, and caught it first. It had a long stem, reaching down to the bottom of the water, and for a moment he tugged at it in vain, but at last it gave way so suddenly, that he tumbled back with the flower into the bottom of the boat. Then Rosamond, almost wild at the danger it was in as he struggled to rise, hurried to save it, but somehow between them it came in pieces, and all its petals of fretted silver were scattered about the boat. When the boy got up, and saw the ruin his companion had occasioned, he burst into tears, and having the long stalk of the flower still in his hand, struck her with it across the face. It did not hurt her much, for he was a very little fellow, but it was wet and slimy. She tumbled rather than rushed at him, seized him in her arms, tore him from his frightened grasp, and flung him into the water. His head struck on the boat as he fell, and he sank at once to the bottom, where he lay looking up at her with white face and open eyes.

The moment she saw the consequences of her deed she was filled with horrible dismay. She tried hard to reach down to him through the water, but it was far deeper than it looked, and she could not. Neither could she get her eyes to leave the white face: its eyes fascinated and fixed hers; and there she lay leaning over the boat and staring at the death she had made. But a voice crying, "Ally! Ally!" shot to her heart, and springing to her feet she saw a lovely lady come running down the grass to the brink of the water with her hair flying about her head.

"Where is my Ally?" she shrieked.

But Rosamond could not answer, and only stared at the lady, as she had before stared at her drowned boy.

Then the lady caught sight of the dead thing at the bottom of the water, and rushed in, and, plunging down, struggled and groped until she reached it. Then she rose and stood up with the dead body of her little son in her arms, his head hanging back, and the water streaming from him.

"See what you have made of him, Rosamond!" she said, holding the body out to her; "and this is your second trial, and also a failure."

The dead child melted away from her arms, and there she stood, the wise woman, on her own hearth, while Rosamond found herself beside the little well on the floor of the cottage, with one arm wet up to the shoulder. She threw herself on the heather-bed and wept from relief and vexation both.

The wise woman walked out of the cottage, shut the door, and left her alone. Rosamond was sobbing, so that she did not hear her go. When at length she looked up, and saw that the wise woman was gone, her misery returned afresh and tenfold, and she wept and wailed. The hours passed, the shadows of evening began to fall, and the wise woman entered.

XIII.

SHE went straight to the bed, and taking Rosamond in her arms, sat down with her by the fire.

"My poor child!" she said. "Two terrible failures! And the more the harder! They get stronger and stronger. What is to be done?"

"Couldn't you help me?" said Rosamond piteously.

"Perhaps I could, now you ask me," answered the wise woman. "When you are ready to try again, we shall see."

"I am very tired of myself," said the princess. "But I can't rest till I try again."

"That is the only way to get rid of your weary, shadowy self, and find your strong, true self. Come, my child; I will help you all I can, for now I *can* help you."

Yet again she led her to the same door, and seemed to the princess to send her yet again alone into the room. She was in a forest, a place half wild, half tended. The trees were grand, and full of the loveliest birds, of all glowing, gleaming and radiant colors, which, unlike the brilliant birds we know in our world, sang deliciously, every one according to his color. The trees were not at all crowded, but their leaves were so thick, and their boughs spread so far, that it was only here and there a sunbeam could get straight through. All the gentle creatures of a forest were there, but no creatures that killed, not even a weasel to kill the rabbits, or a beetle to eat the snails out of their striped shells. As to the butterflies, words would but wrong them if they tried to tell how gorgeous they were. The princess's delight was so great that she neither laughed nor ran, but walked about with a solemn countenance and stately step.

"But where are the flowers?" she said to herself at length.

They were nowhere. Neither on the high trees, nor on the few shrubs that grew here and there amongst them, were there any blossoms; and in the grass that grew everywhere there was not a single flower to be seen.

"Ah, well!" said Rosamond again to herself; "where all the birds and butterflies are living flowers, we can do without the other sort."

Still she could not help feeling that flowers were wanted to make the beauty of the forest complete.

Suddenly she came out on a little open glade; and there, on the root of a great oak, sat the loveliest little girl, with her lap full of flowers of all colors, but of such kinds as Rosamond had never before seen. She was playing with them—burying her hands in them, tumbling them about, and every now and then picking one from the rest, and throwing it away. All the time she never smiled, except with her eyes, which were as full as they could hold of the laughter of the spirit—a laughter which in this world is never heard, only sets the eyes alight with a liquid shining. Rosamond drew nearer, for the wonderful creature would have drawn a tiger to her side, and tamed him on the way. A few yards from her, she came upon one of her cast-away flowers and stooped to pick it up, as well she might where none grew save in her own longing. But to her amazement she found, instead of a flower thrown away to wither, one fast rooted and quite at home. She left it, and went to another; but it also was fast in the soil, and growing comfortably in the warm grass. What could it mean? One after another she tried, until at length she was satisfied that it was the same with every flower the little girl threw from her lap.

She watched then until she saw her throw one, and instantly bounded to the spot. But the flower had been quicker than she: there it grew, fast fixed in the earth, and, she thought looked at her roguishly. Something evil moved in her, and she plucked it.

"Don't! don't!" cried the child. "My flowers cannot live in your hands."

Rosamond looked at the flower. It was withered already. She threw it from her, offended. The child rose, with difficulty keeping her lapful together, picked it up, carried it back, sat down again, spoke to it, kissed it, sang to it—oh, such a sweet childish little song!—The princess never could recall a word of it—and threw it away. Up rose its little head, and there it was, busy growing again!

Rosamond's bad temper soon gave way: the beauty and sweetness of the child had overcome it; and, anxious to make friends with her, she drew near, and said:

"Won't you give me a little flower, please, you beautiful child?"

"There they are; they are all for you," answered the child, pointing with her outstretched arm and forefinger all round.

"But you told me, a minute ago, not to touch them."

"Yes, indeed, I did."

"They can't be mine, if I'm not to touch them."

"If, to call them yours, you must kill them, then they are not yours, and never, never can be yours. They are nobody's when they are dead."

"But you don't kill them."

"I don't pull them; I throw them away. I live them."

"How is it that you make them grow?"

"I say, 'You darling!' and throw it away and there it is."

"Where do you get them?"

"In my lap."

"I wish you would let me throw one away."

"Have you got any in your lap? Let me see."

"No; I have none."

"Then you can't throw one away, if you haven't got one."

"You are mocking me!" cried the princess.

"I am not mocking you," said the child, looking her full in the face, with reproach in her large blue eyes.

"Oh, that's where the flowers come from!" said the princess to herself, the moment she saw them, hardly knowing what she meant

Then the child rose as if hurt, and quickly threw away all the flowers she had in her lap, but one by one, and without any sign of anger. When they were all gone, she stood a moment, and then, in a kind of chanting cry, called, two or three times, "Peggy! Peggy! Peggy!"

A low, glad cry, like the whinny of a horse, answered, and, presently, out of the wood on the opposite side of the glade, came gently trotting the loveliest little snow-white pony, with great shining blue wings, half lifted from his shoulders. Straight towards the little girl, neither hurrying nor lingering, he trotted with light elastic tread.

Rosamond's love for animals broke into a perfect passion of delight at the vision. She rushed to meet the pony with such haste, that, although clearly the best trained animal under the sun, he started back, plunged, reared, and struck out with his fore-feet ere he had time to observe what sort of a creature it was that had so startled him. When he perceived it was a little girl, he dropped instantly upon all fours, and content with avoiding her, resumed his quiet trot in the direction of his mistress. Rosamond stood gazing after him in miserable disappointment.

When he reached the child, he laid his head on her shoulder, and she put her arm up round his neck; and after she had talked to him a little, he turned and came trotting back to the princess.

Almost beside herself with joy, she began caressing him in the rough way which, notwithstanding her love for them, she was in the habit of using with animals; and she was not gentle enough, in herself even, to see that he did not like it and was only putting up with it for the sake of his mistress. But when, that she might jump upon his back, she laid hold of one of his wings and ruffled some of the blue feathers, he wheeled suddenly about gave his long tail a sharp whisk which threw her flat on the grass, and, trotting back to his mistress, bent down his head before her as if asking excuse for ridding himself of the unbearable.

The princess was furious. She had forgotten all her past life up to the time when she first saw the child her: beauty had made her forget, and yet she was now on the very borders of hating her. What she might have done, or rather tried to do, had not Peggy's tail struck her down with such force that for a moment she could not rise, I cannot tell.

But while she lay half stunned, her eyes fell on a little flower just under them. It stared up in her face like the living thing it was, and she could not take her eyes off its face. It was like a primrose trying to express doubt instead of confidence. It seemed to put her half in mind of something, and she felt as if shame were coming. She put out her hand to pluck it; but the moment her fingers touched it, the flower withered up, and hung as dead on its stalks as if a flame of fire had passed over it.

Then a shudder thrilled through the heart of the princess, and she thought with herself, saying: "What sort of a creature am I that the flowers wither when I touch them, and the ponies despise me with their tails? What a wretched, coarse, ill-bred creature I must be! There is that lovely child given life instead of death to the flowers, and a moment ago I was hating her! I am made horrid, and I shall be horrid, and I hate myself, and yet I can't help being myself!"

She heard the sound of galloping feet, and there was the pony, with the child seated betwixt his wings, coming straight on at full speed for where she lay.

"I don't care," she said. "They may trample me under their feet if they like. I am tired and sick of myself—a creature at whose touch the flowers wither!"

On came the winged pony. But while yet some distance off, he gave a great bound, spread out his living sails of blue, rose yards and yards above her in the air, and alighted as gently as a bird, just a few feet on the other side of her. The child slipped down and came and knelt over her.

"Did my pony hurt you?" she said. "I am so sorry!"

"Yes, he hurt me," answered the princess, "but not more than I deserved, for I took liberties with him, and he did not like it."

"Oh, you dear!" said the little girl. "I love you for talking so of my Peggy. He is a good pony, though a little playful sometimes. Would you like a ride upon him?"

"You darling beauty!" cried Rosamond, sobbing. "I do love you so, you are so good. How did you become so sweet?"

"Would you like to ride my pony?" repeated the child, with a heavenly smile in her eyes.

"No, no; he is fit only for you. My clumsy body would hurt him," said Rosamond.

"You don't mind me having such a pony?" said the child.

"What! Mind it?" cried Rosamond, almost indignantly. Then remembering certain thoughts that had but a few moments before passed through her mind, she looked on the ground and was silent.

"You don't mind it then?" repeated the child.

"I am very glad there is such a you and such a pony, and that such a you has got such a pony," said Rosamond, still looking on the ground. "But I do wish the flowers would not die when I touch them. I was cross to see you make them grow, but now I should be content if only I did not make them wither."

As she spoke, she stroked the little girl's bare feet, which were by her, half buried in the soft moss, and as she ended she laid her cheek on them and kissed them.

"Dear princess!" said the little girl, "the flowers will not always wither at your touch. Try now—only do not pluck it. Flowers ought never to be plucked except to give away. Touch it gently."

A silvery flower, something like a snowdrop, grew just within her reach. Timidly she stretched out her hand and touched it. The flower trembled, but neither shrank nor withered.

"Touch it again," said the child.

It changed color a little, and Rosamond fancied it grew larger.

"Touch it again," said the child.

It opened and grew until it was as large as a narcissus, and changed and deepened in color till it was a red glowing gold.

Rosamond gazed motionless. When the transfiguration of the flower was perfected, she sprang to her feet with clasped hands, but for very ecstasy of joy stood speechless, gazing at the child.

"Did you never see me before, Rosamond?" she asked.

"No, never," answered the princess. "I never saw anything half so lovely."

"Look at me," said the child.

And as Rosamond looked, the child began, like the flower, to grow larger. Quickly through every gradation of growth she passed, until she stood before her a woman perfectly beautiful, neither old nor young; for hers was the old age of everlasting youth.

Rosamond was utterly enchanted, and stood gazing without word or movement until she could endure no more delight. Then her mind collapsed to the thought—had the pony grown too? She glanced round. There was no pony, no grass, no flowers, no bright-birded forest—but the cottage of the wise woman—and before her, on the hearth of it the goddess-child, the only thing unchanged.

She gasped with astonishment.

"You must set out for your father's palace immediately," said the lady.

"But where is the wise woman?" asked Rosamond, looking all about.

"Here," said the lady.

And Rosamond, looking again, saw the wise woman, folded as usual in her long dark cloak.

"And it was you all the time?" she cried in delight and kneeled before her, burying her face in her garments.

"It always is me, all the time," said the wise woman, smiling.

"But which is the real you?" asked Rosamond; "This or that?"

"Or a thousand others?" returned the wise woman. "But the one you have just seen is the likest to the real me that you are able to see just yet—but—And that me you could not have seen a little while ago. But, my darling child," she went on, lifting her up and clasping her to her bosom, "you must not think, because you have seen me once, that therefore you are capable of seeing me at all times. No; there are many things in you yet that must be changed before that can be. Now, however, you will seek me. Every time you feel you want me, that is a sign I am wanting you. There are yet many rooms in my house you may have to go through; but when you need no more of them, then you will be able to throw flowers like the little girl you saw in the forest."

The princess gave a sigh.

"Do you think," the wise woman went on, "that the things you have seen in my house are mere empty shows. You do not know, you cannot yet think, how living and true they are. Now you must go."

She led her once more into the great hall, and there showed her the picture of her father's capital, and his palace with the brazen gates.

"There is your home," she said. "Go to it."

The princess understood, and a flush of shame rose to her forehead. She turned to the wise woman and said:

"Will you forgive *all* my naughtiness, and *all* the trouble I have given you?"

"If I had not forgiven you, I would never have taken the trouble to punish you. If I had not loved you, do you think I would have carried you away in my cloak?"

"How could you love such an ugly, ill-tempered, rude, hateful little wretch?"

"I saw, through it all, what you were going to be," said the wise woman, kissing her. "But remember you have yet only *begun* to be what I saw."

"I will try to remember," said the princess, holding her cloak, and looking up in her face.

"Go, then," said the wise woman.

Rosamond turned away on the instant, ran to the picture, stepped over the frame of it, heard a door close gently, gave one glance back, saw behind her the loveliest palace-front of alabaster, gleaming in the pale-yellow light of an early summer-morning, looked again to the eastward, saw the faint outline of her father's city against the sky, and ran off to reach it.

It looked much further off now than when it seemed a picture, but the sun was not yet up, and she had the whole of a summer day before her.

XIV.

THE soldiers sent out by the king, had no great difficulty in finding Agnes's father and mother, of whom they demanded if they knew anything of such a young princess as they described. The honest pair told them the truth in every point—that, having lost their own child and found another, they had taken her home, and treated her as their own; that she had indeed called herself a princess, but they had not believed her, because she did not look like one; that, even if they had, they did not know how they could have done differently, seeing they were poor people who could not afford to keep any idle person about the place; that they had done their best to teach her good ways, and had not parted with her until her bad temper rendered it impossible to put up with her any longer; that, as to the king's proclamation, they heard little of the world's news on their lonely hill, and it had never reached them; that if it had, they did not know how either of them could have gone such a distance from home, and left their sheep or their cottage, one or the other, uncared for.

"You must learn, then, how both of you can go, and your sheep must take care of your cottage," said the lawyer, and commanded the soldier to bind them hand and foot.

Heedless of their entreaties to be spared such an indignity, the soldiers obeyed, bore them to a cart, and set out for the king's palace, leaving the cottage door open, the fire burning, the pot of potatoes boiling upon it, the sheep scattered over the hill, and the dogs not knowing what to do.

Hardly were they gone, however, before the wise woman walked up, with Prince behind her, peeped into the cottage, locked the door, put the key in her pocket, and then walked away up the hill. In a few minutes there arose a great battle between Prince and the dog which filled his former place—a well-meaning but dull fellow, who could fight better than feed. Prince was not long in showing him that he was meant for his master, and then, by his effort, and directions to the other dogs, the sheep were soon gathered again and out of danger from foxes and bad dogs. As soon as this was done, the wise woman left them in charge of Prince, while she went to the next farm to arrange for the folding of the sheep and the feeding of the dogs.

When the soldiers reached the palace, they were ordered to carry their prisoners at once into the presence of the king and queen, in the throne room. Their two thrones stood upon a high dais at one end, and on the floor at the foot of the dais, the soldiers laid their helpless prisoners. The queen commanded that they should be unbound, and ordered them to stand up. They obeyed with the dignity of insulted innocence, and their bearing offended their foolish majesties.

Meantime the princess, after a long day's journey, arrived at the palace, and walked up to the sentry at the gate.

"Stand back," said the sentry.

"I wish to go in, if you please," said the princess gently.

"Ha! ha! ha!" laughed the sentry, for he was one of those dull people who form their judgment from a person's clothes, without even looking in his eyes; and as the princess happened to be in rags, her request was amusing, and the booby thought himself quite clever for laughing at her so thoroughly.

"I am the princess," Rosamond said quietly.

"*What* princess?" bellowed the man.

"The princess Rosamond. Is there another?" she answered and asked.

But the man was so tickled at the wonderous idea of a princess in rags, that he scarcely heard what she said for laughing. As soon as he recovered a little, he proceeded to chuck the princess under the chin, saying: "You're a pretty girl, my dear, though you ain't no princess."

Rosamond drew back with dignity.

"You have spoken three untruths at once," she said. "I am *not* pretty, and I *am* a princess, and if I were dear to you, as I ought to be, you would not laugh at me because I am badly dressed, but stand aside, and let me to my father and mother."

The tone of her speech, and the rebuke she gave him, made the man look at her; and looking at her, he began to tremble inside his foolish body, and wonder whether he might not have made a mistake. He raised his hand in salute, and said: "I beg your pardon, miss, but I have express orders to admit no child whatever within the palace gates. They tell me his majesty the king says he is sick of children."

"He may well be sick of me!" thought the princess; "But it can't mean that he does not want me home again. I don't think you can very well call me a child," she said, looking the sentry full in the face.

"You ain't very big, miss," answered the soldier, "but so be you say you ain't a child, I'll take the risk. The king can only kill me, and a man must die once."

He opened the gate, stepped aside, and allowed her to pass. Had she lost her temper, as even one but the wise woman would have expected of her, he certainly would not have done so.

She ran into the palace, the door of which had been left open by the porter when he followed the soldiers and prisoners to the throne-room and bounded up the stairs to look for her father and mother. As she passed the door of the throne-room she heard an unusual noise in it, and running to the king's private entrance, over which hung a heavy curtain, she peeped past the edge of it, and saw, to her amazement, the shepherd and shepherdess standing like culprits before the king and queen, and the same moment heard the king say: "Peasants, where is the princess Rosamond?"

"Truly, sire, we do not know," answered the shepherd.

"You ought to know," said the king.

"Sire, we could keep her no longer."

"You confess, then," said the king suppressing the outbreak of the wrath that boiled up in him, "that you turned her out of your house."

For the king had been informed by a swift messenger of all that had passed long before the arrival of the prisoners.

"We did, sire; but not only could we keep her no longer, but we knew not that she was the princess."

"You ought to have known, the moment you cast your eyes upon her," said the king. "Any one who does not know a princess the moment he sees her, ought to have his eyes put out."

"Indeed he ought," said the queen.

To this they returned no answer, for they had none ready.

"Why did you not bring her at once to the palace," pursued the king, "whether you knew her to be a princess or not? My proclamation left nothing to your judgment. It said *every child*."

"We heard nothing of the proclamation, sire."

"You ought to have heard," said the king. "It is enough that I make proclamations; it is for you to read them. Are they not written in letters of gold upon the brazen gates of this palace?"

"A poor shepherd, your majesty—how often must he leave his flock, and go hundreds of miles to look whether there may not be something in letters of gold upon the brazen gates? We did not know that your majesty had made a proclamation, or even that the princess was lost."

"You ought to have known," said the king.

The shepherd held his peace.

"But," said the queen, taking up the word, "all this is as nothing, when I think how you misused the darling."

The only ground the queen had for saying thus, was what Agnes had told her as to how the princess was dressed; and her condition seemed to the queen so miserable, that she had imagined all sorts of oppression and cruelty.

But this was more than the shepherdess, who had not yet spoken, could bear.

"She would have been dead, and *not* buried, long ago, madam, if I had not carried her home in my two arms."

"Why does she say her *two* arms?" said the king to himself. "Has she more than two? Is there treason in that?"

"You dressed her in cast-off clothes," said the queen.

"I dressed her in my own sweet child's Sunday clothes. And this is what I get for it!" cried the shepherdess, bursting into tears.

"And what did you do with the clothes you took off her? Sell them?"

"Put them in the fire, madam. They were not fit for the poorest child in the mountains. They were so ragged that you could see her skin through them in twenty different places."

"You cruel woman, to torture a mother's feelings so!" cried the queen, and in her turn burst into tears.

"And I'm sure," sobbed the shepherdess, "I took every pains to teach her what it was right for her to know. I taught her to tidy the house, and"—

"Tidy the house?" moaned the queen. "My poor wretched

offspring!"

"And peel the potatoes, and"—

"Peel the potatoes!" cried the queen. "Oh, horror!"

"And black her master's boots," said the shepherdess.

"Black her master's boots!" shrieked the queen. "Oh, my white-handed princess! Oh, my ruined baby!"

"What I want to know," said the king, paying no heed to this maternal duel, but patting the top of his sceptre as if it had been the hilt of a sword which he was about to draw, "is, where the princess is now."

The shepherd made no answer, for he had nothing to say more than he had said already.

"You have murdered her!" shouted the king. "You shall be tortured till you confess the truth; and then you shall be tortured to death, for you are the most abominable wretches in the whole wide world."

"Who accuses me of crime?" cried the shepherd, indignant.

"I accuse you," said the king: "but you shall see, face to face, the chief witness to your villainy. Officer, bring the girl."

Silence filled the hall while they waited. The king's face was swollen with anger. The queen hid hers behind her handkerchief. The shepherd and shepherdess bent their eyes on the ground, wondering. It was with difficulty Rosamond could keep her place, but so wise had she already become that she saw it would be far better to let everything come out before she interfered.

At length the door opened, and in came the officer, followed by Agnes, looking white as death and mean as sin.

The shepherdess gave a shriek, and darted towards her with arms spread wide; the shepherd followed, but not so eagerly.

"My child! My lost darling! My Agnes!" cried the shepherdess.

"Hold them asunder," shouted the king. "Here is more villainy!

What! Have I a scullery-maid in my house born of such parents? The parents of such a child must be capable of any thing. Take all three of them to the rack. Stretch them till their joints are torn asunder, and give them no water. Away with them!"

The soldiers approached to lay hands on them. But, behold! A girl all in rags, with such a radiant countenance that it was right lovely to see, darted between, and careless of the royal presence, flung herself upon the shepherdess, crying, "Do not touch her. She is my good, kind mistress."

But the shepherdess could hear or see no one but her Agnes, and pushed her away. Then the princess turned, with the tears in her eyes, to the shepherd, and threw her arms about his neck and pulled down his head and kissed him. And the tall shepherd lifted her to his bosom and kept her there, but his eyes were fixed on his Agnes.

"What is the meaning of this?" cried the king, starting up from his throne. "How did that ragged girl get in here? Take her away with the rest. She is one of them, too."

But the princess made the shepherd set her down, and before any one could interfere she had run up the steps of the dais and then the steps of the king's throne like a squirrel, flung herself upon the king, and begun to smother him with kisses.

All stood astonished, except the three peasants, who did not even see what took place. The shepherdess kept calling to her Agnes, but she was so ashamed that she did not dare even lift her eyes to meet her mother's, and the shepherd kept gazing on her in silence. As for the king, he was so breathless and aghast with astonishment, that he was too feeble to fling the ragged child from him, as he tried to do. But she left him, and running down the steps of the one throne and up those of the other, began kissing the queen next. But the queen cried out: "Get away, you great rude child! Will nobody take her to the rack?"

Then the princess, hardly knowing what she did for joy that she had come in time, ran down the steps of the throne and the dais, and placing herself between the shepherd and shepherdess, took a hand of each, and stood looking at the king and queen.

Their faces began to change. At last they began to know her. But she was so altered—so lovelily altered, that it was no wonder they should not have known her at the first glance; but it was the fault of the pride and anger and injustice with which their hearts were filled, that they did not know her at the second.

The king gazed and the queen gazed, both half risen from their thrones, and looking as if about to tumble down upon her, if only they could be right sure that the ragged girl was their own child. A mistake would be such a dreadful thing!

"My darling!" at last shrieked the mother, a little doubtfully.

"My pet of pets?" cried the father, with an interrogative twist of tone.

Another moment, and they were halfway down the steps of the dais.

"Stop!" said the voice of command from somewhere in the hall, and, king and queen as they were, they stopped at once halfway, then drew themselves up, stared, and began to grow angry again, but durst not go farther.

The wise woman was coming slowly up through the crowd that filled the hall. Everyone made way for her. She came straight on until she stood in front of the king and queen.

"Miserable man and woman!" she said, in words they alone could hear, "I took your daughter away when she was worthy of such parents; I bring her back, and they are unworthy of her. That you did not know her when she came to you is a small wonder, for you have been blind in soul all your lives: now be blind in body until your better eyes are unsealed."

She threw her cloak open. It fell to the ground, and the radiance that flashed from her robe of snowy whiteness, from her face of awful beauty, and from her eyes that shone like pools of sunlight, smote them blind.

Rosamond saw them give a great start, shudder, waver to and fro, then sit down on the steps of the dais; and she knew they were punished, but knew not how. She rushed up to them, and catching a hand of each, said: "Father, dear father! Mother dear! I will ask the wise woman to forgive you."

"Oh, I am blind! I am blind!" they cried together.

"Dark as night! Stone blind!"

Rosamond left them, sprang down the steps, and kneeling at her feet, cried, "Oh, my lovely wise woman! Do let them see. Do open their eyes, dear, good, wise woman."

The wise woman bent down to her, and said, so that none else could hear: "I will one day. Meanwhile you must be their servant, as I have been yours. Bring them to me, and I will make them welcome."

Rosamond rose, went up the steps again to her father and mother, where they sat like statues with closed eyes, halfway from the top of the dais where stood their empty thrones, seated herself between them, took a hand of each, and was still.

All this time very few in the room saw the wise woman. The moment she threw off her cloak she vanished from the sight of almost all who were present. The woman who swept and dusted the hall and brushed the thrones, saw her, and the shepherd had a glimmering vision of her; but no one else that I know of caught a glimpse of her. The shepherdess did not see her. Nor did Agnes, but she felt the presence upon her like the heat of a furnace seven times heated.

As soon as Rosamond had taken her place between her father and mother, the wise woman lifted her cloak from the floor, and threw it again around her. Then everybody saw her, and Agnes felt as if a soft dewy cloud had come between her and the torrid rays of a vertical sun. The wise woman turned to the shepherd and shepherdess.

"For you," she said, "you are sufficiently punished by the work of your own hands. Instead of making your daughter obey you, you left her to be a slave to herself; you coaxed when you ought to have compelled; you praised when you ought to have been silent; you fondled when you ought to have punished; you threatened when you ought to have inflicted—and there she stands, the full-grown result of your foolishness! She is your crime and your punishment. Take her home with you, and live hour after hour with the pale-heated disgrace you call your daughter. What she is, the worm at her heart has begun to teach her. When life is no longer endurable, come to me."

"Madam," said the shepherd, "may I not go with you now?"

"You shall," said the wise woman.

"Husband! Husband!" cried the shepherdess, "How are we two to get home without you?"

"I will see to that," said the wise woman. "But little of home you will find it until you have come to me. The king carried you hither, and he shall carry you back. But your husband shall not go with you. He cannot now if he would."

The shepherdess looked and saw that the shepherd stood in a deep sleep. She went to him and sought to rouse him, but neither tongue nor hands were of the slightest avail.

The wise woman turned to Rosamond.

"My child," she said, "I shall never be far from you. Come to me when you will. Bring them to me."

Rosamond smiled and kissed her hand, but kept her place by her parents. They also were now in a deep sleep like the shepherd.

The wise woman took the shepherd by the hand, and led him away.

And that is all my double story. How double it is, if you care to know, you must find out. If you think it is not finished—I never knew a story that was. I could tell you a great deal more concerning them all, but I have already told more than is good for those who read but with their foreheads, and enough for those whom it has made look a little solemn, and sigh as they close the book.

THE CASTLE: A PARABLE

* * *

ON the top of a high cliff, forming part of the base of a great mountain, stood a lofty castle. When or how it was built, no man knew; nor could any one pretend to understand its architecture. Everyone who looked upon it felt that it was lordly and noble; and where one part seemed not to agree with another, the wise and modest dared not to call them incongruous, but presumed that the whole might be constructed on some higher principle of architecture than they yet understood. What helped them to this conclusion was that no one had ever seen the whole of the edifice; that, even of the portion best known, some part or other was always wrapt in thick folds of mist from the mountain; and that, when the sun shone upon this mist, the parts of the building that appeared through the vaporous veil, were strangely glorified in their indistinctness, so that they seemed to belong to some aerial abode in the land of the sunset; and the beholders could hardly tell whether they had ever seen them before, or whether they were now for the first time partially revealed.

Nor, although it was inhabited, could certain information be procured as to its internal construction. Those who dwelt in it often discovered rooms they had never entered before; yea, once or twice, whole suites of apartments, of which only dim legends had been handed down from former times. Some of them expected to find, one day, secret places, filled with treasures of wondrous jewels, amongst which they hoped to light upon Solomon's ring, which had for ages disappeared from the earth, but which had controlled the spirits, and the possession of which made a man simply what a man should be, the king of the world. Now and then, a narrow, winding stair, hitherto untrodden, would bring them forth on a new turret, whence new prospects of the circumjacent country were spread out before them. How many more of these there might be, or how much loftier, no one could tell. Nor could the foundations of the castle in the rock on which it was built be determined with the smallest approach to precision. Those of the family who had given themselves to exploring in that direction, found such a labyrinth of vaults and passages, and endless successions of down-going stairs, out of one underground space into a yet lower, that they came to the conclusion that at least the whole mountain was perforated and honeycombed in this fashion. They had a dim consciousness, too, of the presence, in those awful regions, of beings whom they could not comprehend. Once, they came upon the brink of a great black gulf, in which the eye could see nothing but darkness: they recoiled in horror; for the conviction flashed upon them that that gulf went down into the very central spaces of the earth, of which they had hitherto been wandering only in the upper crust; nay, that the seething blackness before them had relations mysterious, and beyond human comprehension, with the far-off voids of space, into which the stars dare not enter.

At the foot of the cliff whereon the castle stood, lay a deep lake, inaccessible save by a few avenues, being surrounded on all sides with precipices, which made the water look very black, although it was as pure as the night-sky. From a door in the castle, which was not to be otherwise entered, a broad flight of steps, cut in the rock, went down to the lake, and disappeared below its surface. Some thought the steps went to the very bottom of the water.

Now in this castle there dwelt a large family of brothers and sisters. They had never seen their father or mother. The younger had been educated by the elder, and these by an unseen care and ministration, about the sources of which they had, somehow or other, troubled themselves very little, for what people are accustomed to, they regard as coming from nobody; as if help and progress and joy and love were the natural crops of Chaos or old Night. But Tradition said that one day—it was utterly uncertain *when*—their father would come, and leave them no more; for he was still alive, though where he lived nobody knew. In the meantime all the rest had to obey their eldest brother, and listen to his counsels.

But almost all the family was very fond of liberty, as they called it; and liked to run up and down, hither and thither, roving about, with neither law nor order, just as they pleased. So they could not endure their brother's tyranny, as they called it. At one time they said that he was only one of themselves, and therefore they would not obey him; at another, that he was not like them, and could not understand them, and *therefore* they would not obey him. Yet sometimes, when he came and looked them full in the face, they were terrified, and dared not disobey, for he was stately, and stern, and strong. Not one of them loved him heartily, except the eldest sister, who was very beautiful and silent and whose eyes shone as if light lay somewhere deep behind them. Even she, although she loved him, thought him very hard sometimes; for when he had once said a thing plainly, he could not be persuaded to think it over again. So even she forgot him sometimes, and went her own ways, and enjoyed herself without him. Most of them regarded him as a sort of watchman, whose business it was to keep them in order; and so they were indignant and disliked him. Yet they all had a secret feeling that they ought to be subject to him; and after any particular act of disregard, none of them could think, with any peace, of the old story about the return of their father to his house. But indeed they never thought much about it, or about their father at all; for how could those who cared so little for their brother, whom they saw every day, care for their father whom they had never seen? One chief cause of complaint against him was that he interfered with their favourite studies and pursuits; whereas he only sought to make them give up trifling with earnest things, and seek for truth, and not for amusement, from the many wonders around them. He did not want them to turn to other studies, or to eschew pleasures; but, in those studies, to seek the highest things most, and other things in proportion to their true worth and nobleness. This could not fail to be distasteful to those who did not care for what was higher than they. And so matters went on for a time. They thought they could do better without their brother; and their brother knew they could not do at all without him, and tried to fulfil the charge committed into his hands.

At length, one day, for the thought seemed to strike them simultaneously, they conferred together about giving a great entertainment in their grandest rooms to any of their neighbours who chose to come, or indeed to any inhabitants of the earth or air who would visit them. They were too proud to reflect that some company might defile even the dwellers in what was undoubtedly the finest palace on the face of the earth. But what made the thing worse was that the old tradition said that these rooms were to be kept entirely for the use of the owner of the castle. And, indeed, whenever they entered them, such was the effect of their loftiness and grandeur upon their minds, that they always thought of the old story, and could not help believing it. Nor would the brother permit them to forget it now; but, appearing suddenly amongst them, when they had no expectation of being interrupted by him, he rebuked them, both for the indiscriminate nature of their imitation, and for the intention of introducing any one, not to speak of some who would doubtless make their appearance on the evening in question, into the rooms kept sacred for the use of the unknown father. But by this time their talk with each other had so excited their expectations of enjoyment, which had previously been strong enough, that anger sprung up within them at the thought of being deprived of their hopes, and they looked each other in the eyes; and the look said: "We are many, and he is one—let us get rid of him, for he is always finding fault, and thwarting us in the most innocent pleasures—as if we would wish to do anything wrong!" So without a word spoken, they rushed upon him; and although he was stronger than any of them, and struggled hard at first, yet they overcame him at last. Indeed some of them thought he yielded to their violence long before they had the mastery of him; and this very submission terrified the more tender-hearted among them. However, they bound him; carried him down many stairs, and, having remembered an iron staple in the wall of a certain vault with a thick rusty chain attached to it, they bore him thither, and made the chain fast around him. There they left him, shutting the great gnarring brazen door of the vault as they departed for the upper regions of the castle.

Now all was in a tumult of preparation. Everyone was talking of the coming festivity; but no one spoke of the deed they had done. A sudden paleness overspread the face, now of one, and now of another; but it passed away, and no one took any notice of it; they only plied the task of the moment the more energetically. Messengers were sent far and near, not to individuals or families, but publishing in all places of concourse a general invitation to any who chose to come on a certain day, and partake for certain succeeding days, of the hospitality of the dwellers in the castle. Many were the preparations immediately begun for complying with the invitation.

But the noblest of their neighbours refused to appear; not from pride, but because of the unsuitableness and carelessness of such a mode. With some of them it was an old condition in the tenure of their estates, that they should go to no one's dwelling except visited in person, and expressly solicited. Others, knowing what sorts of persons would be there, and that, from a certain physical antipathy, they could scarcely breathe in their company, made up their minds at once not to go. Yet multitudes, many of them beautiful and innocent as well as gay, resolved to appear.

Meanwhile the great rooms of the castle were got in readiness—that is, they proceeded to deface them with decorations; for there was a solemnity and stateliness about them in their ordinary condition, which was at once felt to be unsuitable for the light-hearted company so soon to move about in them with the self-same carelessness with which men walk abroad within the great heavens and hills and clouds. One day, while the workmen were busy, the eldest sister, of whom I have already spoken, happened to enter, she knew not why. Suddenly the great idea of the mighty halls dawned upon her, and filled her soul. The so-called decorations vanished from her view, and she felt as if she stood in her father's presence. She was at once elevated and humbled. As suddenly the idea faded and fled, and she beheld but the gaudy festoons and draperies and paintings which disfigured the grandeur. She wept and sped away. Now it was too late to interfere, and things must take their course. She would have been but a Cassandra-prophetess to those who saw but the pleasure before them. She had not been present when her brother was imprisoned; and indeed for some days had been so wrapt in her own business, that she had taken but little heed of anything that was going on. But they all expected her to show herself when the company was gathered; and they had applied to her for advice at various times during their operations.

At length the expected hour arrived, and the company began to assemble. It was a warm summer evening. The dark lake reflected the rose-coloured clouds in the west, and through the flush rowed many gaily-painted boats, with various coloured flags, towards the massy rock on which the castle stood. The trees and flowers seemed already asleep, and breathing forth their sweet dream-breath. Laughter and low voices rose from the breast of the lake to the ears of the youths and maidens looking forth expectant from the lofty windows. They went down to the broad platform at the top of the stairs in front of the door to receive their visitors. By degrees the festivities of the evening commenced. The same smiles flew forth both at eyes and lips, darting like beams through the gathering crowd. Music, from unseen sources, now rolled in billows, now crept in ripples through the sea of air that filled the lofty rooms. And in the dancing halls, when hand took hand, and form and motion were moulded and swayed by the indwelling music, it governed not these alone, but, as the ruling spirit of the place, every new burst of music for a new dance swept before it a new and accordant odour, and dyed the flames that glowed in the lofty lamps with a new and accordant stain. The floors bent beneath the feet of the time-keeping dancers. But twice in the evening some of the inmates started, and the pallor occasionally common to the household overspread their faces, for they felt underneath them a counter-motion to the dance, as if the floor rose slightly to answer their feet. And all the time their brother lay below in the dungeon, like John the Baptist in the castle of Herod, when the lords and captains sat around, and the daughter of Herodias danced before them. Outside, all around the castle, brooded the dark night unheeded; for the clouds had come up from all sides, and were crowding together overhead. In the unfrequent pauses of the music, they might have heard, now and then, the gusty rush of a lonely wind, coming and going no one could know whence or whither, born and dying unexpected and unregarded. But when the festivities were at their height, when the external and passing confidence which is produced between superficial natures by a common pleasure, was at the full, a sudden crash of thunder quelled the music, as the thunder quells the noise of the uplifted sea. The windows were driven in, and torrents of rain, carried in the folds of a rushing wind, poured into the halls. The lights were swept away; and the great rooms, now dark within, were darkened yet more by the dazzling shoots of flame from the vault of blackness overhead. Those that ventured to look out of the windows saw, in the blue brilliancy of the quick-following jets of lightning, the lake at the foot of the rock, ordinarily so still and so dark, lighted up, not on the surface only, but down to half its depth; so that, as it tossed in the wind, like a tortured sea of writhing flames, or incandescent half-molten serpents of brass, they could not tell whether a strong phosphorescence did not issue from the transparent body of the waters, as if earth and sky lightened together, one consenting source of flaming utterance.

Sad was the condition of the late plastic mass of living form that had flowed into shape at the will and law of the music. Broken into individuals, the common transfusing spirit withdrawn, they stood drenched, cold, and benumbed, with clinging garments; light, order, harmony, purpose departed, and chaos restored; the issuings of life turned back on their sources, chilly and dead. And in every heart reigned that falsest of despairing convictions, that this was the only reality, and that was but a dream. The eldest sister stood with clasped hands and downbent head, shivering and speechless, as if waiting for something to follow. Nor did she wait long. A terrible flash and thunder-peal made the castle rock; and in the pausing silence that followed, her quick sense heard the rattling of a chain far off, deep down; and soon the sound of heavy footsteps, accompanied with the clanking of iron, reached her ear. She felt that her brother was at hand. Even in the darkness, and amidst the bellowing of another deep-bosomed cloud-monster, she knew that he had entered the room. A moment after, a continuous pulsation of angry blue light began, which, lasting for some moments, revealed him standing amidst them, gaunt, haggard, and motionless; his hair and beard untrimmed, his face ghastly, his eyes large and hollow. The light seemed to gather around him as a centre. Indeed some believed that it throbbed and radiated from his person, and not from the stormy heavens above them. The lightning had rent the wall of his prison, and released the iron staple of his chain, which he had wound about him like a girdle. In his hand he carried an iron fetter-bar, which he had found on the floor of the vault. More terrified at this aspect than at all the violence of the storm, the visitors, with many a shriek and cry, rushed out into the tempestuous night. By degrees, the storm died away. Its last flash revealed the forms of the brothers and sisters lying prostrate, with their faces on the floor, and that fearful shape standing motionless amidst them still.

Morning dawned, and there they lay, and there he stood. But at a word from him, they arose and went about their various duties, though listlessly enough. The eldest sister was the last to rise; and when she did, it was only by a terrible effort that she was able to reach her room, where she fell again on the floor. There she remained lying for days. The brother caused the doors of the great suite of rooms to be closed, leaving them just as they were, with all the childish adornment scattered about, and the rain still falling in through the shattered windows. "Thus let them lie," said he, "till the rain and frost have cleansed them of paint and drapery: no storm can hurt the pillars and arches of these halls."

The hours of this day went heavily. The storm was gone, but the rain was left; the passion had departed, but the tears remained behind. Dull and dark the low misty clouds brooded over the castle and the lake, and shut out all the neighbourhood. Even if they had climbed to the loftiest known turret, they would have found it swathed in a garment of clinging vapour, affording no refreshment to the eye, and no hope to the heart. There was one lofty tower that rose sheer a hundred feet above the rest, and from which the fog could have been seen lying in a grey mass beneath; but that tower they had not yet discovered, nor another close beside it, the top of which was never seen, nor could be, for the highest clouds of heaven clustered continually around it. The rain fell continuously, though not heavily, without; and within, too, there were clouds from which dropped the tears which are the rain of the spirit. All the good of life seemed for the time departed, and their souls lived but as leafless trees that had forgotten the joy of the summer, and whom no wind prophetic of spring had yet visited. They moved about mechanically, and had not strength enough left to wish to die.

The next day the clouds were higher, and a little wind blew through such loopholes in the turrets as the false improvements of the inmates had not yet filled with glass, shutting out, as the storm, so the serene visitings of the heavens. Throughout the day, the brother took various opportunities of addressing a gentle command, now to one and now to another of his family. It was obeyed in silence. The wind blew fresher through the loopholes and the shattered windows of the great rooms, and found its way, by unknown passages, to faces and eyes hot with weeping. It cooled and blessed them. When the sun arose the next day, it was in a clear sky.

By degrees, everything fell into the regularity of subordination. With the subordination came increase of freedom. The steps of the more youthful of the family were heard on the stairs and in the corridors more light and quick than ever before. Their brother had lost the terrors of aspect produced by his confinement, and his

THE CASTLE: A PARABLE

commands were issued more gently, and oftener with a smile, than in all their previous history. By degrees his presence was universally felt through the house. It was no surprise to any one at his studies, to see him by his side when he lifted up his eyes, though he had not before known that he was in the room. And although some dread still remained, it was rapidly vanishing before the advances of a firm friendship. Without immediately ordering their labours, he always influenced them, and often altered their direction and objects. The change soon evident in the household was remarkable. A simpler, nobler expression was visible on all the countenances. The voices of the men were deeper, and yet seemed by their very depth more feminine than before; while the voices of the women were softer and sweeter, and at the same time more full and decided. Now the eyes had often an expression as if their sight was absorbed in the gaze of the inward eyes; and when the eyes of two met, there passed between those eyes the utterance of a conviction that both meant the same thing. But the change was, of course, to be seen more clearly, though not more evidently, in individuals.

One of the brothers, for instance, was very fond of astronomy. He had his observatory on a lofty tower, which stood pretty clear of the others, towards the north and east. But hitherto, his astronomy, as he had called it, had been more of the character of astrology. Often, too, he might have been seen directing a heaven-searching telescope to catch the rapid transit of a fiery shooting-star, belonging altogether to the earthly atmosphere, and not to the serene heavens. He had to learn that the signs of the air are not the signs of the skies. Nay, once, his brother surprised him in the act of examining through his longest tube a patch of burning heath upon a distant hill. But now he was diligent from morning till night in the study of the laws of the truth that has to do with stars; and when the curtain of the sun-light was about to rise from before the heavenly worlds which it had hidden all day long, he might be seen preparing his instruments with that solemn countenance with which it becometh one to look into the mysterious harmonics of nature. Now he learned what law and order and truth are, what consent and harmony mean; how the individual may find his own end in a higher end, where law and freedom mean the same thing, and the purest certainty exists without the slightest constraint. Thus he stood on the earth, and looked to the heavens.

Another, who had been much given to searching out the hollow places and recesses in the foundations of the castle, and who was often to be found with compass and ruler working away at a chart of the same which he had been in process of constructing, now came to the conclusion that only by ascending the upper regions of his abode, could he become capable of understanding what lay beneath; and that, in all probability, one clear prospect, from the top of the highest attainable turret, over the castle as it lay below, would reveal more of the idea of its internal construction, than a year spent in wandering through its subterranean vaults. But the fact was that the desire to ascend wakening within him had made him forget what was beneath; and having laid aside his chart for a time at least, he was now to be met in every quarter of the upper parts, searching and striving upward, now in one direction, now in another; and seeking, as he went, the best outlooks into the clear air of outer realities.

And they began to discover that they were all mediating different aspects of the same thing; and they brought together their various discoveries, and recognized the likeness between them; and the one thing often explained the other, and combining with it helped to a third. They grew in consequence more and more friendly and loving; so that every now and then, one turned to another and said, as in surprise, "Why, you are my brother!" and "Why, you are my sister!" And yet they had always known it.

The change reached to all. One, who lived on the air of sweet sounds, and who was almost always to be found seated by her harp or some other instrument had, till the late storm, been generally merry and playful, though sometimes sad. But for a long time after that she was often found weeping, and playing little simple airs which she had heard in childhood—backward longings, followed by fresh tears. Before long, however, a new element manifested itself in her music. It became yet more wild, and sometimes retained all its sadness, but it was mingled with anticipation and hope. The past and the future merged in one; and while memory yet brought the rain-cloud, expectation threw the rainbow across its bosom—and all was uttered in her music, which rose and swelled, now to defiance, now to victory; then died in a torrent of weeping.

As to the eldest sister, it was many days before she recovered from the shock. At length, one day, her brother came to her, took her by the hand, led her to an open window, and told her to seat herself by it, and look out. She did so; but at first saw nothing more than an unsympathizing blaze of sunlight. But as she looked, the horizon widened out, and the dome of the sky ascended, till the grandeur seized upon her soul, and she fell on her knees and wept. Now the heavens seemed to bend lovingly over her, and to stretch out wide cloud-arms to embrace her; the earth lay like the bosom of an infinite love beneath her, and the wind kissed her cheek with an odour of roses. She sprang to her feet and turned, in an agony of hope, expecting to behold the face of the father, but there stood only her brother, looking calmly though lovingly on her emotion. She turned again to the window. On the hilltops rested the sky: Heaven and Earth were one; and the prophecy awoke in her soul, that from betwixt them would the steps of the father approach.

Hitherto she had seen but beauty; now she beheld truth. Often had she looked on such clouds as these, and loved the strange ethereal curves into which the winds moulded them; and had smiled as her little pet sister told her what curious animals she saw in them, and tried to point them out to her. Now they were as troops of angels, jubilant over her new birth, for they sang, in her soul, of beauty, and truth, and love. She looked down, and her little sister knelt beside her.

She was a curious child, with black, glittering eyes, and dark hair; at the mercy of every wandering wind; a frolicsome, daring girl, who laughed more than she smiled. She was generally in attendance on her sister, and was always finding and bringing her strange things. She never pulled a primrose, but she knew the haunts of all the orchis tribe, and brought from them bees and butterflies innumerable, as offerings to her sister. Curious moths and glow-worms were her greatest delight; and she loved the stars, because they were like the glow-worms. But the change had affected her too; for her sister saw that her eyes had lost their glittering look, and had become more liquid and transparent. And from that time she often observed that her gaiety was more gentle, her smile more frequent, her laugh less bell-like; and although she was as wild as ever, there was more elegance in her motions, and more music in her voice. And she clung to her sister with far greater fondness than before.

The land reposed in the embrace of the warm summer days. The clouds of heaven nestled around the towers of the castle; and the hearts of its inmates became conscious of a warm atmosphere—of a presence of love. They began to feel like the children of a household, when the mother is at home. Their faces and forms grew daily more and more beautiful, till they wondered as they gazed on each other. As they walked in the gardens of the castle, or in the country around, they were often visited, especially the eldest sister, by sounds that no one heard by themselves, issuing from woods and waters; and by forms of love that lightened out of flowers, and grass, and great rocks. Now and then the young children would come in with a slow, stately step, and, with great eyes that looked as if they would devour all the creation, say that they had met the father amongst the trees, and that he had kissed them; "And," added one of them once, "I grew so big!" But when others went out to look, they could see no one. And some said it must have been the brother, who grew more and more beautiful, and loving, and reverend, and who had lost all traces of hardness, so that they wondered they could ever have thought him stern and harsh. But the eldest sister held her peace, and looked up, and her eyes filled with tears. "Who can tell," thought she, "but the little children know more about it than we?"

Often, at sunrise, might be heard their hymn of praise to their unseen father, whom they felt to be near, though they saw him not. Some words thereof once reached my ear through the folds of the music in which they floated, as in an upward snowstorm of sweet sounds. And these are some of the words I heard—but there was much I seemed to hear, which I could not understand, and some things which I understood but cannot utter again.

"We thank thee that we have a father, and not a maker; that thou hast begotten us, and not moulded us as images of clay; that we have come forth of thy heart, and have not been fashioned by thy hands. It *must* be so. Only the heart of a father is able to create. We rejoice in it, and bless thee that we know it. We thank thee for thyself. Be what thou art—our root and life, our beginning and end, our all in all. Come home to us. Thou livest; therefore we live. In thy light we see. Thou art—that is all our song."

Thus they worship, and love, and wait. Their hope and expectation grow ever stronger and brighter, that one day, ere long, the father will show himself amongst them, and thenceforth dwell in his own house for evermore. What was once but an old legend has become the one desire of their hearts.

And the loftiest hope is the surest of being fulfilled.

THE BROKEN SWORDS

* * *

THE eyes of three, two sisters and a brother, gazed for the last time on a great pale-golden star, that followed the sun down the steep west. It went down to arise again; and the brother about to depart might return, but more than the usual doubt hung upon his future. For between the white dresses of the sisters, shone his scarlet coat and golden swordknot which he had put on for the first time, more to gratify their pride than his own vanity. The brightening moon, as if prophetic of a future memory, had already begun to dim the scarlet and the gold, and to give them a pale, ghostly hue. In her thoughtful light the whole group seemed more like a meeting in the land of shadows, than a parting in the substantial earth. But which should be called the land of realities? The region where appearance, and space, and time drive between, and stop the flowing currents of the soul's speech? Or that region where heart meets heart, and appearance has become the slave to utterance, and space and time are forgotten?

Through the quiet air came the far-off rush of water, and the near cry of the land-rail. Now and then a chilly wind blew unheeded through the startled and jostling leaves that shaded the ivy-seat. Else, there was calm everywhere, rendered yet deeper and more intense by the dusky sorrow that filled their hearts. For, far away, hundreds of miles beyond the hearing of their ears, roared the great war-guns; next week their brother must sail with his regiment to join the army; and tomorrow he must leave his home. The sisters looked on him tenderly, with vague fears about his fate. Yet little they divined it. That the face they loved might lie pale and bloody, in a heap of slain, was the worst image of it that arose before them; but this, had they seen the future, they would, in ignorance of the further future, have infinitely preferred to that which awaited him. And even while they looked on him, a dim feeling of the unsuitableness of his lot filled their minds. For, indeed, to all judgments it must have seemed unsuitable that the home-boy, the loved of his mother, the pet of his sisters, who was happy, womanlike (as Coleridge says), if he possessed the signs of love, having never yet sought for its proofs—that he should be sent amongst soldiers, to command and be commanded; to kill, or perhaps to be himself crushed out of the fair earth in the uproar that brings back for the moment the reign of Night and Chaos. No wonder that to his sisters it seemed strange and sad. Yet such was their own position in the battle of life, in which their father had died with doubtful conquest, that when their old military uncle sent the boy an ensign's commission, they did not dream of refusing the only path open, as they thought, to an honourable profession, even though it might lead to the trench-grave. They heard it as the voice of destiny, wept, and yielded.

If they had possessed a deeper insight into his character, they would have discovered yet further reason to doubt the fitness of the profession chosen for him; and if they had ever seen him at school, it is possible the doubt of fitness might have strengthened into a certainty of incongruity. His comparative inactivity amongst his schoolfellows, though occasioned by no dulness of intellect, might have suggested the necessity of a quiet life, if inclination and liking had been the arbiters in the choice. Nor was this inactivity the result of defective animal spirits either, for sometimes his mirth and boyish frolic were unbounded; but it seemed to proceed from an over-activity of the inward life, absorbing, and in some measure checking, the outward manifestation. He had so much to do in his own hidden kingdom, that he had not time to take his place in the polity and strife of the commonwealth around him. Hence, while other boys were acting, he was thinking. In this point of difference, he felt keenly the superiority of many of his companions; for another boy would have the obstacle overcome, or the adversary subdued, while he was meditating on the propriety, or on the means, of effecting the desired end. He envied their promptitude, while they never saw reason to envy his wisdom; for his conscience, tender and not strong, frequently transformed slowness of determination into irresolution: while a delicacy of the sympathetic nerves tended to distract him from any predetermined course, by the diversity of their vibrations, responsive to influences from all quarters, and destructive to unity of purpose.

Of such a one, the *a priori* judgment would be that he ought to be left to meditate and grow for some time, before being called upon to produce the fruits of action. But add to these mental conditions a vivid imagination, and a high sense of honour, nourished in childhood by the reading of the old knightly romances, and then put the youth in a position in which action is imperative, and you have elements of strife sufficient to reduce that fair kingdom of his to utter anarchy and madness. Yet so little do we know ourselves, and so different are the symbols with which the imagination works its algebra, from the realities which those symbols represent, that as yet the youth felt no uneasiness, but contemplated his new calling with a glad enthusiasm and some vanity; for all his prospect lay in the glow of the scarlet and the gold. Nor did this excitement receive any check till the day before his departure, on which day I have introduced him to my readers, when, accidentally taking up a newspaper of a week old, his eye fell on these words— "*Already crying women are to be met in the streets.*" With this cloud afar on his horizon, which, though no bigger than a man's hand, yet cast a perceptible shadow over his mind, he departed next morning. The coach carried him beyond the consecrated circle of home laws and impulses, out into the great tumult, above which rises ever and anon the cry of Cain, "Am I my brother's keeper?"

Every tragedy of higher order, constructed in Christian times, will correspond more or less to the grand drama of the Bible; wherein the first act opens with a brilliant sunset vision of Paradise, in which childish sense and need are served with all the profusion of the indulgent nurse. But the glory fades off into grey and black, and night settles down upon the heart which, rightly uncontent with the childish, and not having yet learned the childlike, seeks knowledge and manhood as a thing denied by the Maker, and yet to be gained by the creature; so sets forth alone to climb the heavens, and instead of climbing, falls into the abyss. Then follows the long dismal night of feverish efforts and delirious visions, or, it may be, helpless despair; till at length a deeper stratum of the soul is heaved to the surface; and amid the first dawn of morning, the youth says within him, "I have sinned against my *Maker*—I will arise and go to my *Father.*" More or less, I say, will Christian tragedy correspond to this—a fall and a rising again; not a rising only, but a victory; not a victory merely, but a triumph. Such, in its way and degree, is my story. I have shown, in one passing scene, the home paradise; now I have to show a scene of a far differing nature.

The young ensign was lying in his tent, weary, but wakeful. All day long the cannon had been bellowing against the walls of the city, which now lay with wide, gaping breach, ready for the morrow's storm, but covered yet with the friendly darkness. His regiment was ordered to be ready with the earliest dawn to march up to the breach. That day, for the first time, there had been blood on his sword—there the sword lay, a spot on the chased hilt still. He had cut down one of the enemy in a skirmish with a sally party of the besieged, and the look of the man as he fell, haunted him. He felt, for the time, that he dared not pray to the Father, for the blood of a brother had rushed forth at the stroke of his arm, and there was one fewer of living souls on the earth because he lived thereon. And tomorrow he must lead a troop of men up to that poor disabled town, and turn them loose upon it, not knowing what might follow in the triumph of enraged and victorious foes, who for weeks had been subjected, by the constancy of the place, to the greatest privations. It was true the general had issued his commands against all disorder and pillage; but if the soldiers once yielded to temptation, what might not be done before the officers could reclaim them! All the wretched tales he had read of the sack of cities rushed back on his memory. He shuddered as he lay. Then his conscience began to speak, and to ask what right he had to be there. Was the war a just one? He could not tell; for this was a bad time for settling nice questions. But there he was, right or wrong, fighting and shedding blood on God's earth, beneath God's heaven.

Over and over he turned the question in his mind; again and again the spouting blood of his foe, and the death-look in his eye, rose before him; and the youth who at school could never fight with a companion because he was not sure that he was in the right, was alone in the midst of undoubting men of war, amongst whom he was driven helplessly along, upon the waves of a terrible necessity. What wonder that in the midst of these perplexities his courage should fail him! What wonder that the consciousness of fainting should increase the faintness! Or that the dread of fear and its consequences should hasten and invigorate its attacks! To crown all, when he dropped into a troubled slumber at length, he found himself hurried, as on a storm of fire, through the streets of the captured town, from all the windows of which looked forth familiar faces, old and young, but distorted from the memory of his boyhood by fear and wild despair. On one spot lay the body of his father, with his face to the earth; and he woke at the cry of horror and rage that burst from his own lips, as he saw the rough, bloody hand of a soldier twisted in the loose hair of his elder sister, and the younger fainting in the arms of a scoundrel belonging to his own regiment.

He slept no more. As the grey morning broke, the troops appointed for the attack assembled without sound of trumpet or drum, and were silently formed in fitting order. The young ensign was in his place, weary and wretched after his miserable night. Before him he saw a great, broad-shouldered lieutenant, whose brawny hand seemed almost too large for his sword-hilt and in any one of whose limbs played more animal life than in the whole body of the pale youth. The firm-set lips of this officer, and the fire of his eye, showed a concentrated resolution, which, by the contrast increased the misery of the ensign, and seemed, as if the stronger absorbed the weaker, to draw out from him the last fibres of self-possession: the sight of unattainable determination, while it increased the feeling of the arduousness of that which required such determination, threw him into the great gulf which lay between him and it. In this disorder of his nervous and mental condition, with a doubting conscience and a shrinking heart, is it any wonder that the terrors which lay before him at the gap in those bristling walls, should draw near, and, making sudden inroad upon his soul, overwhelm the government of a will worn out by the tortures of an unassured spirit? What share fear contributed to unman him, it was impossible for him, in the dark, confused conflict of differing emotions, to determine; but

THE BROKEN SWORDS

doubtless a natural shrinking from danger, there being no excitement to deaden its influence, and no hope of victory to encourage to the struggle, seeing victory was dreadful to him as defeat, had its part in the sad result. Many men who have courage, are dependent on ignorance and a low state of the moral feeling for that courage; and a further progress towards the development of the higher nature would, for a time at least entirely overthrow it. Nor could such loss of courage be rightly designated by the name of cowardice.

But alas! The colonel happened to fix his eyes upon him as he passed along the file; and this completed his confusion. He betrayed such evident symptoms of perturbation, that that officer ordered him under arrest; and the result was that, chiefly for the sake of example to the army, he was, upon trial by court-martial, expelled from the service, and had his sword broken over his head. Alas for the delicate-minded youth! Alas for the home-darling!

Long after, he found at the bottom of his chest the pieces of the broken sword, and remembered that at the time, he had lifted them from the ground and carried them away. But he could not recall under what impulse he had done so. Perhaps the agony he suffered, passing the bounds of mortal endurance, had opened for him a vista into the eternal, and had shown him, if not the injustice of the sentence passed upon him, yet his freedom from blame, or, endowing him with dim prophetic vision, had given him the assurance that some day the stain would be wiped from his soul, and leave him standing clear before the tribunal of his own honour. Some feeling like this, I say, may have caused him, with a passing gleam of indignant protest, to lift the fragments from the earth, and carry them away; even as the friends of a so-called traitor may bear away his mutilated body from the wheel. But if such was the case, the vision was soon overwhelmed and forgotten in the succeeding anguish. He could not see that, in mercy to his doubting spirit, the question which had agitated his mind almost to madness, and which no results of the impending conflict could have settled for him, was thus quietly set aside for the time; nor that, painful as was the dark, dreadful existence that he was now to pass in self-torment and moaning, it would go by, and leave his spirit clearer far, than if, in his apprehension, it had been stained with further blood-guiltiness, instead of the loss of honour. Years after, when he accidentally learned that on that very morning the whole of his company, with parts of several more, had, or ever they began to mount the breach, been blown to pieces by the explosion of a mine, he cried aloud in bitterness, "Would God that my fear had not been discovered before I reached that spot!" But surely it is better to pass into the next region of life having reaped some assurance, some firmness of character, determination of effort, and consciousness of the worth of life, in the present world; so approaching the future steadily and faithfully, and if in much darkness and ignorance, yet not in the oscillations of moral uncertainty.

Close upon the catastrophe followed a torpor, which lasted he did not know how long, and which wrapped in a thick fog all the succeeding events. For some time he can hardly be said to have had any conscious history. He awoke to life and torture when halfway across the sea towards his native country, where was no home any longer for him. To this point, and no farther, could his thoughts return in after years. But the misery which he then endured is hardly to be understood, save by those of like delicate temperament with himself. All day long he sat silent in his cabin; nor could any effort of the captain, or others on board, induce him to go on deck till night came on, when, under the starlight, he ventured into the open air. The sky soothed him then, he knew not how. For the face of nature is the face of God, and must bear expressions that can influence, though unconsciously to them, the most ignorant and hopeless of His children. Often did he watch the clouds in hope of a storm, his spirit rising and falling as the sky darkened or cleared; he longed, in the necessary selfishness of such suffering, for a tumult of waters to swallow the vessel; and only the recollection of how many lives were involved in its safety besides his own, prevented him from praying to God for lightning and tempest, borne on which he might dash into the haven of the other world. One night, following a sultry calm day, he thought that Mercy had heard his unuttered prayer. The air and sea were intense darkness, till a light as intense for one moment annihilated it, and the succeeding darkness seemed shattered with the sharp reports of the thunder that cracked without reverberation. He who had shrunk from battle with his fellowmen, rushed to the mainmast, threw himself on his knees, and stretched forth his arms in speechless energy of supplication; but the storm passed away overhead, and left him kneeling still by the uninjured mast. At length the vessel reached her port. He hurried on shore to bury himself in the most secret place he could find. *Out of sight* was his first, his only thought. Return to his mother he would not, he could not; and, indeed, his friends never learned his fate, until it had carried him far beyond their reach.

For several weeks he lurked about like a malefactor, in low lodging houses in narrow streets of the seaport to which the vessel had borne him, heeding no one, and but little shocked at the strange society and conversation with which, though only in bodily presence, he had to mingle. These formed the subjects of reflection in after times; and he came to the conclusion that, though much evil and much misery exist, sufficient to move prayers and tears in those who love their kind, yet there is less of both than those looking down from a more elevated social position upon the weltering heap of humanity, are ready to imagine; especially if they regard it likewise from the pedestal of self-congratulation on which a meagre type of religion has elevated them. But at length his little stock of money was nearly expended, and there was nothing that he could do, or learn to do, in this seaport. He felt impelled to seek manual labour, partly because he thought it more likely he could obtain that sort of employment, without a request for reference as to his character, which would lead to inquiry about his previous history; and partly, perhaps, from an instinctive feeling that hard bodily labour would tend to lessen his inward suffering.

He left the town, therefore, at nightfall of a July day, carrying a little bundle of linen, and the remains of his money, somewhat augmented by the sale of various articles of clothing and convenience, which his change of life rendered superfluous and unsuitable. He directed his course northwards, travelling principally by night—so painfully did he shrink from the gaze even of footfarers like himself; and sleeping during the day in some hidden nook of wood or thicket, or under the shadow of a great tree in a solitary field. So fine was the season, that for three successive weeks he was able to travel thus without inconvenience, lying down when the sun grew hot in the forenoon, and generally waking when the first faint stars were hesitating in the great darkening heavens that covered and shielded him. For above every cloud, above every storm, rise up, calm, clear, divine, the deep infinite skies; they embrace the tempest even as the sunshine; by their permission it exists within their boundless peace: therefore it cannot hurt, and must pass away, while there they stand as ever, domed up eternally, lasting, strong, and pure.

Several times he attempted to get agricultural employment; but the whiteness of his hands and the tone of his voice not merely suggested unfitness for labour, but generated suspicion as to the character of one who had evidently dropped from a rank so much higher, and was seeking admittance within the natural masonic boundaries and secrets and privileges of another. Disheartened somewhat, but hopeful, he journeyed on. I say hopeful; for the blessed power of life in the universe, in fresh air and sunshine absorbed by active exercise, in winds, yea in rain, though it fell but seldom, had begun to work its natural healing, soothing effect, upon his perturbed spirit. And there was room for hope in his new endeavour. As his bodily strength increased, and his health, considerably impaired by inward suffering, improved, the trouble of his soul became more endurable—and in some measure to endure is to conquer and destroy. In proportion as the mind grows in the strength of patience, the disturber of its peace sickens and fades away. At length, one day, a widow lady in a village through which his road led him, gave him a day's work in her garden. He laboured hard and well, notwithstanding his soon-blistered hands, received his wages thankfully, and found a resting-place for the night on the low part of a hay-stack from which the upper portion had been cut away. Here he ate his supper of bread and cheese, pleased to have found such comfortable quarters, and soon fell fast asleep.

When he awoke, the whole heavens and earth seemed to give a full denial to sin and sorrow. The sun was just mounting over the horizon, looking up the clear, cloud-mottled sky. From millions of waterdrops hanging on the bending stalks of grass, sparkled his rays in varied refraction, transformed here to a gorgeous burning ruby, there to an emerald, green as the grass, and yonder to a flashing, sunny topaz. The chanting priest-lark had gone up from the low earth, as soon as the heavenly light had begun to enwrap and illumine the folds of its tabernacle; and had entered the high heavens with his offering, whence, unseen, he now dropped on the earth the sprinkled sounds of his overflowing blessedness. The poor youth rose but to kneel, and cry, from a bursting heart, "Hast Thou not, O Father, some care for me? Canst Thou not restore my lost honour? Can anything befall Thy children for which Thou hast no help?

Surely, if the face of Thy world lie not, joy and not grief is at the heart of the universe, is there none for me?"

The highest poetic feeling of which we are now conscious, springs not from the beholding of perfected beauty, but from the mute sympathy which the creation with all its children manifests with us in the groaning and travailing which look for the sonship. Because of our need and aspiration, the snowdrop gives birth in our hearts to a loftier spiritual and poetic feeling, than the rose most complete in form, colour, and odour. The rose is of Paradise—the snowdrop is of the striving, hoping, longing Earth. Perhaps our highest poetry is the expression of our aspirations in the sympathetic forms of visible nature. Nor is this merely a longing for a restored Paradise; for even in the ordinary history of men, no man or woman that has fallen, can be restored to the position formerly held. Such must rise to a yet higher place, whence they can behold their former standing far beneath their feet. They must be restored by the attainment of something better than they ever possessed before, or not at all. If the law be a weariness, we must escape it by taking refuge with the spirit for not otherwise can we fulfil the law than by being above the law. To escape the overhanging rocks of Sinai, we must climb to its secret top.

> *"Is thy strait horizon dreary?*
> *Is thy foolish fancy chill?*
> *Change the feet that have grown weary*
> *For the wings that never will."*

Thus, like one of the wandering knights searching the wide earth for the Sangreal, did he wander on, searching for his lost honour, or rather (for that he counted gone forever) seeking unconsciously for the peace of mind which had departed from him, and taken with it not the joy merely, but almost the possibility, of existence.

At last when his little store was all but exhausted, he was employed by a market gardener, in the neighbourhood of a large country town, to work in his garden, and sometimes take his vegetables to market. With him he continued for a few weeks, and wished for no change; until, one day driving his cart through the town, he saw approaching him an elderly gentleman, whom he knew at once, by his gait and carriage, to be a military man. Now he had never seen his uncle the retired officer, but it struck him that this might be he; and under the tyranny of his passion for concealment, he fancied that, if it were he, he might recognise him by some family likeness— not considering the improbability of his looking at him. This fancy, with the painful effect which the sight of an officer, even in plain clothes, had upon him, recalling the torture of that frightful day, so overcame him, that he found himself at the other end of an alley before he recollected that he had the horse and cart in charge. This increased his difficulty; for now he dared not return, lest his inquiries after the vehicle, if the horse had strayed from the direct line, should attract attention, and cause interrogations which he would be unable to answer. The fatal want of self-possession seemed again to ruin him. He forsook the town by the nearest way, struck across the country to another line of road, and before he was missed, was miles away, still in a northerly direction.

But although he thus shunned the face of man, especially of any one who reminded him of the past, the loss of his reputation in their eyes was not the cause of his inward grief. That would have been comparatively powerless to disturb him, had he not lost his own respect. He quailed before his own thoughts; he was dishonoured in his own eyes. His perplexity had not yet sufficiently cleared away to allow him to see the extenuating circumstances of the case; not to say the fact that the peculiar mental condition in which he was at the time, removed the case quite out of the class of ordinary instances of cowardice. He condemned himself more severely than any of his judges would have dared; remembering that portion of his mental sensations which had savoured of fear, and forgetting the causes which had produced it. He judged himself a man stained with the foulest blot that could cleave to a soldier's name, a blot which nothing but death, not even death, could efface. But, inwardly condemned and outwardly degraded, his dread of recognition was intense; and feeling that he was in more danger of being discovered where the population was sparser, he resolved to hide himself once more in the midst of poverty; and, with this view, found his way to one of the largest of the manufacturing towns.

He reached it during the strike of a great part of the workmen; so that, though he found some difficulty in procuring employment, as might be expected from his ignorance of machine-labour, he yet was sooner successful than he would otherwise have been. Possessed of a natural aptitude for mechanical operations, he soon became a tolerable workman; and he found that his previous education assisted to the fitting execution of those operations even which were most purely mechanical.

He found also, at first, that the unrelaxing attention requisite for the mastering of the many niceties of his work, of necessity drew his mind somewhat from its brooding over his misfortune, hitherto almost ceaseless. Every now and then, however, a pang would shoot suddenly to his heart, and turn his face pale, even before his consciousness had time to inquire what was the matter. So by degress, as attention became less necessary, and the nervo-mechanical action of his system increased with use, his thoughts again returned to their old misery. He would wake at night in his poor room, with the feeling that a ghostly nightmare sat on his soul; that a want—a loss—miserable, fearful—was present; that something of his heart was gone from him; and through the darkness he would hear the snap of the breaking sword, and lie for a moment overwhelmed beneath the assurance of the incredible fact. Could it be true that *he* was a coward? That *his* honour was gone, and in its place a stain? That *he* was a thing for men—and worse, for women—to point the finger at, laughing bitter laughter? Never lover or husband could have mourned with the same desolation over the departure of the loved; the girl alone, weeping scorching tears over *her* degradation, could resemble him in his agony, as he lay on his bed, and wept and moaned.

His sufferings had returned with the greater weight, that he was no longer upheld by the "divine air" and the open heavens, whose sunlight now only reached him late in an afternoon, as he stood at his loom, through windows so coated with dust that they looked like frosted glass; showing, as it passed through the air to fall on the dirty floor, how the breath of life was thick with dust of iron and wood, and films of cotton; amidst which his senses were now too much dulled by custom to detect the exhalations from greasy wheels and overtasked humankind. Nor could he find comfort in the society of his fellow labourers. True, it was a kind of comfort to have those near him who could not know of his grief; but there was so little in common between them, that any interchange of thought was impossible. At least, so it seemed to him. Yet sometimes his longing for human companionship would drive him out of his dreary room at night, and send him wandering through the lower part of the town, where he would gaze wistfully on the miserable faces that passed him, as if looking for someone—some angel, even there—to speak goodwill to his hungry heart.

Once he entered one of those gin-palaces, which, like the golden gates of hell, entice the miserable to worse misery, and seated himself close to a half-tipsy, good-natured wretch, who made room for him on a bench by the wall. He was comforted even by this proximity to one who would not repel him. But soon the paintings of warlike action—of knights, and horses, and mighty deeds done with battle-axe, and broad-sword, which adorned the panels all round, drove him forth even from this heaven of the damned; yet not before the impious thought had arisen in his heart, that the brilliantly painted and sculptural roof, with the gilded vine-leaves and bunches of grapes trained up the windows, all lighted with the great shining chandeliers, was only a microcosmic repetition of the bright heavens and the glowing earth, that overhung and surrounded the misery of man. But the memory of how kindly they had comforted and elevated him, at one period of his painful history, not only banished the wicked thought, but brought him more quiet, in the resurrection of a past blessing, than he had known for some time. The period, however, was now at hand when a new grief, followed by a new and more elevated activity, was to do its part towards the closing up of the fountain of bitterness.

Amongst his fellow labourers, he had for a short time taken some interest in observing a young woman, who had lately joined them. There was nothing remarkable about her, except what at first sight seemed a remarkable plainness. A slight scar over one of her rather prominent eyebrows, increased this impression of plainness. But the first day had not passed, before he began to see that there was something not altogether common in those deep eyes; and the plain look vanished before a closer observation, which also discovered, in the forehead and the lines of the mouth, traces of sorrow or other suffering. There was an expression, too, in the whole face, of fixedness of purpose, without any hardness of determination. Her countenance altogether seemed the index to an interesting mental history. Signs of mental trouble were always an attraction to him; in this case so great, that he overcame his shyness, and spoke to her one evening as they left the works. He often walked home with her after that; as, indeed, was natural, seeing that she occupied an attic in the same poor lodging house in which he lived himself. The street did not bear the best character; nor, indeed, would the occupations of all the inmates of the house have stood investigation; but so retiring and quiet was this girl, and so seldom did she go abroad after work hours, that he had not discovered till then that she lived in the same street, not to say the same house, with himself.

He soon learned her history—a very common one as outward events, but not surely insignificant because common. Her father and mother were both dead, and hence she had to find her livelihood alone, and amidst associations which were always disagreeable, and sometimes painful. Her quick womanly instinct must have discovered that he too had a history; for though, his mental prostration favouring the operation of outward influences, he had greatly approximated in appearance to those amongst whom he laboured, there were yet signs, besides the educated accent of his speech, which would have distinguished him to an observer; but she put no questions to him, nor made any approach towards seeking a return of the confidence she reposed in him. It was a sensible alleviation to his sufferings to hear her kind voice, and look in her gentle face, as they walked home together; and at length the expectation of this pleasure began to present itself, in the midst of the busy, dreary work-hours, as the shadow of a heaven to close up the dismal, uninteresting day.

But one morning he missed her from her place, and a keener pain passed through him than he had felt of late; for he knew that the Plague was abroad, feeding in the low stagnant places of human abode; and he had but too much reason to dread that she might be now struggling in its grasp. He seized the first opportunity of slipping out and hurrying home. He sprang upstairs to her room. He found the door locked, but heard a faint moaning within. To avoid disturbing her, while determined to gain an entrance, he went down for the key of his own door, with which he succeeded in unlocking hers, and so crossed her threshold for the first time. There she lay on her bed, tossing in pain, and beginning to be delirious. Careless of his own life, and feeling that he could not die better than in helping the only friend he had; certain, likewise, of the difficulty of finding a nurse for one in this disease and of her station in life; and sure, likewise, that there could be no question of propriety either in the circumstances with which they were surrounded, nor in this case of terrible fever almost as hopeless for her as dangerous to him, he instantly began the duties of a nurse, and returned no more to his employment. He had a little money in his possession, for he could not in the way in which he lived, spend all his wages; so he proceeded to make her as comfortable as he could, with all the pent-up tenderness of a loving heart finding an outlet at length. When a boy at home, he had often taken the place of nurse, and he felt quite capable of performing its duties. Nor was his boyhood far behind yet, although the trials he had come through made it appear an age since he had lost his light heart. So he never left her bedside, except to procure what was necessary for her. She was too ill to oppose any of his measures, or to seek to prohibit his presence. Indeed, by the time he had returned with the first medicine, she was insensible; and she continued so through the whole of the following week, during which time he was constantly with her.

That action produces feeling is as often true as its converse; and it is not surprising that, while he smoothed the pillow for her head, he should have made a nest in his heart for the helpless girl. Slowly and unconsciously he learned to love her. The chasm between his early associations and the circumstances in which he found her, vanished as he drew near to the simple, essential womanhood. His heart saw hers and loved it; and he knew that, the centre once gained, he could, as from the fountain of life, as from the innermost secret of the holy place, the hidden germ of power and possibility, transform the outer intellect and outermost manners as he pleased. With what a thrill of joy, a feeling for a long time unknown to him, and till now never known in this form or with this intensity, the thought arose in his heart that here lay one who some day would love him; that he should have a place of refuge and rest; one to lie in his bosom and not despise him! "For," said he to himself, "I will call forth her soul from where it sleeps, like an unawakened echo, in an unknown cave; and like a child, of whom I once dreamed, that was mine, and to my delight turned in fear from all besides, and clung to me, this soul of hers will run with bewildered, half-sleeping eyes, and tottering steps, but with a cry of joy on its lips, to me as the life-giver. She will cling to me and worship me. Then will I tell her, for she must know all, that I am low and contemptible; that I am an outcast from the world, and that if she receive me, she will be to me as God. And I will fall down at her feet and pray her for comfort, for life, for restoration to myself; and she will throw herself beside me, and weep and love me, I know. And we will go through life together, working hard, but for each other, and when we die, she shall lead me into paradise as the prize her angel-hand found cast on a desert shore, from the storm of winds and waves which I was too weak to resist—and raised, and tended, and saved." Often did such thoughts as these pass through his mind while watching her bed; alternated, checked, and sometimes destroyed, by the fears which attended her precarious condition, but returning with every apparent betterment or hopeful symptom.

I will not stop to decide the nice question, how far the intention was right, of causing her to love him before she knew his story. If in the whole matter there was too much thought of self, my only apology is the sequel. One day, the ninth from the commencement of her illness, a letter arrived, addressed to her, which he, thinking he might prevent some inconvenience thereby, opened and read, in the confidence of that love which already made her and all belonging to her appear his own. It was from a soldier—*her lover*. It was plain that they had been betrothed before he left for the continent a year ago; but this was the first letter which he had written to her. It breathed changeless love, and hope, and confidence in her. He was so fascinated that he read it through without pause.

Laying it down, he sat pale, motionless, almost inanimate. From the hard-won sunny heights, he was once more cast down into the shadow of death. The second storm of his life began, howling and raging, with yet more awful lulls between. "Is she not *mine*?" he said, in agony. "Do I not feel that she is mine? Who will watch over her as I? Who will kiss her soul to life as I? Shall she be torn away from me, when my soul seems to have dwelt with hers forever in an eternal house? But have I not a right to her? Have I not given my life for hers? Is he not a soldier, and are there not many chances that he may never return? And it may be that, although they were engaged in word, soul has never touched soul with them; their love has never reached that point where it passes from the mortal to the immortal, the indissoluble: and so, in a sense, she may be yet free. Will he do for her what I will do? Shall this precious heart of hers, in which I see the buds of so many beauties, be left to wither and die?"

But here the voice within him cried out, "Art thou the disposer of destinies? Wilt thou, in a universe where the visible God hath died for the Truth's sake, do evil that a good, which He might neglect or overlook, may be gained? Leave thou her to Him, and do thou right." And he said within himself, "Now is the real trial for my life! Shall I conquer or no?" And his heart awoke and cried, "I will. God forgive me for wronging the poor soldier! A brave man, brave at least is better for her than I."

THE BROKEN SWORDS

A great strength arose within him, and lifted him up to depart. "Surely I may kiss her once," he said. For the crisis was over, and she slept. He stooped towards her face, but before he had reached her lips he saw her eyelids tremble; and he who had longed for the opening of those eyes, as of the gates of heaven, that she might love him, stricken now with fear lest she should love him, fled from her, before the eyelids that hid such strife and such victory from the unconscious maiden had time to unclose. But it was agony—quietly to pack up his bundle of linen in the room below, when he knew she was lying awake above, with her dear, pale face, and living eyes! What remained of his money, except a few shillings, he put up in a scrap of paper, and went out with his bundle in his hand, first to seek a nurse for his friend, and then to go he knew not whither. He met the factory people with whom he had worked, going to dinner, and amongst them a girl who had herself but lately recovered from the fever, and was yet hardly able for work. She was the only friend the sick girl had seemed to have amongst the women at the factory, and she was easily persuaded to go and take charge of her. He put the money in her hand, begging her to use it for the invalid, and promising to send the equivalent of her wages for the time he thought she would have to wait on her. This he easily did by the sale of a ring, which, besides his mother's watch, was the only article of value he had retained. He begged her likewise not to mention his name in the matter; and was foolish enough to expect that she would entirely keep the promise she had made him.

Wandering along the street, purposeless now and bereft, he spied a recruiting party at the door of a public house; and on coming nearer, found, by one of those strange coincidences which do occur in life, and which have possibly their root in a hidden and wondrous law, that it was a party, perhaps a remnant, of the very regiment in which he had himself served, and in which his misfortune had befallen him. Almost simultaneously with the shock which the sight of the well-known number on the soldiers' knapsacks gave him, arose in his mind the romantic, ideal thought, of enlisting in the ranks of this same regiment, and recovering, as a private soldier and unknown, that honour which as officer he had lost. To this determination, the new necessity in which he now stood for action and change of life, doubtless contributed, though unconsciously. He offered himself to the sergeant; and, notwithstanding that his dress indicated a mode of life unsuitable as the antecedent to a soldier's, his appearance, and the necessity for recruits combined, led to his easy acceptance.

The English armies were employed in expelling the enemy from an invaded and helpless country. Whatever might be the political motives which had induced the government to this measure, the young man was now able to feel that he could go and fight, individually and for his part, in the cause of liberty. He was free to possess his own motives for joining in the execution of the schemes of those who commanded his commanders.

With a heavy heart, but with more of inward hope and strength than he had ever known before, he marched with his comrades to the seaport and embarked. It seemed to him that because he had done right in his last trial, here was a new glorious chance held out to his hand. True, it was a terrible change to pass from a woman in whom he had hoped to find healing, into the society of rough men, to march with the, "*mit gleichem Tritt und Schritt,*" up to the bristling bayonets or the horrid vacancy of the cannon mouth. But it was the only cure for the evil that consumed his life.

He reached the army in safety, and gave himself, with religious assiduity, to the smallest duties of his new position. No one had a brighter polish on his arms, or whiter belts than he. In the necessary movements, he soon became precise to a degree that attracted the attention of his officers; while his character was remarkable for all the virtues belonging to a perfect soldier.

One day, as he stood sentry, he saw the eyes of his colonel intently fixed on him. He felt his lip quiver, but he compressed and stilled it, and tried to look as unconscious as he could; which effort was assisted by the formal bearing required by his position. Now the colonel, such had been the losses of the regiment, had been promoted from a lieutenancy in the same, and had belonged to it at the time of the ensign's degradation. Indeed, had not the changes in the regiment been so great, he could hardly have escaped so long without discovery. But the poor fellow would have felt that his name was already free of reproach, if he had seen what followed on the close inspection which had awakened his apprehensions, and which, in fact, had convinced the colonel of his identity with the disgraced ensign. With a hasty and less soldierly step than usual, the colonel entered his tent, threw himself on his bed, and wept like a child. When he rose he was overheard to say these words—and these only escaped his lips: "He is nobler than I."

But this officer showed himself worthy of commanding such men as this private; for right nobly did he understand and meet his feelings. He uttered no word of the discovery he had made, till years afterwards; but it soon began to be remarked that whenever anything arduous, or in any manner distinguished, had to be done, this man was sure to be of the party appointed. In short, as often as he could, the colonel "set him in the forefront of the battle." Passing through all with wonderful escape, he was soon as much noticed for his reckless bravery, as hitherto for his precision in the discharge of duties, bringing only commendation and not honour. But his final lustration was at hand.

A great part of the army was hastening, by forced marches, to raise the siege of a town which was already on the point of falling into the hands of the enemy. Forming one of a reconnoitring party, which preceded the main body at some considerable distance, he and his companions came suddenly upon one of the enemy's outposts, occupying a high, and on one side precipitous rock, a short way from the town, which it commanded. Retreat was impossible, for they were already discovered, and the bullets were falling amongst them like the first of a hailstorm. The only possibility of escape remaining for them was a nearby hopeless improbability. It lay in forcing the post on this steep rock; which if they could do before assistance came to the enemy, they might, perhaps, be able to hold out, by means of its defences, till the arrival of the army. Their position was at once understood by all; and, by a sudden, simultaneous impulse, they found themselves halfway up the steep ascent, and in the struggle of a close conflict, without being aware of any order to that effect from their officer. But their courage was of no avail; the advantages of the place were too great; and in a few minutes the whole party was cut to pieces, or stretched helpless on the rock. Our youth had fallen amongst the foremost; for a musket ball had grazed his skull, and laid him insensible.

But consciousness slowly returned, and he succeeded at last in raising himself and looking around him. The place was deserted. A few of his friends, alive, but grievously wounded, lay near him. The rest were dead. It appeared that, learning the proximity of the English forces from this rencontre with part of their advanced guard, and dreading lest the town, which was on the point of surrendering, should after all be snatched from their grasp, the commander of the enemy's forces had ordered an immediate and general assault; and had for this purpose recalled from their outposts the whole of his troops thus stationed, that he might make the attempt with the utmost strength he could accumulate.

As the youth's power of vision returned, he perceived, from the height where he lay, that the town was already in the hands of the enemy. But looking down into the level space immediately below him, he started to his feet at once; for a girl, bare-headed, was fleeing towards the rock, pursued by several soldiers. "Aha!" said he, divining her purpose—the soldiers behind and the rock before her—"I will help you to die!" And he stooped and wrenched from the dead fingers of a sergeant the sword which they clenched by the bloody hilt. A new throb of life pulsed through him to his very fingertips; and on the brink of the unseen world he stood, with the blood rushing through his veins in a wild dance of excitement. One who lay near him wounded, but recovered afterwards, said that he looked like one inspired. With a keen eye he watched the chase. The girl drew nigh; and rushed up the path near which he was standing. Close on her footsteps came the soldiers, the distance gradually lessening between them.

Not many paces higher up, was a narrower part of the ascent, where the path was confined by great stones, or pieces of rock. Here had been the chief defence in the preceding assault, and in it lay many bodies of his friends. Thither he went and took his stand.

On the girl came, over the dead, with rigid hands and flying feet, the bloodless skin drawn tight on her features, and her eyes awfully large and wild. She did not see him though she bounded past so near that her hair flew in his eyes. "Never mind!" said he, "We shall meet soon." And he stepped into the narrow path just in time to face her pursuers—between her and them. Like the red lightning, the bloody sword fell, and a man beneath it. Cling! Clang! went the echoes in the rocks—and another man was down; for, in his excitement he was destroying angel to the breathless pursuers. His stature rose, his chest dilated; and as the third foe fell dead, the girl was safe; for her body lay a broken, empty, but undesecrated temple, at the foot of the rock. That moment his sword flew in shivers from his grasp. The next instant he fell, pierced to the heart; and his spirit rose triumphant, free, strong, and calm, above the stormy world, which at length lay vanquished beneath him.

THE WOW O'RIVVEN

* * *

ELSIE Scott had let her work fall on her knees, and her hands on her work, and was looking out of the wide, low window of her room, which was on one of the ground floors of the village street. Through a gap in the household shrubbery of fuchsias and myrtles filling the windowsill, one passing on the foot-pavement might get a momentary glimpse of her pale face, lighted up with two blue eyes, over which some inward trouble had spread a faint gauze-like haziness. But almost before her thoughts had had time to wander back to this trouble, a shout of children's voices, at the other end of the street, reached her ear. She listened a moment. A shadow of displeasure and pain crossed her countenance; and rising hastily, she betook herself to an inner apartment and closed the door behind her.

Meantime the sounds drew nearer; and by and by, an old man, whose strange appearance and dress showed that he had little capacity either for good or evil, passed the window. His clothes were comfortable enough in quality and condition, for they were the annual gift of a benevolent lady in the neighbourhood; but being made to accommodate his taste, both known and traditional, they were somewhat peculiar in cut and adornment. Both coat and trousers were of a dark grey cloth; but the former, which, in its shape, partook of the military, had a straight collar of yellow, and narrow cuffs of the same; while upon both sleeves, about the place where a corporal wears his stripes, was expressed, in the same yellow cloth, a somewhat singular device. It was as close an imitation of a bell, with its tongue hanging out of its mouth, as the tailor's skill could produce from a single piece of cloth. The origin of the military cut of his coat was well known. His preference for it arose in the time of the wars of the first Napoleon, when the threatened invasion of the country caused the organization of many volunteer regiments. The martial show and exercises captivated the poor man's fancy; and from that time forward nothing pleased his vanity and consequently conciliated his good-will more than to style him by his favourite title—the *Colonel*. But the badge on his arm had a deeper origin, which will be partially manifest in the course of the story—if story it can be called. It was, indeed, the baptism of the fool, the outward and visible sign of his relation to the infinite and unseen. His countenance, however, although the features were not of any peculiarly low or animal type, showed no corresponding sign of the consciousness of such a relation, being as vacant as human countenance could well be.

The cause of Elsie's annoyance was that the fool was annoyed; he was followed by a troop of boys, who turned his rank into scorn, and assailed him with epithets hateful to him. Although the most harmless of creatures when let alone, he was dangerous when roused; and now he stooped repeatedly to pick up stones and hurl them at his tormentors, who took care, while abusing him, to keep at a considerable distance, lest he should get hold of them. Amidst the sounds of derision that followed him, might be heard the words frequently repeated—"*Come hame, come hame.*" But in a few minutes the noise ceased, either from the interference of some friendly inhabitant, or that the boys grew weary, and departed in search of other amusement. By and by, Elsie might be seen again at her work in the window; but the cloud over her eyes was deeper, and her whole face more sad.

Indeed, so much did the persecution of this poor man affect her, that an onlooker would have been compelled to seek the cause in some yet deeper sympathy than that commonly felt for the oppressed, even by women. And such a sympathy existed, strange as it may seem, between the beautiful girl (for many called her *a bonnie lassie*) and this "tatter of humanity." Nothing would have been further from the thoughts of those that knew them, than the supposition of any correspondence or connection between them; yet this sympathy sprang in part from a real similarity in their history and present condition.

All the facts that were known about *Feel Jock's* origin were these: that seventy years ago, a man who had gone with his horse and cart some miles from the village, to fetch home a load of peat from a desolate moss, had heard, while toiling along as rough a road, on as lonely a hillside as any in Scotland, the cry of a child; and, searching about had found the infant hardly wrapt in rags, and untended, as if the earth herself had just given him birth,—that desert moor, wide and dismal, broken and watery, the only bosom for him to lie upon, and the cold, clear night-heaven his only covering. The man had brought him home, and the parish had taken parish-care of him. He had grown up, and proved what he now was—almost an idiot. Many of the townspeople were kind to him, and employed him in fetching water for them from the river or wells in the neighbourhood, paying him for his trouble in victuals, or whisky, of which he was very fond. He seldom spoke; and the sentences he could utter were few; yet the tone, and even the words of his limited vocabulary, were sufficient to express gratitude and some measure of love towards those who were kind to him, and hatred of those who teased and insulted him. He lived a life without aim, and apparently to no purpose; in this resembling most of his more gifted fellow men, who, with all the tools and materials necessary for building a noble mansion, are yet content with a clay hut.

Elsie, on the contrary, had been born in a comfortable farmhouse, amidst homeliness and abundance. But at a very early age, she had lost both father and mother; not so early, however, but that she had faint memories of warm, soft times on her mother's bosom, and of refuge in her mother's arms from the attacks of geese, and the pursuit of pigs. Therefore, in aftertimes, when she looked forward to heaven, it was as much a reverting to the old heavenly times of childhood and mother's love, as an anticipation of something yet to be revealed. Indeed, without some such memory, how should we ever picture to ourselves a perfect rest? But sometimes it would seem as if the more a heart was made capable of loving, the less it had to love; and poor Elsie, in passing from a mother's to a brother's guardianship, felt a change of spiritual temperature too keen. He was not a bad man, or incapable of benevolence when touched by the sight of want in anything of which he would himself have felt the privation; but he was so coarsely made, that only the purest animal necessities affected him; and a hard word, or unfeeling speech, could never have reached the quick of his nature through the hide that enclosed it. Elsie, on the contrary, was excessively and painfully sensitive, as if her nature constantly portended an invisible multitude of half-spiritual, half-nervous antennae, which shrank and trembled in every current of air at all below their own temperature. The effect of this upon her behaviour was such that she was called odd; and the poor girl felt she was not like other people, yet could not help it. Her brother, too, laughed at her without the slightest idea of the pain he occasioned, or the remotest feeling of curiosity as to what the inward and consistent causes of the outward abnormal condition might be. Tenderness was the divine comforting she needed; and it was altogether absent from her brother's character and behaviour.

Her neighbours looked on her with some interest, but they rather shunned than courted her acquaintance; especially after the return of certain nervous attacks, to which she had been subject in childhood, and which were again brought on by the events I must relate. It is curious how certain diseases repel, by a kind of awe, the sympathies of the neighbours: as if, by the fact of being subject to them, the patient were removed into another realm of existence, from which, like the dead with the living, she can hold communion with those around her only partially, and with a mixture of dread pervading the intercourse. Thus some of the deepest, purest wells of spiritual life, are, like those in old castles, choked up by the decay of the outer walls. But what tended more than anything, perhaps, to keep up the painful unrest of her soul (for the beauty of her character was evident in the fact that the irritation seldom reached her *mind*), was a circumstance at which, in its present connection, some of my readers will smile, and others feel a shudder corresponding in kind to that of Elsie.

Her brother was very fond of a rather small, but ferocious-looking bulldog, which followed close at his heels, wherever he went, with hanging head and slouching gait, never leaping or racing about like other dogs. When in the house, he always lay under his master's chair. He seemed to dislike Elsie, and she felt an unspeakable repugnance to him. Though she never mentioned her aversion, her brother easily saw it by the way in which she avoided the animal; and attributing it entirely to fear—which indeed had a great share in the matter—he would cruelly aggravate it, by telling her stories of the fierce hardihood and relentless persistency of this kind of animal. He dared not yet further increase her terror by offering to set the creature upon her, because it was doubtful whether he might be able to restrain him; but the mental suffering which he occasioned by this heartless conduct, and for which he had no sympathy, was as severe as many bodily sufferings to which he would have been sorry to subject her. Whenever the poor girl happened inadvertently to pass near the dog, which was seldom, a low growl made her aware of his proximity, and drove her to a quick retreat. He was, in fact, the animal impersonation of the animal opposition which she had continually to endure. Like chooses like; and the bulldog *in* her brother made choice of the bulldog *out of* him for his companion. So her day was one of shrinking fear and multiform discomfort.

But a nature capable of so much distress, must of necessity be *capable* of a corresponding amount of pleasure; and in her case this was manifest in the fact that sleep and the quiet of her own room restored her wonderfully. If she was only let alone, a calm mood, filled with images of pleasure, soon took possession of her mind.

Her acquaintance with the fool had commenced some ten years previous to the time I write of, when she was quite a little girl, and had come from the country with her brother, who, having taken a small farm close to the town, preferred residing in the town to occupying the farmhouse, which was not comfortable. She looked at first with some terror on his uncouth appearance, and with much wonderment on his strange dress. This wonder was heightened by a conversation she overheard one day in the street, between the fool and a little pale-faced boy, who, approaching him respectfully, said, "Weel, cornel!" "Weel, laddie!" was the reply. "Fat dis the wow say, cornel?" "Come hame, come hame!" answered the *colonel*, with both accent and quantity heaped on the word *hame*. What the *wow* could be, she had no idea; only, as the years passed on, the strange word became in her mind indescribably associated with the strange shape in yellow cloth on his sleeves. Had she been a native of the town, she could not have failed to know its import, so familiar was everyone with it, although it did not belong to the local vocabulary; but, as it was, years passed away before she discovered its meaning. And

THE WOW O'RIVVEN

when, again and again, the fool, attempting to convey his gratitude for some kindness she had shown him, mumbled over the words—"*The wow o' Rivven—the wow o' Rivven*," the wonder would return as to what could be the idea associated with them in his mind, but she made no advance towards their explanation.

That, however, which most attracted her to the old man, was his persecution by the children. They were to him what the bulldog was to her—the constant source of irritation and annoyance. They could hardly hurt him, nor did he appear to dread other injury from them than insult, to which, fool though he was, he was keenly alive. Human gad-flies that they were! They sometimes stung him beyond endurance, and he would curse them in the impotence of his anger. Once or twice Elsie had been so far carried beyond her constitutional timidity, by sympathy for the distress of her friend, that she had gone out and talked to the boys, even scolded them, so that they slunk away ashamed, and began to stand as much in dread of her as of the clutches of their prey. So she, gentle and timid to excess, acquired among them the reputation of a termagant [a turbulent girl]. Popular opinion among children, as among men, is often just, but as often very unjust; for the same manifestations may proceed from opposite principles; and, therefore, as indices to character, may mislead as often as enlighten.

Next door to the house in which Elsie resided, dwelt a tradesman and his wife, who kept an indefinite sort of shop, in which various kinds of goods were exposed for sale. Their youngest son was about the same age as Elsie; and while they were rather more than children, and less than young people, he spent many of his evenings with her, somewhat to the loss of position in his classes at the parish school. They were, indeed, much attached to each other; and, peculiarly constituted as Elsie was, one may imagine what kind of heavenly messenger a companion stronger than herself must have been to her. In fact, if she could have framed the undefinable need of her child-like nature into an articulate prayer, it would have been—"Give me someone to love me stronger than I." Any love was helpful, yes, in its degree, saving to her poor troubled soul; but the hope, as they grew older together, that the powerful, yet tender-hearted youth, really loved her, and would one day make her his wife, was like the opening of heavenly eyes of life and love in the hitherto blank and deathlike face of her existence. But nothing had been said of love, although they met and parted like lovers.

Doubtless, if the circles of their thought and feeling had continued as now to intersect each other, there would have been no interruption to their affection; but the time at length arrived when the old couple, seeing the rest of their family comfortably settled in life, resolved to make a gentleman of the youngest; and so sent him from school to college. The facilities existing in Scotland for providing a professional training enabled them to educate him as a surgeon. He parted from Elsie with some regret; but, far less dependent on her than she was on him, and full of the prospects of the future, he felt none of that sinking at the heart which seemed to lay her whole nature open to a fresh inroad of all the terrors and sorrows of her peculiar existence. No correspondence took place between them. New pursuits and relations, and the development of his tastes and judgments, entirely altered the position of poor Elsie in his memory. Having been, during their intercourse, far less of a man than she of a woman, he had no definite idea of the place he had occupied in her regard; and in his mind she receded into the background of the past, without his having any idea that she would suffer thereby, or that he was unjust towards her; while, in her thoughts, his image stood in the highest and clearest relief. It was the centre-point from which and towards which all lines radiated and converged; and although she could not but be doubtful about the future, yet there was much hope mingled with her doubts.

But when, at the close of two years, he visited his native village, and she saw before her, instead of the homely youth who had left her that winter evening, one who, to her inexperienced eyes, appeared a finished gentleman, her heart sank within her, as if she had found Nature herself false in her ripening processes, destroying the beautiful promise of a former year by changing instead of developing her creations. He spoke kindly to her, but not cordially. To her ear the voice seemed to come from a great distance out of the past; and while she looked upon him, that optical change passed over her vision, which all have experienced after gazing abstractedly on any object for a time: his form grew very small, and receded to an immeasurable distance; till, her imagination mingling with the twilight haze of her senses, she seemed to see him standing far off on a hill, with the bright horizon of sunset for a background to his clearly defined figure.

She knew no more till she found herself in bed in the dark; and the first message that reached her from the outer world, was the infernal growl of the bulldog from the room below. Next day she saw her lover walking with two ladies, who would have thought it some degree of condescension to speak to her; and he passed the house without once looking towards it.

One who is sufficiently possessed by the demon of nervousness to be glad of the magnetic influences of a friend's company in a public promenade, or of a horse beneath him in passing through a churchyard, will have some faint idea of how utterly exposed and defenceless poor Elsie now felt on the crowded thoroughfare of life. And so the insensibility which had overtaken her, was not the ordinary swoon with which Nature relieves the overstrained nerves, but the return of the epileptic fits of her early childhood; and if the condition of the poor girl had been pitiable before, it was tenfold more so now. Yet she did not complain, but bore all in silence, though it was evident that her health was giving way. But now, help came to her from a strange quarter; though many might not be willing to accord the name of help to that which rather hastened than retarded the progress of her decline.

She had gone to spend a few of the summer days with a relative in the country, some miles from her home, if home it could be called. One evening, towards sunset, she went out for a solitary walk. Passing from the little garden gate, she went along a bare country road for some distance, and then turning aside by a footpath through a thicket of low trees, she came out in a lonely little churchyard on the hillside. Hardly knowing whether or not she had intended to go there, she seated herself on a mound covered with long grass, one of many. Before her stood the ruins of an old church which was taking centuries to crumble. Little remained but the gable-wall, immensely thick, and covered with ancient ivy. The rays of the setting sun fell on a mound at its foot, not green like the rest, but of a rich, red-brown in the rosy sunset, and evidently but newly heaped up. Her eyes, too, rested upon it. Slowly the sun sank below the near horizon.

As the last brilliant point disappeared, the ivy darkened, and a wind arose and shook all its leaves, making them look cold and troubled; and to Elsie's ear came a low faint sound, as from a far-off bell. But close beside her—and she started and shivered at the sound— rose a deep, monotonous, almost sepulchral voice, *"Come hame, come hame! The wow, the wow!"*

At once she understood the whole. She sat in the churchyard of the ancient parish church of Ruthven; and when she lifted up her eyes, there she saw, in the half-ruined belfry, the old bell, all but hidden with ivy, which the passing wind had roused to utter one sleepy tone; and there, beside her, stood the fool with the bell on his arm; and to him and to her the *wow o' Rivven* said, "*Come hame, come hame!*" Ah, what did she want in the whole universe of God but a home? And though the ground beneath was hard, and the sky overhead far and boundless, and the hillside lonely and companionless, yet somewhere within the visible, and beyond these the outer surfaces of creation, there might be a home for her; as round the wintry house the snows lie heaped up cold and white and dreary all the long forenight, while within, beyond the closed shutters, and giving no glimmer through the thick stone walls, the fires are blazing joyously, and the voices and laughter of young unfrozen children are heard, and nothing belongs to winter but the grey hairs on the heads of the parents, within whose warm hearts child-like voices are heard, and child-like thoughts move to and fro. The kernel of winter itself is spring, or a sleeping summer.

It was no wonder that the fool, cast out of the earth on a far more desolate spot than this, should seek to return within her bosom at this place of open doors, and should call it *home*. For surely the surface of the earth had no home for him. The mound at the foot of the gable contained the body of one who had shown him kindness. He had followed the funeral that afternoon from the town, and had remained behind with the bell. Indeed, it was his custom, though Elsie had not known it, to follow every funeral going to this, his favourite churchyard of Ruthven; and, possibly in imitation of its booming, for it was still tolled at the funerals, he had given the old bell the name of *the wow*, and had translated its monotonous clangour into the articulate sounds—*come hame, come hame*. What precise meaning he attached to the words, it is impossible to say; but it was evident that the place possessed a strange attraction for him, drawing him towards it by the cords of some spiritual magnetism. It is possible that in the mind of the idiot there may have been some feeling about this churchyard and bell, which, in the mind of another, would have become a grand poetic thought; a feeling as if the ghostly old bell hung at the church door of the invisible world, and ever and anon rang out joyous notes (though they sounded sad in the ears of the living), calling to the children of the unseen to *come hame, come hame.* She sat for some time in silence; for the bell did not ring again, and the fool spoke no more; till the dews began to fall, when she rose and went home, followed by her companion, who passed the night in the barn.

From that hour Elsie was furnished with a visual image of the rest she sought; an image which, mingling with deeper and holier thoughts, became, like the bow set in the cloud, the earthly pledge and sign of the fulfilment of heavenly hopes. Often when the wintry fog of cold discomfort and homelessness filled her soul, all at once the picture of the little churchyard—with the old gable and belfry, and the slanting sunlight steeping down to the very roots of the long grass on the graves—arose in the darkened chamber (*camera obscura*) of her soul; and again she heard the faint Aeolian sound of the bell, and the voice of the prophet-fool who interpreted the oracle; and the inward weariness was soothed by the promise of a long sleep. Who can tell how many have been counted fools simply because they were prophets; or how much of the madness in the world may be the utterance of thoughts true and just, but belonging to a region differing from ours in its nature and scenery!

But to Elsie looking out of her window came the mocking tones of the idle boys who had chosen as the vehicle of their scorn the very words which showed the relation of the fool to the eternal, and revealed in him an element higher far than any yet developed in them. They turned his glory into shame, like the enemies of David when they mocked the would-be king. And the best in a man is often that which is most condemned by those who have not attained to his goodness. The words, however, even as repeated by the boys, had not solely awakened indignation at the persecution of the old man: they had likewise comforted her with the thought of the refuge that awaited both him and her.

But the same evening a worse trial was in store for her. Again she sat near the window, oppressed by the consciousness that her brother had come in. He had gone upstairs, and his dog had remained at the door, exchanging surly compliments with some of his own kind, when the fool came strolling past, and, I do not know from what cause, the dog flew at him. Elsie heard his cry and looked up. Her fear of the brute vanished in a moment before her sympathy for her friend. She darted from the house, and rushed towards the dog to drag him off the defenceless idiot, calling him by his name in a tone of anger and dislike. He left the fool, and, springing at Elsie, seized her by the arm above the elbow with such a grip that, in the midst of her agony, she fancied she heard the bone crack. But she uttered no cry, for the most apprehensive are sometimes the most courageous. Just then, however, her former lover was coming along the street, and, catching a glimpse of what had happened, was on the spot in an instant, took the dog by the throat with a grip not inferior to his own, and having thus compelled him to relax his hold, dashed him on the ground with a force that almost stunned him, and then with a super-added kick sent him away limping and howling; whereupon the fool, attacking him furiously with a stick would certainly have finished him, had not his master descried his plight and come to his rescue.

Meantime the young surgeon had carried Elsie into the house; for, as soon as she was rescued from the dog, she had fallen down in one of her fits, which were becoming more and more frequent of themselves, and little needed such a shock as this to increase their violence. He was dressing her arm when she began to recover; and when she opened her eyes, in a state of half-consciousness, the first object she beheld was his face bending over her. Recalling nothing of what had occurred, it seemed to her, in the dreamy condition in which the fit had left her, the same face, unchanged, which had once shone in upon her tardy springtime, and promised to ripen it into summer. She forgot it had departed and left her in the wintry cold. And so she uttered wild words of love and trust; and the youth, while stung with remorse at his own neglect, was astonished to perceive the poetic forms of beauty in which the soul of the uneducated maiden burst into flower. But as her senses recovered themselves, the face gradually changed to her, as if the slow alteration of two years had been phantasmagorically compressed into a few moments; and the glow departed from the maiden's thoughts and words, and her soul found itself at the narrow window of the present, from which she could behold but a dreary country. From the street came the iambic cry of the fool, "*Come hame, come hame.*"

Tycho Brahe, I think, is said to have kept a fool, who frequently sat at his feet in his study, and to whose mutterings he used to listen in the pauses of his own thought. The shining soul of the astronomer drew forth the rainbow of harmony from the misty spray of words ascending ever from the dark gulf into which the thoughts of the idiot were ever falling. He beheld curious concurrences of words therein, and could read strange meanings from them—sometimes even received wondrous hints for the direction of celestial inquiry, from what to any other, and it may be to the fool himself, was but a ceaseless and aimless babble. Such power lieth in words. It is not then to be wondered at that the sounds I have mentioned should fall on the ears of Elsie, at such a moment as a message from God himself. This then—all this dreariness—was but a passing show like the rest, and there lay somewhere for her a reality—a home. The tears burst up from her oppressed heart. She received the message, and prepared to go home. From that time her strength gradually sank, but her spirits as steadily rose.

The strength of the fool, too, began to fail, for he was old. He bore all the signs of age, even to the grey hairs, which betokened no wisdom. But one cannot say what wisdom might be in him, or how far he had not fought his own battle, and been victorious. Whether any notion of a continuance of life and thought dwelt in his brain, it is impossible to tell; but he seemed to have the idea that this was not his home; and those who saw him gradually approaching his end, might well anticipate for him a higher life in the world to come. He had passed through this world without ever awaking to such a consciousness of being as is common to mankind. He had spent his years like a weary dream through a long night, a strange, dismal, unkindly dream; and now the morning was at hand. Often in his dream had he listened with sleepy senses to the ringing of the bell, but that bell would awake him at last. He was like a seed buried too deep in the soil, to which the light has never penetrated, and which, therefore, has never forced its way upwards to the open air, never experienced the resurrection of the dead. But seeds will grow ages after they have fallen into the earth; and, indeed, with many kinds, and within some limits, the older the seed before it germinates, the more plentiful the fruit. And may it not be believed of many human beings, that the great Husbandman having sown them like seeds in the soil of human affairs, there they lie buried a life long; and only after the upturning of the soil by death, reach a position in which the awakening of their aspiration and the consequent growth become possible. Surely he has made nothing in vain.

A violent cold and cough brought him at last near to his end, and hearing that he was ill, Elsie ventured one bright spring day to go to see him. When she entered the miserable room where he lay, he held out his hand to her with something like a smile, and muttered feebly and painfully, "I'm gaein' to the wow, nae to come back again." Elsie could not restrain her tears; while the old man, looking fixedly at her, though with meaningless eyes, muttered for the last time, "*Come hame! Come hame!*" and sank into a lethargy, from which nothing could rouse him, till, next morning, he was waked by friendly death from the long sleep of this world's night. They bore him to his favourite churchyard, and buried him within the site of the old church, below his loved bell, which had ever been to him as the cuckoo-note of a coming spring. Thus he at length obeyed its summons, and went home.

Elsie lingered till the first summer days lay warm on the land. Several kind hearts in the village, hearing of her illness, visited her and ministered to her. Wondering at her sweetness and patience, they regretted they had not known her before. How much consolation might not their kindness have imparted, and how much might not their sympathy have strengthened her on her painful road! But they could not long have delayed her going home. Nor, mentally constituted as she was, would this have been at all to be desired. Indeed it was chiefly the expectation of departure that quieted and soothed her tremulous nature. It is true that a deep spring of hope and faith kept singing on in her heart, but this alone, without the anticipation of speedy release, could only have kept her mind at peace. It could not have reached, at least for a long time, the border land between body and mind, in which her disease lay.

One still night of summer, the nurse who watched by her bedside heard her murmur through her sleep, "I hear it: *come hame—come hame*. I'm comin', I'm comin'—I'm gaein' hame to the wow, nae to come back." She awoke at the sound of her own words, and begged the nurse to convey to her brother her last request that she might be buried by the side of the fool, within the old church of Ruthven. Then she turned her face to the wall, and in the morning was found quiet and cold. She must have died within a few minutes after her last words. She was buried according to her request; and thus she too went home.

Side by side rest the aged fool and the young maiden; for the bell called them and they obeyed; and surely they found the fire burning bright, and heard friendly voices, and felt sweet lips on theirs, in the home to which they went. Surely both intellect and love were waiting them there.

Still the old bell hangs in the old gable; and whenever another is borne to the old churchyard, it keeps calling to those who are left behind, with the same sad, but friendly and unchanging voice—
"*Come hame! Come hame! Come hame!*"

"Thy sun shall no more go down; neither shall thy moon withdraw itself: for the LORD shall be thine everlasting light, and the days of thy mourning shall be ended" (Isaiah 60:20).

BIRTH, DREAMING, DEATH

* * *

THE SCHOOLMASTER'S STORY

IN a little room, scantily furnished, lighted, not from the window, for it was dark without, and the shutters were closed, but from the peaked flame of a small, clear-burning lamp, sat a young man, with his back to the lamp and his face to the fire. No book or paper on the table indicated labour just forsaken; nor could one tell from his eyes, in which the light had all retreated inwards, whether his consciousness was absorbed in thought, or reverie only. The window curtains, which scarcely concealed the shutters, were of coarse texture, but of brilliant scarlet, for he loved bright colours; and the faint reflection they threw on his pale, thin face, made it look more delicate than it would have seemed in pure daylight. Two or three bookshelves, suspended by cords from a nail in the wall, contained a collection of books, poverty-stricken as to numbers, with but few to fill up the chronological gap between the Greek New Testament and stray volumes of the poets of the present century. But his love for the souls of his individual books was the stronger that there was no possibility of its degenerating into avarice for the bodies or outsides whose aggregate constitutes the piece of house-furniture called a library.

"Some years before, the young man (my story is so short, and calls in so few personages, that I need not give him a name) had aspired, under the influence of religious and sympathetic feeling, to be a clergyman; but Providence, either in the form of poverty, or of theological difficulty, had prevented his prosecuting his studies to that end. And now he was *only* a village schoolmaster; but is it not better to be a teacher *of* babes than a preacher *to* men, at any time; not to speak of those troublous times of transition, wherein a difference of degree must so often assume the appearance of a difference of kind? That man is more happy—I will not say more blessed—who, loving boys and girls, is loved and revered by them, than he who, ministering unto men and women, is compelled to pour his words into the filter of religious suspicion, whence the water is allowed to pass away unheeded, and only the residuum is retained for the analysis of ignorant party-spirit.

"He had married a simple village girl, in whose eyes he was nobler than the noblest—to whom he was the mirror, in which the real forms of all things around were reflected. Who dares pity my poor village schoolmaster? I fling his pity away. Had he not found in her love the verdict of God, that he was worth loving? Did he not in her possess the eternal and the unchangeable? Were not her eyes openings through which he looked into the great depths that could not be measured or represented? She was his public, his society, his critic. He found in her the heaven of his rest God gave unto him immortality, and he was glad. For his ambition, it had died of its own mortality. He read the words of Jesus, and the words of great prophets whom he has sent; and learned that the wind-tossed anemone is a word of God as real and true as the unbending oak beneath which it grows—that reality is an absolute existence precluding degrees. If his mind was, as his room, scantily furnished, it was yet lofty; if his light was small, it was brilliant. God lived, and he lived. Perhaps the highest moral height which a man can reach, and at the same time the most difficult of attainment, is the willingness to be

✱ BIRTH, DREAMING, DEATH

nothing relatively, so that he attain that positive excellence which the original conditions of his being render not merely possible, but imperative. It is nothing to a man to be greater or less than another; to be esteemed or otherwise by the public or private world in which he moves. Does he, or does he not, behold and love and live the unchangeable, the essential, the divine? This he can only do according as God has made him. He can behold and understand God in the least degree, as well as in the greatest, only by the godlike within him; and he that loves thus the good and great has no room, no thought, no necessity for comparison and difference. The truth satisfies him. He lives in its absoluteness. God makes the glow-worm as well as the star; the light in both is divine. If mine be an earth-star to gladden the wayside, I must cultivate humbly and rejoicingly its green earth-glow, and not seek to blanch it to the whiteness of the stars that lie in the fields of blue. For to deny God in my own being is to cease to behold him in any. God and man can meet only by the man's becoming that which God meant him to be. Then he enters into the house of life, which is greater than the house of fame. It is better to be a child in a green field than a knight of many orders in a state ceremonial.

"All night long he had sat there, and morning was drawing nigh. He has not heard the busy wind all night, heaping up snow against the house, which will make him start at the ghostly face of the world when at length he opens the shutters, and it stares upon him so white. For up in a little room above, white-curtained, like the great earth without, there has been a storm, too, half the night—moanings and prayers—and some forbidden tears; but now, at length, it is over; and through the portals of two mouths instead of one, flows and ebbs the tide of the great air-sea which feeds the life of man. With the sorrow of the mother, the new life is purchased for the child; our very being is redeemed from nothingness with the pains of a death of which we know nothing.

"An hour has gone by since the watcher below has been delivered from the fear and doubt that held him. He has seen the mother and the child—the first she has given to life and him, and has returned to his lonely room, quiet and glad.

"But not long did he sit thus before thought of doubt awoke in his mind. He remembered his scanty income, and the somewhat feeble health of his wife. One of two small debts he had contracted seemed absolutely to press on his bosom; and the newborn child—'Oh! How doubly welcome,' he thought, 'if I were but half as rich again as I am!'—brought with it, as its own love, so its own care. The dogs of need, that so often hunt us up to heaven, seemed hard upon his heels; and he prayed to God with fervour; and as he prayed he fell asleep in his chair, and as he slept he dreamed. The fire and the lamp burned on as before, but threw no rays into his soul; yet now, for the first time, he seemed to become aware of the storm without; for his dream was as follows:

"He lay in his bed, and listened to the howling of the wintry wind. He trembled at the thought of the pitiless cold, and turned to sleep again, when he thought he heard a feeble knocking at the door. He rose in haste, and went down with a light. As he opened the door, the wind, entering with a gust of frosty particles, blew out his candle; but he found it unnecessary, for the grey dawn had come. Looking out, he saw nothing at first; but a second look, turned downwards, showed him a little half-frozen child, who looked quietly, but beseechingly, in his face. His hair was filled with drifted snow, and his little hands and cheeks were blue with cold. The heart of the schoolmaster swelled to bursting with the spring-flood of love and pity that rose up within it. He lifted the child to his bosom, and carried him into the house, where, in the dream's incongruity, he found a fire blazing in the room in which he now slept. The child

* BIRTH, DREAMING, DEATH

said never a word. He set him by the fire, and made haste to get hot water, and put him in a warm bath. He never doubted that this was a stray orphan who had wandered to him for protection, and he felt that he could not part with him again; even though the train of his previous troubles and doubts once more passed through the mind of the dreamer, and there seemed no answer to his perplexities for the lack of that cheap thing, gold—yea, silver. But when he had undressed and bathed the little orphan, and having dried him on his knees, set him down to reach something warm to wrap him in, the boy suddenly looked up in his face, as if revived, and said with a heavenly smile, 'I am the child Jesus.' 'The child Jesus!' said the dreamer, astonished. 'Thou art like any other child.' 'No, do not say so,' returned the boy; 'but say, *Any other child is like me.*' And the child and the dream slowly faded away; and he awoke with these words sounding in his heart—'Whosoever shall receive one of such children in my name, receiveth me; and whosoever shall receive me, receiveth not me, but him that sent me.' It was the voice of God saying to him; 'Thou wouldst receive the child whom I sent thee out of the cold, stormy night; receive the new child out of the cold waste into the warm, human house, as the door by which it can enter God's house, its home. If better could be done for it, or for thee, would I have sent it hither? Through thy love, my little one must learn my love and be blessed. And thou shalt not keep it without thy reward. For thy necessities—in thy little house, is there not yet room? In thy barrel, is there not yet meal? And thy purse is not empty quite. Thou canst not eat more than a mouthful at once. I have made thee so. Is it any trouble to me to take care of thee? Only I prefer to feed thee from my own hand, and not from thy store.' And the schoolmaster sprang up in joy, ran up stairs, kissed his wife, and clasped the baby in his arms in the name of the child Jesus. And in that embrace, he knew that he received God to his heart. Soon, with a tender, beaming face, he was wading through the snow to the schoolhouse, where he spent a happy day amidst the rosy faces and bright eyes of his boys and girls. These, likewise, he loved the more dearly and joyfully for that dream, and those words in his heart; so that amidst their true child-faces, (all going well with them, as not infrequently happened in his schoolroom), he felt as if all the elements of Paradise were gathered around him, and knew that he was God's child, doing God's work.

"But while that dream was passing through the soul of the husband, another visited the wife, as she lay in the faintness and trembling joy of the new motherhood. For although she that has been mother before, is not the less a new mother to the new child, her former relation not covering with its wings the fresh bird in the nest of her bosom, yet there must be a peculiar delight in the thoughts and feelings that come with the first-born. As she lay half in a sleep, half in a faint, with the vapours of a gentle delirium floating through her brain, without losing the sense of existence she lost the consciousness of its form, and thought she lay, not a young mother in her bed, but a nosegay of wild flowers in a basket, crushed, flattened and half-withered. With her in the basket lay other bunches of flowers, whose odours, some rare as well as rich, revealed to her the sad contrast in which she was placed. Beside her lay a cluster of delicately curved, faintly tinged, tea-scented roses; while she was only blue hyacinth bells, pale primroses, amethyst anemones, closed blood-coloured daisies, purple violets, and one sweet-scented, pure white orchis. The basket lay on the counter of a well-known little shop in the village, waiting for purchasers. By and by her own husband entered the shop, and approached the basket to choose a nosegay. 'Ah!' thought she, 'Will he choose me? How dreadful if he should not, and I should be left lying here, while he takes another! But how should he choose me? They are all so beautiful; and even

*   BIRTH, DREAMING, DEATH

my scent is nearly gone. And he cannot know that it is I lying here. Alas! Alas!' But as she thought thus, she felt his hand clasp her, heard the ransom-money fall, and felt that she was pressed to his face and lips, as he passed from the shop. He *had* chosen her, he *had* known her. She opened her eyes: her husband's kiss had awakened her. She did not speak, but looked up thankfully in his eyes, as if he had, in fact, like one of the old knights, delivered her from the transformation of some evil magic, by the counter-enchantment of a kiss, and restored her from a half-withered nosegay to be a woman, a wife, a mother. The dream comforted her much, for she had often feared that she, the simple, so-called uneducated girl, could not be enough for the great schoolmaster. But soon her thoughts flowed into another channel; the tears rose in her dark eyes, shining clear from beneath a stream that was not of sorrow; and it was only weakness that kept her from uttering audible words like these: 'Father in heaven, shall I trust my husband's love, and doubt thine? Wilt thou meet less richly the fearing hope of thy child's heart, than he in my dream met the longing of his wife's? He was perfected in my eyes by the love he bore me—shall I find thee less complete? Here I lie on thy world, faint, and crushed, and withered; and my soul often seems as if it had lost all the odours that should float up in the sweet-smelling savour of thankfulness and love to thee. But thou hast only to take me, only to choose me, only to clasp me to thy bosom, and I shall be a beautiful singing angel, singing to God, and comforting my husband while I sing. Father, take me, possess me, fill me!'

"So she lay patiently waiting for the summertime of restored strength that drew slowly nigh. With her husband and her child near her, in her soul, and God everywhere, there was for her no death, and no hurt. When she said to herself, 'How rich I am!' it was with the riches that pass not away—the riches of the Son of man; for in her treasures, the human and the divine were blended—were one.

"But there was a hard trial in store for them. They had learned to receive what the Father sent: they had now to learn that what he gave he gave eternally, after his own being—his own glory. For ere the mother awoke from her first sleep, the baby, like a frolicsome child-angel, that but tapped at his mother's window and fled, the baby died; died while the mother slept away the pangs of its birth; died while the father was teaching other babes out of the joy of his new fatherhood.

"When the mother woke, she lay still in her joy—the joy of a doubled life; and knew not that death had been there, and had left behind only the little human coffin.

"'Nurse, bring me the baby,' she said at last. 'I want to see it.'

"But the nurse pretended not to hear.

"'I want to nurse it. Bring it.'

"She had not yet learned to say *him*; for it was her first baby.

"But the nurse went out of the room, and remained some minutes away. When she returned, the mother spoke more absolutely, and the nurse was compelled to reply—at last.

"'Nurse, do bring me the baby; I am quite able to nurse it now.'

"'Not yet if you please, ma'am. Really you must rest a while first. Do try to go to sleep.'

"The nurse spoke steadily, and looked her, too, straight in the face; and there was a constraint in her voice, a determination to be calm, that at once roused the suspicion of the mother, for though her first-born was dead, and she had given birth to what was now, as far as the eye could reach, the waxen image of a son, a child had come from God, and had departed to him again; and she *was* his mother.

"And the fear fell upon her heart that it might be as it was; and, looking at her attendant with a face blanched yet more with fear

* BIRTH, DREAMING, DEATH

than with suffering, she said: "'Nurse, is the baby—?'

"She could not say *dead*; for to utter the word would be at once to make it possible that the only fruit of her labour had been pain and sorrow.

"But the nurse saw that further concealment was impossible; and, without another word, went and fetched the husband, who, with face pale as the mother's, brought the baby, dressed in its white clothes, and laid it by its mother's side, where it lay too still.

"'Oh, ma'am, do not take on so,' said the nurse, as she saw the face of the mother grow like the face of the child, as if she were about to rush after him into the dark.

"But she was not 'taking on' at all. She only felt that pain at her heart, which is the farewell kiss of a long-cherished joy. Though cast out of paradise into a world that looked very dull and weary, yet, used to suffering, and always claiming from God the consolation it needed, and satisfied with that, she was able, presently, to look up in her husband's face, and try to reassure him of her well-being by a dreary smile.

"'Leave the baby,' she said; and they left it where it was. Long and earnestly she gazed on the perfect tiny features of the little alabaster countenance, and tried to feel that this was the child she had been so long waiting for. As she looked, she fancied she heard it breathe, and she thought—'What if it should be only asleep!' but, alas! The eyes would not open, and when she drew it close to her, she shivered to feel it so cold. At length, as her eyes wandered over and over the little face, a look of her husband dawned unexpectedly upon it; and, as if the wife's heart awoke the mother's, she cried out, 'Baby! Baby!' and burst into tears, during which weeping she fell asleep.

"When she awoke, she found the babe had been removed while she slept. But the unsatisfied heart of the mother longed to look again on the form of the child; and again, though with remonstrance from the nurse, it was laid beside her. All day and all night long, it remained by her side, like a little frozen thing that had wandered from its home, and now lay dead by the door.

"Next morning the nurse protested that she must part with it, for it made her fret; but she knew it quieted her, and she would rather keep her little lifeless babe. At length the nurse appealed to the father; and the mother feared he would think it necessary to remove it; but to her joy and gratitude he said, 'No, no; let her keep it as long as she likes.' And she loved her husband the more for that; for he understood her.

"Then she had the cradle brought near the bed, all ready as it was for a live child that had open eyes, and therefore needed sleep— needed the lids of the brain to close, when it was filled full of the strange colours and forms of the new world. But this one needed no cradle, for it slept on. It needed, instead of the little curtains to darken it to sleep, a great sunlight to wake it up from the darkness, and the ever-satisfied rest. Yet she laid it in the cradle, which she had set near her, where she could see it, with the little hand and arm laid out on the white coverlet. If she could only keep it so! Could not something be done, if not to awake it yet to turn it to stone, and let it remain so forever? No; the body must go back to its mother, the earth, and the *form* which is immortal, being the thought of God, must go back to its Father—the Maker. And as it lay in the white cradle, a white coffin was being made for it. And the mother thought: 'I wonder which trees are growing coffins for my husband and me.'

"But ere the child, that had the prayer of Job in his grief, and had died from its mother's womb, was carried away to be buried, the mother prayed over it this prayer: 'O God, if thou wilt not let me be a mother, I have one refuge: I will go back and be a child: I will be thy child more than ever. My mother-heart will find relief in childhood towards its Father. For is it not the same nature that makes the true mother and the true child? Is it not the same thought blossoming upward and blossoming downward? So there is God the Father and God the Son. Thou wilt keep my little son for me. He has gone home to be nursed for me. And when I grow well, I will be more simple, and truthful, and joyful in thy sight. And now thou art taking away my child, my plaything from me. But I think how pleased I should be, if I had a daughter, and she loved me so well that she only smiled when I took her plaything from her. Oh! I will not disappoint thee—thou shalt have thy joy. Here I am, do with me what thou wilt; I will only smile.'

"And how fared the heart of the father? At first, in the bitterness of his grief, he called the loss of his child a punishment for his doubt and unbelief; and the feeling of punishment made the stroke more keen, and the heart less willing to endure it. But better thoughts woke within him ere long.

"The old woman who swept out his schoolroom, came in the evening to inquire after the mistress, and to offer her condolences on the loss of the baby. She came likewise to tell the news, that a certain old man of little respectability had departed at last, unregretted by a single soul in the village but herself, who had been his nurse through the last tedious illness.

"The schoolmaster thought with himself:

"'Can that soiled and withered leaf of a man, and my little snow-flake of a baby, have gone the same road? Will they meet by the way? Can they talk about the same thing—anything? They must part on the borders of the shining land, and they could hardly speak by the way.'

"'He will live four-and-twenty hours, nurse,' the doctor had said.

"'No, doctor; he will die to-night,' the nurse had replied; during which whispered dialogue, the patient had lain breathing quietly, for the last of suffering was nearly over.

He was at the close of an ill-spent life, not so much selfishly towards others as indulgently towards himself. He had failed of true joy by trying often and perseveringly to create a false one; and now, about to knock at the gate of the other world, he bore with him no burden of the good things of this; and one might be tempted to say of him, that it were better he had not been born. The great majestic mystery lay before him—but when would he see its majesty?

"He was dying thus, because he had tried to live as Nature said he should not live; and he had taken his own wages—for the law of the Maker is the necessity of his creature. His own children had forsaken him, for they were not perfect as their Father in heaven, who maketh his sun to shine on the evil and on the good. Instead of doubling their care as his need doubled, they had thought of the disgrace he brought on them, and not of the duty they owed him; and now, left to die alone for them, he was waited on by this hired nurse, who, familiar with death-beds, knew better than the doctor, knew that he could live only a few hours.

"Stooping to his ear, she had told him, as gently as she could, for she thought she ought not to conceal it, that he must die that night. He had lain silent for a few moments; then had called her, and, with broken and fading voice, had said, 'Nurse, you are the only friend I have; give me one kiss before I die.' And the woman-heart had answered the prayer.

"'And,' said the old woman, 'he put his arms round my neck, and gave me a long kiss, such a long kiss! And then he turned his face away, and never spoke again.'

"So, with the last unction of a woman's kiss, with this baptism for the dead, he had departed.

* BIRTH, DREAMING, DEATH

"'Poor old man! He had not quite destroyed his heart yet,' thought the schoolmaster. 'Surely it was the child-nature that woke in him at the last when the only thing left for his soul to desire, the only thing he could think of as a preparation for the dread something, was a kiss. Strange conjunction, yet simple and natural! Eternity—a kiss. Kiss me; for I am going to the Unknown! Poor old man!' the schoolmaster went on in his thoughts, 'I hope my baby has met him, and put his tiny hand in the poor old shaking hand, and so led him across the borders into the shining land, and up to where Jesus sits, and said to the Lord: "Lord, forgive this old man, for he knew not what he did." And I trust the Lord has forgiven him.'

"And then the bereaved father fell on his knees, and cried out:

"'Lord, thou has not punished me. Thou wouldst not punish for a passing thought of troubled unbelief, with which I strove. Lord, take my child and his mother and me, and do what thou wilt with us. I know thou givest not, to take again.'

"And ere the schoolmaster could call his Protestantism to his aid, he had ended his prayer with the cry:

"'And O God! Have mercy upon the poor old man, and lay not his sins to his charge.'

"For, though a woman's kiss may comfort a man to eternity, it is not all he needs. And the thought of his lost child had made the soul of the father compassionate."

He ceased, and we sat silent.

THE LIGHT PRINCESS

* * *

I. WHAT! NO CHILDREN?

ONCE upon a time, so long ago that I have quite forgotten the date, there lived a king and queen who had no children.

And the king said to himself, "All the queens of my acquaintance have children, some three, some seven, and some as many as twelve; and my queen has not one. I feel ill-used." So he made up his mind to be cross with his wife about it. But she bore it all like a good patient queen as she was. Then the king grew very cross indeed. But the queen pretended to take it all as a joke, and a very good one too.

"Why don't you have any daughters, at least?" said he. "I don't say *sons*; that might be too much to expect."

"I am sure, dear king, I am very sorry," said the queen.

"So you ought to be," retorted the king; "you are not going to make a virtue of *that*, surely."

But he was not an ill-tempered king, and in any matter of less moment would have let the queen have her own way with all his heart. This, however, was an affair of state.

The queen smiled.

"You must have patience with a lady, you know, dear king," said she.

She was, indeed a very nice queen, and heartily sorry that she could not oblige the king immediately.

The king tried to have patience, but he succeeded very badly. It was more than he deserved, therefore, when, at last, the queen gave him a daughter—as lovely a little princess as ever cried.

II. WON'T I, JUST?

THE day grew near when the infant must be christened. The king wrote all the invitations with his own hand. Of course somebody was forgotten.

Now it does not generally matter if somebody *is* forgotten, only you must mind who. Unfortunately, the king forgot without intending to forget; and so the chance fell upon the Princess Makemnoit, which was awkward. For the princess was the king's own sister; and he ought not to have forgotten her. But she had made herself so disagreeable to the old king, their father, that he had forgotten her in making his will; and so it was no wonder that her brother forgot her in writing his invitations. But poor relations don't do anything to keep you in mind of them. Why don't they? The king could not see into the garret she lived in, could he?

She was a sour, spiteful creature. The wrinkles of contempt crossed the wrinkles of peevishness, and made her face as full of wrinkles as a pat of butter. If ever a king could be justified in forgetting anybody, this king was justified in forgetting his sister, even at a christening. She looked very odd, too. Her forehead was as large as all the rest of her face, and projected over it like a precipice. When she was angry, her little eyes flashed blue. When she hated anybody, they shone yellow and green. What they looked like when she loved anybody, I do not know; for I never heard of her loving anybody but herself, and I do not think she could have managed that if she had not somehow got used to herself. But what made it highly imprudent in the king to forget her was—that she was awfully clever. In fact, she was a witch; and when she bewitched anybody, he very soon had enough of it; for she beat all the wicked fairies in wickedness, and all the clever ones in cleverness. She despised all the modes we read of in history, in which offended fairies and witches have taken their revenges; and therefore, after waiting and waiting in vain for an invitation, she made up her mind at last to go without one, and make the whole family miserable, like a princess as she was.

So she put on her best gown, went to the palace, was kindly received by the happy monarch, who forgot that he had forgotten her, and took her place in the procession to the royal chapel. When they were all gathered about the font, she contrived to get next to it, and throw something into the water; after which she maintained a very respectful demeanour till the water was applied to the child's face. But at that moment she turned round in her place three times, and muttered the following words, loud enough for those beside her to hear:

> *"Light of spirit, by my charms,*
> *Light of body every part,*
> *Never weary human arms—*
> *Only crush thy parents' heart!"*

They all thought she had lost her wits, and was repeating some foolish nursery rhyme; but a shudder went through the whole of them notwithstanding. The baby, on the contrary, began to laugh and crow; while the nurse gave a start and a smothered cry, for she thought she was struck with paralysis: she could not feel the baby in her arms. But she clasped it tight and said nothing.

The mischief was done.

III. SHE CAN'T BE OURS

HER atrocious aunt had deprived the child of all her gravity. If you ask me how this was effected I answer, "In the easiest way in the world. She had only to destroy gravitation." For the princess was a philosopher, and knew all the *ins* and *outs* of the laws of gravitation as well as the *ins* and *outs* of her bootlace. And being a witch as well, she could abrogate those laws in a moment; or at least so clog their wheels and rust their bearings, that they would not work at all. But we have more to do with what followed than with how it was done.

The first awkwardness that resulted from this unhappy privation was that the moment the nurse began to float the baby up and down, she flew from her arms towards the ceiling. Happily, the resistance of the air brought her ascending career to a close within a foot of it. There she remained, horizontal as when she left her nurse's arms, kicking and laughing amazingly. The nurse in terror flew to the bell, and begged the footman, who answered it to bring up the house-steps directly. Trembling in every limb, she climbed upon the steps, and had to stand upon the very top, and reach up, before she could catch the floating tail of the baby's long clothes.

When the strange fact came to be known, there was a terrible commotion in the palace. The occasion of its discovery by the king was naturally a repetition of the nurse's experience. Astonished that he felt no weight when the child was laid in his arms, he began to wave her up and—not down; for she slowly ascended to the ceiling as before, and there remained floating in perfect comfort and satisfaction, as was testified by her peals of tiny laughter. The king stood staring up in speechless amazement, and trembled so that his beard shook like grass in the wind. At last, turning to the queen, who was just as horror-struck as himself, he said, gasping, staring, and stammering, "She *can't* be ours, queen!"

Now the queen was much cleverer than the king, and had begun already to suspect that "this effect defective came by cause."

"I am sure she is ours," answered she. "But we ought to have taken better care of her at the christening. People who were never invited ought not to have been present."

"Oh, ho!" said the king, tapping his forehead with his forefinger, "I have it all. I've found out. Don't you see it, queen? Princess Makemnoit has bewitched her."

"That's just what I say," answered the queen.

"I beg your pardon, my love; I did not hear you. John! bring the steps I get on my throne with."

For he was a little king with a great throne, like many other kings.

The throne-steps were brought, and set upon the dining table, and John got upon the top of them. But he could not reach the little princess, who lay like a baby-laughter-cloud in the air, exploding continuously.

"Take the tongs, John," said his majesty; and getting up on the table, he handed them to him.

John could reach the baby now, and the little princess was handed down by the tongs.

IV. WHERE IS SHE?

ONE fine summer day, a month after these her first adventures, during which time she had been very carefully watched, the princess was lying on the bed in the queen's own chamber, fast asleep. One of the windows was open, for it was noon, and the day was so sultry that the little girl was wrapped in nothing less ethereal than slumber itself. The queen came into the room, and not observing that the baby was on the bed, opened another window. A frolicsome fairy wind, which had been watching for a chance of mischief, rushed in at the one window, and taking its way over the bed where the child was lying, caught her up, and rolling and floating her along like a piece of flue, or a dandelion seed, carried her with it through the opposite window, and away. The queen went down-stairs, quite ignorant of the loss she had herself occasioned.

When the nurse returned, she supposed that her majesty had carried her off, and, dreading a scolding, delayed making inquiry about her. But hearing nothing, she grew uneasy, and went at length to the queen's boudoir, where she found her majesty.

"Please, your majesty, shall I take the baby?" said she.

"Where is she?" asked the queen.

"Please forgive me. I know it was wrong."

"What do you mean?" said the queen, looking grave.

"Oh! Don't frighten me, your majesty!" exclaimed the nurse, clasping her hands.

The queen saw that something was amiss, and fell down in a faint. The nurse rushed about the palace, screaming, "My baby! My baby!"

Everyone ran to the queen's room. But the queen could give no orders. They soon found out however, that the princess was missing, and in a moment the palace was like a beehive in a garden; and in one minute more the queen was brought to herself by a great shout and a clapping of hands. They had found the princess fast asleep under a rose-bush, to which the elvish little wind-puff had carried her, finishing its mischief by shaking a shower of red rose-leaves all over the little white sleeper. Startled by the noise the servants made, she woke, and furious with glee, scattered the rose-leaves in all directions, like a shower of spray in the sunset.

She was watched more carefully after this, no doubt; yet it would be endless to relate all the odd incidents resulting from this peculiarity of the young princess. But there never was a baby in a house, not to say a palace, that kept the household in such constant good humour, at least below-stairs. If it was not easy for her nurses to hold her, at least she made neither their arms nor their hearts ache. And she was so nice to play at ball with! There was positively no danger of letting her fall. They might throw her down, or knock her down, or push her down, but couldn't *let* her down. It is true, they might let her fly into the fire or the coal-hole, or through the window; but none of these accidents had happened as yet. If you heard peals of laughter resounding from some unknown region, you might be sure enough of the cause. Going down into the kitchen, or *the room*, you would find Jane and Thomas, and Robert and Susan, all and sum, playing at ball with the little princess. She was the ball herself, and did not enjoy it the less for that. Away she went flying from one to another, screeching with laughter. And the servants loved the ball itself better even than the game. But they had to take some care how they threw her, for if she received an upward direction she would never come down again without being fetched.

V. WHAT IS TO BE DONE?

BUT above-stairs it was different. One day, for instance, after breakfast the king went into his counting house, and counted out his money.

The operation gave him no pleasure.

"To think," said he to himself, "that every one of these gold sovereigns weighs a quarter of an ounce, and my real, live, flesh-and-blood princess weighs nothing at all!"

And he hated his gold sovereigns, as they lay with a broad smile of self-satisfaction all over their yellow faces.

The queen was in the parlour, eating bread and honey. But at the second mouthful she burst out crying, and could not swallow it.

The king heard her sobbing. Glad of anybody, but especially of his queen, to quarrel with, he clashed his gold sovereigns into his money-box, clapped his crown on his head, and rushed into the parlour.

"What is all this about?" exclaimed he. "What are you crying for, queen?"

"I can't eat it," said the queen, looking ruefully at the honey-pot.

"No wonder!" retorted the king. "You've just eaten your breakfast—two turkey eggs, and three anchovies."

"Oh, that's not it!" sobbed her majesty. "It's my child, my child!"

"Well, what's the matter with your child? She's neither up the chimney nor down the draw-well. Just hear her laughing."

Yet the king could not help a sigh, which he tried to turn into a cough, saying, "It is a good thing to be light-hearted, I am sure, whether she be ours or not."

"It is a bad thing to be light-headed," answered the queen, looking with prophetic soul far into the future.

"'Tis a good thing to be light-handed," said the king.

"'Tis a bad thing to be light-fingered," answered the queen.

"'Tis a good thing to be light-footed," said the king.

"'Tis a bad thing—" began the queen; but the king interrupted her.

"In fact," said he, with the tone of one who concludes an argument in which he has had only imaginary opponents, and in which, therefore, he has come off triumphant—"in fact, it is a good thing altogether to be light-bodied."

"But it is a bad thing altogether to be light-minded," retorted the queen, who was beginning to lose her temper.

This last answer quite discomfited his majesty, who turned on his heel, and betook himself to his counting house again. But he was not halfway towards it, when the voice of his queen overtook him.

"And it's a bad thing to be light-haired," screamed she,

determined to have more last words, now that her spirit was roused.

The queen's hair was black as night; and the king's had been, and his daughter's was, golden as morning. But it was not this reflection on his hair that arrested him; it was the double use of the word *light*. For the king hated all witticisms, and punning especially. And besides, he could not tell whether the queen meant light-*haired* or light-*heired*; for why might she not aspirate her vowels when she was exasperated herself?

He turned upon his other heel, and rejoined her. She looked angry still, because she knew that she was guilty, or, what was much the same, knew that he thought so.

"My dear queen," said he, "duplicity of any sort is exceedingly objectionable between married people of any rank, not to say kings and queens; and the most objectionable form duplicity can assume is that of punning."

"There!" said the queen, "I never made a jest, but I broke it in the making. I am the most unfortunate woman in the world!"

She looked so rueful, that the king took her in his arms; and they sat down to consult.

"Can you bear this?" said the king.

"No, I can't," said the queen.

"Well, what's to be done?" said the king.

"I'm sure I don't know," said the queen. "But might you not try an apology?"

"To my older sister, I suppose you mean?" said the king.

"Yes," said the queen.

"Well, I don't mind," said the king.

So he went the next morning to the house of the princess, and, making a very humble apology, begged her to undo the spell. But the princess declared, with a grave face, that she knew nothing at all about it. Her eyes, however, shone pink, which was a sign that she was happy. She advised the king and queen to have patience, and to mend their ways. The king returned disconsolate. The queen tried to comfort him.

"We will wait till she is older. She may then be able to suggest something herself. She will know at least how she feels, and explain things to us."

"But what if she should marry?" exclaimed the king, in sudden consternation at the idea.

"Well, what of that?" rejoined the queen.

"Just think! If she were to have children! In the course of a hundred years the air might be as full of floating children as of gossamers in autumn."

"That is no business of ours," replied the queen. "Besides, by that time they will have learned to take care of themselves."

A sigh was the king's only answer.

He would have consulted the court physicians; but he was afraid they would try experiments upon her.

VI. SHE LAUGHS TOO MUCH

MEANTIME, notwithstanding awkward occurrences, and griefs that she brought upon her parents, the little princess laughed and grew—not fat, but plump and tall. She reached the age of seventeen, without having fallen into any worse scrape than a chimney; by rescuing her from which, a little bird-nesting urchin got fame and a black face. Nor, thoughtless as she was, had she committed anything worse than laughter at everybody and everything that came in her way. When she was told, for the sake of experiment, that General Clanrunfort was cut to pieces with all his troops, she laughed; when she heard that the enemy was on his way to besiege her papa's capital, she laughed hugely; but when she was told that the city would certainly be abandoned to the mercy of the enemy's soldiery—why, then she laughed immoderately. She never could be brought to see the serious side of anything. When her mother cried, she said: "What queer faces mamma makes! And she squeezes water out of her cheeks! Funny mamma!" And when her papa stormed at her, she laughed, and danced round and round him, clapping her hands, and crying, "Do it again, papa. Do it again! It's such fun! Dear, funny papa!"

And if he tried to catch her, she glided from him in an instant, not in the least afraid of him, but thinking it part of the game not to be caught. With one push of her foot, she would be floating in the air above his head; or she would go dancing backwards and forwards and sideways, like a great butterfly. It happened several times, when her father and mother were holding a consultation about her in private, that they were interrupted by vainly repressed outbursts of laughter over their heads; and looking up with indignation, saw her floating at full length in the air above them, whence she regarded them with the most comical appreciation of the position.

One day an awkward accident happened. The princess had come out upon the lawn with one of her attendants, who held her by the hand. Spying her father at the other side of the lawn, she snatched her hand from the maid's, and sped across to him. Now when she wanted to run alone, her custom was to catch up a stone in each hand, so that she might come down again after a bound. Whatever she wore as part of her attire had no effect in this way; even gold, when it thus became as it were a part of herself, lost all its weight for the time. But whatever she only held in her hands retained its downward tendency. On this occasion she could see nothing to catch up but a huge toad, that was walking across the lawn as if he had a hundred years to do it in. Not knowing what disgust meant, for this was one of her peculiarities, she snatched up the toad and bounded away. She had almost reached her father, and he was holding out his arms to receive her, and take from her lips the kiss which hovered on them like a butterfly on a rosebud, when a puff of wind blew her aside into the arms of a young page, who had just been receiving a message from his majesty. Now it was no great peculiarity in the princess that, once she was set agoing, it always cost her time and trouble to check herself. On this occasion there was not time. She *must* kiss—and she kissed the page. She did not mind it much; for she had no shyness in her composition; and she knew, besides, that she could not help it. So she only laughed, like a musical box. The poor page fared the worst. For the princess, trying to correct the unfortunate tendency of the kiss, put out her hands to keep her off the page; so that along with the kiss, he received, on the other cheek, a slap with the huge black toad, which she poked right into his eye. He tried to laugh, too, but the attempt resulted in such an odd contortion of countenance, as showed that there was no danger of his pluming himself on the kiss. As for the king, his dignity was greatly hurt, and he did not speak to the page for a whole month.

I may here remark that it was very amusing to see her run, if her mode of progression would properly be called running. For first she would make a bound; then, having alighted, she would run a few steps, and make another bound. Sometimes she would fancy she had reached the ground before she actually had, and her feet would go backwards and forwards, running upon nothing at all, like those of a chicken on its back. Then she would laugh like the very spirit of fun; only in her laugh there was something missing. What it was, I find myself unable to describe. I think it was a certain tone, depending upon the possibility of sorrow—*morbidezza*, perhaps. She never smiled.

VII. TRY METAPHYSICS

AFTER a long avoidance of the painful subject, the king and queen resolved to hold a council of three upon it; and so they sent for the princess. In she came, sliding and flitting and gliding from one piece of furniture to another, and put herself at last in an armchair, in a sitting posture. Whether she could be said *to sit*, seeing she received no support from the seat of the chair, I do not pretend to determine.

"My dear child," said the king, "you must be aware by this time that you are not exactly like other people."

"Oh, you dear funny papa! I have got a nose, and two eyes, and all the rest. So have you. So has mamma."

"Now be serious, my dear, for once," said the queen.

"No, thank you, mamma; I had rather not."

"Would you not like to be able to walk like other people?" said the king.

"No indeed, I should think not. You only crawl. You are such slow coaches!"

"How do you feel, my child?" he resumed, after a pause of discomfiture.

"Quite well, thank you."

"I mean, what do you feel like?"

"Like nothing at all, that I know of."

"You must feel like something."

"I feel like a princess with such a funny papa, and such a dear pet of a queen-mamma!"

"Now really!" began the queen; but the princess interrupted her.

"Oh yes," she added, "I remember. I have a curious feeling sometimes, as if I were the only person that had any sense in the whole world."

She had been trying to behave herself with dignity; but now

she burst into a violent fit of laughter, threw herself backwards over the chair, and went rolling about the floor in an ecstasy of enjoyment. The king picked her up easier than one does a down quilt and replaced her in her former relation to the chair. The exact preposition expressing this relation I do not happen to know.

"Is there nothing you wish for?" resumed the king, who had learned by this time that it was useless to be angry with her.

"Oh, you dear papa! Yes," answered she.

"What is it my darling?"

"I have been longing for it—oh, such a time! Ever since last night."

"Tell me what it is."

"Will you promise to let me have it?"

The king was on the point of saying *Yes*, but the wiser queen checked him with a single motion of her head.

"Tell me what it is first," said he.

"No, no. Promise first."

"I dare not. What is it?"

"Mind, I hold you to your promise. It is—to be tied to the end of a string—a very long string indeed, and be flown like a kite. Oh such fun! I would rain rose-water, and hail sugar-plums, and snow whipped-cream, and—and—and—"

A fit of laughing checked her; and she would have been off again over the floor, had not the king started up and caught her just in time. Seeing that nothing but talk could be got out of her, he rang the bell, and sent her away with two of her ladies-in-waiting.

"Now, queen," he said, turning to her majesty, "what *is* to be done?"

"There is but one thing left," answered she. "Let us consult the college of Metaphysicians."

"Bravo!" cried the king; "We will."

THE LIGHT PRINCESS

Now at the head of this college were two very wise Chinese philosophers—by name Hum-Drum, and Kopy-Keck. For them the king sent; and straightway they came. In a long speech he communicated to them what they knew very well already—as who did not? Namely, the peculiar condition of his daughter in relation to the globe on which she dwelt; and requested them to consult together as to what might be the cause and probable cure of her *infirmity*. The king laid stress upon the word, but failed to discover his own pun. The queen laughed; but Hum-Drum and Kopy-Keck heard with humility and retired in silence.

Their consultation consisted chiefly in propounding and supporting, for the thousandth time, each his favourite theories. For the condition of the princess afforded delightful scope for the discussion of every question arising from the division of thought—in fact, of all the Metaphysics of the Chinese Empire. But it is only justice to say that they did not altogether neglect the discussion of the practical question, *what was to be done.*

Hum-Drum was a Materialist, and Kopy-Keck was a Spiritualist. The former was slow and sententious; the latter was quick and flighty: the latter had generally the first word; the former the last.

"I reassert my former assertion," began Kopy-Keck, with a plunge. "There is not a fault in the princess, body or soul; only they are wrong put together. Listen to me now, Hum-Drum, and I will tell you in brief what I think. Don't speak. Don't answer me. I *won't* hear you till I have done. At that decisive moment, when souls seek their appointed habitations, two eager souls met, struck, rebounded, lost their way, and arrived each at the wrong place. The soul of the princess was one of those, and she went far astray. She does not belong by rights to this world at all, but to some other planet, probably Mercury. Her proclivity to her true sphere destroys all the natural influence which this orb would otherwise possess over her corporeal frame. She cares for nothing here. There is no relation between her and this world.

"She must therefore be taught, by the sternest compulsion, to take an interest in the earth as the earth. She must study every department of its history—its animal history; its vegetable history; its mineral history; its social history; its moral history; its political history; its scientific history; its literary history; its musical history; its artistical history; above all, its metaphysical history. She must begin with the Chinese dynasty and end with Japan. But first of all she must study geology, and especially the history of the extinct races of animals—their natures, their habits, their loves, their hates, their revenges. She must—"

"Hold, h-o-o-old!" roared Hum-Drum. "It is certainly my turn now. My rooted and insubvertible conviction is, that the causes of the anomalies evident in the princess's condition are strictly and solely physical. But that is only tantamount to acknowledging that they exist. Hear my opinion. From some cause or other, of no importance to our inquiry, the motion of her heart has been reversed. That remarkable combination of the suction and force-pump works the wrong way—I mean in the case of the unfortunate princess: it draws in where it should force out and forces out where it should draw in. The offices of the auricles and the ventricles are subverted. The blood is sent forth by the veins, and returns by the arteries. Consequently it is running the wrong way through all her corporeal organism—lungs and all. Is it then at all mysterious, seeing that such is the case, that on the other particular of gravitation as well, she should differ from normal humanity? My proposal for the cure is this:

"Phlebotomize until she is reduced to the last point of safety. Let it be effected, if necessary, in a warm bath. When she is reduced to a state of perfect asphyxy, apply a ligature to the left ankle, drawing it as tight as the bone will bear. Apply, at the same moment, another of equal tension around the right wrist. By means of plates constructed for the purpose, place the other foot and hand under the receivers of two air-pumps. Exhaust the receivers. Exhibit a pint of French brandy, and await the result."

"Which would presently arrive in the form of grim Death," said Kopy-Keck.

"If it should, she would yet die in doing our duty," retorted Hum-Drum.

But their majesties had too much tenderness for their volatile offspring to subject her to either of the schemes of the equally unscrupulous philosophers. Indeed, the most complete knowledge of the laws of nature would have been unserviceable in her case; for it was impossible to classify her. She was a fifth imponderable body, sharing all the other properties of the ponderable.

VIII. TRY A DROP OF WATER

PERHAPS the best thing for the princess would have been to fall in love. But how a princess who had no gravity could fall into anything is a difficulty—perhaps *the* difficulty. As for her own feelings on the subject, she did not even know that there was such a beehive of honey and stings to be fallen into. But now I come to mention another curious fact about her.

The palace was built on the shores of the loveliest lake in the world; and the princess loved this lake more than father or mother. The root of this preference no doubt, although the princess did not recognise it as such, was, that the moment she got into it, she recovered the natural right of which she had been so wickedly deprived—namely, gravity. Whether this was owing to the fact that water had been employed as the means of conveying the injury, I do not know. But it is certain that she could swim and dive like the duck that her old nurse said she was. The manner in which this alleviation of her misfortune was discovered was as follows.

One summer evening, during the carnival of the country, she had been taken upon the lake by the king and queen, in the royal barge. They were accompanied by many of the courtiers in a fleet of little boats. In the middle of the lake she wanted to get into the lord chancellor's barge, for his daughter, who was a great favourite with her, was in it with her father. Now though the old king rarely condescended to make light of his misfortune, yet, happening on this occasion to be in a particularly good humour, as the barges approached each other, he caught up the princess to throw her into the chancellor's barge. He lost his balance, however, and dropping into the bottom of the barge, lost his hold of his daughter; not, however, before imparting to her the downward tendency of his own person, though in a somewhat different direction; for, as the king fell into the boat, she fell into the water. With a burst of delighted laughter she disappeared in the lake. A cry of horror ascended from the boats. They had never seen the princess go down before. Half the men were under water in a moment; but they had all, one after another, come up to the surface again for breath, when—tinkle, tinkle, babble, and gush! Came the princess's laugh over the water from far away. There she was, swimming like a swan. Nor would she come out for king or queen, chancellor or daughter. She was perfectly obstinate.

But at the same time she seemed more sedate than usual. Perhaps that was because a great pleasure spoils laughing. At all events, after this, the passion of her life was to get into the water, and she was always the better behaved and the more beautiful the more she had of it. Summer and winter it was quite the same; only she could not stay so long in the water when they had to break the ice to let her in. Any day, from morning till evening in summer, she might be descried—a streak of white in the blue water—lying as still as the shadow of a cloud, or shooting along like a dolphin; disappearing, and coming up again far off, just where one did not expect her. She would have been in the lake of a night too, if she could have had her way; for the balcony of her window overhung a deep pool in it; and through a shallow reedy passage she could have swum out into the wide wet water, and no one would have been any the wiser. Indeed, when she happened to wake in the moonlight, she could hardly resist the temptation. But there was the sad difficulty of getting into it. She had as great a dread of the air as some children have of the water. For the slightest gust of wind would blow her away; and a gust might arise in the stillest moment. And if she gave herself a push towards the water and just failed of reaching it, her situation would be dreadfully awkward, irrespective of the wind; for at best there she would have to remain, suspended in her nightgown, till she was seen and angled for by somebody from the window.

"Oh! If I had my gravity," thought she, contemplating the water, "I would flash off this balcony like a long white sea-bird, headlong into the darling wetness. Heigh-ho!"

This was the only consideration that made her wish to be like other people.

Another reason for her being fond of the water was that in it alone she enjoyed any freedom. For she could not walk out without a *cortége*, consisting in part of a troop of light-horses, for fear of the liberties which the wind might take with her. And the king grew more apprehensive with increasing years, till at last he would not allow her to walk abroad at all without some twenty silken cords fastened to as many parts of her dress, and held by twenty noblemen. Of course horseback was out of the question. But she bade goodbye to all this ceremony when she got into the water.

And so remarkable were its effects upon her, especially in restoring her for the time to the ordinary human gravity, that Hum-Drum and Kopy-Keck agreed in recommending the king to bury her alive for three years; in the hope that, as the water did her so much good, the earth would do her yet more. But the king had some vulgar prejudices against the experiment, and would not give his consent. Foiled in this, they yet agreed in another recommendation; which, seeing that one imported his opinions from China and the other from Tibet was very remarkable indeed. They argued that if water of external origin and application could be so efficacious, water from a deeper source might work a perfect cure; in short, that if the poor afflicted princess could by any means be made to cry, she might recover her lost gravity.

But how was this to be brought about? Therein lay all the difficulty—to meet which the philosophers were not wise enough. To make the princess cry was as impossible as to make her weigh. They sent for a professional beggar; commanded him to prepare his most touching oracle of woe; helped him out of the court charade-box, to whatever he wanted for dressing up, and promised great rewards in the event of his success. But it was all in vain. She listened to the mendicant artist's story, and gazed at his marvellous make-up, till she could contain herself no longer, and went into the most undignified contortions for relief, shrieking, positively screeching with laughter.

When she had a little recovered herself, she ordered her attendants to drive him away, and not give him a single copper; whereupon his look of mortified discomfiture wrought her punishment and his revenge, for it sent her into violent hysterics, from which she was with difficulty recovered.

But so anxious was the king that the suggestion should have a fair trial, that he put himself in a rage one day, and, rushing up to her room, gave her an awful whipping. Yet not a tear would flow. She looked grave, and her laughing sounded uncommonly like screaming—that was all. The good old tyrant, though he put on his best gold spectacles to look, could not discover the smallest cloud in the serene blue of her eyes.

IX. PUT ME IN AGAIN

IT must have been about this time that the son of a king, who lived a thousand miles from Lagobel, set out to look for the daughter of a queen. He travelled far and wide, but as sure as he found a princess, he found some fault in her. Of course he could not marry a mere woman, however beautiful; and there was no princess to be found worthy of him. Whether the prince was so near perfection that he had a right to demand perfection itself, I cannot pretend to say. All I know is, that he was a fine, handsome, brave, generous, well-bred, and well-behaved youth, as all princes are.

In his wanderings he had come across some reports about our princess; but as everybody said she was bewitched, he never dreamed that she could bewitch him. For what indeed could a prince do with a princess that had lost her gravity? Who could tell what she might not lose next? She might lose her visibility, or her tangibility; or, in short, the power of making impressions upon the radical sensorium; so that he should never be able to tell whether she was dead or alive. Of course he made no further inquiries about her.

One day he lost sight of his retinue in a great forest. These forests are very useful in delivering princes from their courtiers, like a sieve that keeps back the bran. Then the princes get away to follow their fortunes. In this they have the advantage of the princesses, who are forced to marry before they have had a bit of fun. I wish our princesses got lost in a forest sometimes.

One lovely evening, after wandering about for many days, he found that he was approaching the outskirts of this forest; for the trees had got so thin that he could see the sunset through them; and he soon came upon a kind of heath. Next he came upon signs of human neighbourhood; but by this time it was getting late, and there was nobody in the fields to direct him.

After travelling for another hour, his horse, quite worn out with long labour and lack of food, fell, and was unable to rise again. So he continued his journey on foot. At length he entered another wood—not a wild forest but a civilized wood, through which a footpath led him to the side of a lake. Along this path the prince pursued his way through the gathering darkness. Suddenly he paused, and listened. Strange sounds came across the water. It was, in fact the princess laughing. Now there was something odd in her laugh, as I have already hinted; for the hatching of a real hearty laugh requires the incubation of gravity; and perhaps this was how the prince mistook the laughter for screaming. Looking over the lake, he saw something white in the water; and, in an instant he had torn off his tunic, kicked off his sandals, and plunged in. He soon reached the white object and found that it was a woman. There was not light enough to show that she was a princess, but quite enough to show that she was a lady, for it does not want much light to see that.

Now I cannot tell how it came about, whether she pretended to be drowning, or whether he frightened her, or caught her so as to embarrass her, but certainly he brought her to shore in a fashion ignominious to a swimmer, and more nearly drowned than she had ever expected to be; for the water had got into her throat as often as she had tried to speak.

At the place to which he bore her, the bank was only a foot or two above the water; so he gave her a strong lift out of the water, to lay her on the bank. But, her gravitation ceasing the moment she left the water, away she went up into the air, scolding and screaming.

"You naughty, *naughty*, NAUGHTY, NAUGHTY man!" she cried.

No one had ever succeeded in putting her into a passion before. When the prince saw her ascend, he thought he must have been bewitched, and have mistaken a great swan for a lady. But the princess caught hold of the topmost cone upon a lofty fir. This came off; but she caught at another; and, in fact, stopped herself by gathering cones, dropping them as the stalks gave way. The prince, meantime, stood in the water, staring, and forgetting to get out. But the princess disappearing, he scrambled on shore, and went in the direction of the tree. There he found her climbing down one of the branches towards the stem. But in the darkness of the wood, the prince continued in some bewilderment as to what the phenomenon could be; until, reaching the ground, and seeing him standing there, she caught hold of him, and said: "I'll tell papa."

"Oh no, you won't!" returned the prince.

"Yes, I will," she persisted. "What business had you to pull me down out of the water, and throw me to the bottom of the air? I never did you any harm."

"Pardon me. I did not mean to hurt you."

"I don't believe you have any brains; and that is a worse loss than your wretched gravity. I pity you."

The prince now saw that he had come upon the bewitched princess, and had already offended her. But before he could think what to say next, she burst out angrily, giving a stamp with her foot that would have sent her aloft again but for the hold she had of his arm: "Put me up directly."

"Put you up where, you beauty?" asked the prince.

He had fallen in love with her almost, already; for her anger made her more charming than any one else had ever beheld her; and, as far as he could see, which certainly was not far, she had not a single fault about her, except, of course, that she had not any gravity. No prince, however, would judge of a princess by weight. The loveliness of her foot he would hardly estimate by the depth of the impression it could make in mud.

"Put you up where, you beauty?" asked the prince.

"In the water, you stupid!" answered the princess.

"Come, then," said the prince.

The condition of her dress, increasing her usual difficulty in walking, compelled her to cling to him; and he could hardly persuade himself that he was not in a delightful dream, notwithstanding the torrent of musical abuse with which she overwhelmed him. The prince being therefore in no hurry, they came upon the lake at quite another part, where the bank was twenty-five feet high at least; and when they had reached the edge, he turned towards the princess, and said: "How am I to put you in?"

"That is your business," she answered, quite snappishly. "You took me out—put me in again."

"Very well," said the prince; and, catching her up in his arms, he sprang with her from the rock. The princess had just time to give one delighted shriek of laughter before the water closed over them. When they came to the surface, she found that, for a moment or two, she could not even laugh, for she had gone down with such a rush, that it was with difficulty she recovered her breath. The instant they reached the surface—

"How do you like falling in?" said the prince.

After some effort the princess panted out: "Is that what you call *falling in?*"

"Yes," answered the prince, "I should think it a very tolerable specimen."

"It seemed to me like going up," rejoined she.

"My feeling was certainly one of elevation too," the prince

conceded.

The princess did not appear to understand him, for she retorted his question:

"How do *you* like falling in?" said the princess.

"Beyond everything," answered he; "for I have fallen in with the only perfect creature I ever saw."

"No more of that: I am tired of it," said the princess.

Perhaps she shared her father's aversion to punning.

"Don't you like falling in, then?" said the prince.

"It is the most delightful fun I ever had in my life," answered she. "I never fell before. I wish I could learn. To think I am the only person in my father's kingdom that can't fall!"

Here the poor princess looked almost sad.

"I shall be most happy to fall in with you any time you like," said the prince, devotedly.

"Thank you. I don't know. Perhaps it would not be proper. But I don't care. At all events, as we have fallen in, let us have a swim together."

"With all my heart," responded the prince.

And away they went, swimming, and diving, and floating, until at last they heard cries along the shore, and saw lights glancing in all directions. It was now quite late, and there was no moon.

"I must go home," said the princess. "I am very sorry, for this is delightful."

"So am I," returned the prince. "But I am glad I haven't a home to go to—at least, I don't exactly know where it is."

"I wish I hadn't one either," rejoined the princess; "it is so stupid! I have a great mind," she continued, "to play them all a trick. Why couldn't they leave me alone? They won't trust me in the lake for a single night! You see where that green light is burning? That is the window of my room. Now if you would just swim there with me very quietly, and when we are all but under the balcony, give me such a push—*up* you call it—as you did a little while ago, I should be able to catch hold of the balcony, and get in at the window; and then they may look for me till tomorrow morning!"

"With more obedience than pleasure," said the prince, gallantly; and away they swam, very gently.

"Will you be in the lake tomorrow night?" the prince ventured to ask.

"To be sure I will. I don't think so. Perhaps," was the princess's somewhat strange answer.

But the prince was intelligent enough not to press her further; and merely whispered, as he gave her the parting lift, "Don't tell." The only answer the princess returned was a rougish look. She was already a yard above his head. The look seemed to say, "Never fear. It is too good fun to spoil that way."

So perfectly like other people had she been in the water, that even yet the prince could scarcely believe his eyes when he saw her ascend slowly, grasp the balcony, and disappear through the window. He turned, almost expecting to see her still by his side. But he was alone in the water. So he swam away quietly, and watched the lights roving about the shore for hours after the princess was safe in her chamber. As soon as they disappeared, he landed in search of his tunic and sword, and, after some trouble, found them again. Then he made the best of his way round the lake to the other side. There the wood was wilder, and the shore steeper—rising more immediately towards the mountains which surrounded the lake on all sides, and kept sending it messages of silvery streams from morning to night, and all night long. He soon found a spot whence he could see the green light in the princess's room, and where, even in the broad daylight, he would be in no danger of being discovered from the opposite shore. It was a sort of cave in the rock, where he provided himself a bed of withered leaves, and lay down too tired for hunger to keep him awake. All night long he dreamed that he was swimming with the princess.

X. LOOK AT THE MOON

EARLY the next morning the prince set out to look for something to eat, which he soon found at a forester's hut, where for many following days he was supplied with all that a brave prince could consider necessary. And having plenty to keep him alive for the present, he would not think of wants not yet in existence. Whenever Care intruded, this prince always bowed him out in the most princely manner.

When he returned from his breakfast to his watch-cave, he saw the princess already floating about in the lake, attended by the king and queen—whom he knew by their crowns—and a great company in lovely little boats, with canopies of all the colours of the rainbow, and flags and streamers of a great many more. It was a very bright day, and soon the prince, burned up with the heat, began to long for the cold water and the cool princess. But he had to endure till twilight; for the boats had provisions on board, and it was not till the sun went down that the gay party began to vanish. Boat after boat drew away to the shore, following that of the king and queen, till only one, apparently the princess's own boat, remained. But she did not want to go home even yet, and the prince thought he saw her order the boat to the shore without her. At all events, it rowed away; and now, of all the radiant company, only one white speck remained. Then the prince began to sing.

And this is what he sang:

"*Lady fair,*

Swan-white,
Lift thine eyes,
Banish night
By the might
Of thine eyes.

"*Snowy arms,*
Oars of snow,
Oar her hither,
Plashing low.
Soft and slow,
Oar her hither.

"*Stream behind her*
O'er the lake,
Radiant whiteness!
In her wake
Following, following for her sake,
Radiant whiteness!

"*Cling about her,*
Waters blue.
Part not from her,
But renew
Cold and true
Kisses round her.

"*Lap me round,*
Waters sad
That have left her.
Make me glad,

For ye had
Kissed her ere ye left her."

Before he had finished his song, the princess was just under the place where he sat, and looking up to find him. Her ears had led her truly.

"Would you like a fall, princess?" said the prince, looking down.

"Ah! There you are! Yes, if you please, prince," said the princess, looking up.

"How do you know I am a prince, princess?" said the prince.

"Because you are a very nice young man, prince," said the princess.

"Come up then, princess."

"Fetch me, prince."

The prince took off his scarf, then his sword-belt, then his tunic, and tied them all together, and let them down. But the line was far too short. He unwound his turban, and added it to the rest, when it was all but long enough; and his purse completed it. The princess just managed to lay hold of the knot of money, and was beside him in a moment. This rock was much higher than the other, and the splash and the dive were tremendous. The princess was in ecstasies of delight, and their swim was delicious.

Night after night they met, and swam about in the dark clear lake; where such was the prince's gladness, that (whether the princess's way of looking at things infected him, or he was actually getting lightheaded) he often fancied that he was swimming in the sky instead of the lake. But when he talked about being in heaven, the princess laughed at him dreadfully.

When the moon came, she brought them fresh pleasure. Everything looked strange and new in her light, with an old, withered, yet unfading newness. When the moon was nearly full, one of their great delights was to dive deep in the water, and then, turning round, look up through it at the great blot of light close above them, shimmering and trembling and wavering, spreading and contracting, seeming to melt away, and again grow solid. Then they would shoot up through the blot; and lo! There was the moon, far off, clear and steady and cold, and very lovely, at the bottom of a deeper and bluer lake than theirs, as the princess said.

The prince soon found out that while in the water the princess was very like other people. And besides this, she was not so forward in her questions or pert in her replies at sea as on shore. Neither did she laugh so much; and when she did laugh, it was more gently. She seemed altogether more modest and maidenly in the water than out of it. But when the prince, who had really fallen in love when he fell in the lake, began to talk to her about love, she always turned her head towards him and laughed. After a while she began to look puzzled, as if she were trying to understand what he meant, but could not—revealing a notion that he meant something. But as soon as ever she left the lake, she was so altered, that the prince said to himself, "If I marry her, I see no help for it: we must turn merman and mermaid, and go out to sea at once."

XI. HISS!

THE princess's pleasure in the lake had grown to a passion, and she could scarcely bear to be out of it for an hour. Imagine then her consternation, when, diving with the prince one night, a sudden suspicion seized her that the lake was not so deep as it used to be. The prince could not imagine what had happened. She shot to the surface, and, without a word, swam at full speed towards the higher side of the lake. He followed, begging to know if she was ill, or what was the matter. She never turned her head, or took the smallest notice of his question. Arrived at the shore, she coasted the rocks with minute inspection. But she was not able to come to a conclusion, for the moon was very small, and so she could not see well. She turned therefore and swam home, without saying a word to explain her conduct to the prince, of whose presence she seemed no longer conscious. He withdrew to his cave, in great perplexity and distress.

Next day she made many observations, which, alas, strengthened her fears. She saw that the banks were too dry; and that the grass on the shore, and the trailing plants on the rocks, were withering away. She caused marks to be made along the borders, and examined them, day after day, in all directions of the wind; till at last the horrible idea became a certain fact—that the surface of the lake was slowly sinking.

The poor princess nearly went out of the little mind she had. It was awful to her to see the lake, which she loved more than any living thing, lie dying before her eyes. It sank away, slowly vanishing. The tops of rocks that had never been seen till now, began to appear far down in the clear water. Before long they were dry in the sun. It was fearful to think of the mud that would soon lie there baking and festering, full of lovely creatures dying, and ugly creatures coming to life, like the unmaking of a world. And how hot the sun would be without any lake! She could not bear to swim in it anymore, and began to pine away. Her life seemed bound up with it; and ever as the lake sank, she pined. People said she would not live an hour after the lake was gone.

But she never cried.

Proclamation was made to all the kingdom, that whosoever should discover the cause of the lake's decrease, would be rewarded after a princely fashion. Hum-Drum and Kopy-Keck applied themselves to their physics and metaphysics; but in vain. Not even they could suggest a cause.

Now the fact was that the old princess was at the root of the mischief. When she heard that her niece found more pleasure in the water than any one else had out of it, she went into a rage, and cursed herself for her want of foresight.

"But," said she, "I will soon set all right. The king and the people shall die of thirst; their brains shall boil and frizzle in their skulls before I will lose my revenge."

And she laughed a ferocious laugh, that made the hairs on the back of her black cat stand erect with terror.

Then she went to an old chest in the room, and opening it, took out what looked like a piece of dried seaweed. This she threw into a tub of water. Then she threw some powder into the water, and stirred it with her bare arm, muttering over it words of hideous sound, and yet more hideous import. Then she set the tub aside, and took from the chest a huge bunch of a hundred rusty keys, that clattered in her shaking hands. Then she sat down and proceeded to oil them all. Before she had finished, out from the tub, the water of which had kept on a slow motion ever since she had ceased stirring it, came the head and half the body of a huge gray snake. But the witch did not look round. It grew out of the tub, waving itself backwards and forwards with a slow horizontal motion, till it reached the princess, when it laid its head upon her shoulder, and gave a low hiss in her ear. She started—but with joy; and seeing the head resting on her shoulder, drew it towards her and kissed it. Then she drew it all out of the tub, and wound it round her body. It was one of those dreadful creatures which few have ever beheld—the White Snakes of Darkness.

Then she took the keys and went down to her cellar; and as she unlocked the door she said to herself, "This is worth living for!"

Locking the door behind her, she descended a few steps into the cellar, and crossing it, unlocked another door into a dark, narrow passage. She locked this also behind her, and descended a few more steps. If any one had followed the witch-princess, he would have heard her unlock exactly one hundred doors, and descend a few steps after unlocking each. When she had unlocked the last, she entered a vast cave, the roof of which was supported by huge natural pillars of rock. Now this room was the under side of the bottom of the lake.

She then untwined the snake from her body, and held it by the tail high above her. The hideous creature stretched up its head towards the roof of the cavern, which it was just able to reach. It then began to move its head backwards and forwards, with a slow oscillating motion, as if looking for something. At the same moment the witch began to walk round and round the cavern, coming nearer to the centre every circuit; while the head of the snake described the same path over the roof that she did over the floor, for she kept holding it up. And still it kept slowly oscillating. Round and round the cavern they went, ever lessening the circuit, till at last the snake made a sudden dart, and clung to the roof with its mouth.

"That's right, my beauty!" cried the princess; "drain it dry."

She let it go, left it hanging, and sat down on a great stone, with her black cat, which had followed her all round the cave, by her side. Then she began to knit and mutter awful words. The snake hung like a huge leech, sucking at the stone; the cat stood with his back arched, and his tail like a piece of cable, looking up at the snake; and the old woman sat and knitted and muttered. Seven days and seven nights they remained thus; when suddenly the serpent dropped from the roof as if exhausted, and shrivelled up till it was again like a piece of dried seaweed. The witch started to her feet, picked it up, put it in her pocket, and looked up at the roof. One drop of water was trembling on the spot where the snake had been sucking. As soon as she saw that, she turned and fled, followed by her cat. Shutting the door in a terrible hurry, she locked it and having muttered some frightful words, sped to the next which also she locked and muttered over; and so with all the hundred doors, till she arrived in her own cellar. There she sat down on the floor ready to faint but listening with malicious delight to the rushing of the water, which she could hear distinctly through all the hundred doors.

But this was not enough. Now that she had tasted revenge, she lost her patience. Without further measures, the lake would be too long in disappearing. So the next night, with the last shred of the dying old moon rising, she took some of the water in which she had revived the snake, put it in a bottle, and set out, accompanied by her cat. Before morning she had made the entire circuit of the lake, muttering fearful words as she crossed every stream, and casting into it some of the water out of her bottle. When she had finished the circuit she muttered yet again, and flung a handful of water towards the moon. Thereupon every spring in the country ceased to throb and bubble, dying away like the pulse of a dying man. The next day there was no sound of falling water to be heard along the borders of the lake. The very courses were dry; and the mountains showed no silvery streaks down their dark sides. And not alone had the fountains of mother Earth ceased to flow; for all the babies throughout the country were crying dreadfully—only without tears.

XII. WHERE IS THE PRINCE?

NEVER since the night when the princess left him so abruptly had the prince had a single interview with her. He had seen her once or twice in the lake; but as far as he could discover, she had not been in it anymore at night. He had sat and sung, and looked in vain for his Nereid; while she, like a true Nereid, was wasting away with her lake, sinking as it sank, withering as it dried. When at length he discovered the change that was taking place in the level of the water, he was in great alarm and perplexity. He could not tell whether the lake was dying because the lady had forsaken it; or whether the lady would not come because the lake had begun to sink. But he resolved to know so much at least.

He disguised himself, and, going to the palace, requested to see the lord chamberlain. His appearance at once gained his request; and the lord chamberlain, being a man of some insight perceived that there was more in the prince's solicitation than met the ear. He felt likewise that no one could tell whence a solution of the present difficulties might arise. So he granted the prince's prayer to be made shoe-black to the princess. It was rather cunning in the prince to request such an easy post, for the princess could not possibly soil as many shoes as other princesses.

He soon learned all that could be told about the princess. He went nearly distracted; but after roaming about the lake for days, and diving in every depth that remained, all that he could do was to put an extra polish on the dainty pair of boots that was never called for.

For the princess kept her room, with the curtains drawn to shut out the dying lake. But could not shut it out of her mind for a moment. It haunted her imagination so that she felt as if the lake were her soul, drying up within her, first to mud, then to madness and death. She thus brooded over the change, with all its dreadful accompaniments, till she was nearly distracted. As for the prince, she had forgotten him. However much she had enjoyed his company in the water, she did not care for him without it. But she seemed to have forgotten her father and mother too.

The lake went on sinking. Small slimy spots began to appear, which glittered steadily amidst the changeful shine of the water. These grew to broad patches of mud, which widened and spread, with rocks here and there, and floundering fishes and crawling eels swarming. The people went everywhere catching these, and looking for anything that might have dropped from the royal boats.

At length the lake was all but gone, only a few of the deepest pools remaining unexhausted.

It happened one day that a party of youngsters found themselves on the brink of one of these pools in the very centre of the lake. It was a rocky basin of considerable depth. Looking in, they saw at the bottom something that shone yellow in the sun. A little boy jumped in and dived for it. It was a plate of gold covered with writing. They carried it to the king.

On one side of it stood these words:

> "*Death alone from death can save.*
> *Love is death, and so is brave.*
> *Love can fill the deepest grave.*
> *Love loves on beneath the wave.*"

Now this was enigmatical enough to the king and courtiers. But the reverse of the plate explained it a little. Its writing amounted to this:

> *If the lake should disappear, they must find the hole through which the water ran. But it would be useless to try to stop it by any ordinary means. There was but one effectual mode. The body of a living man should alone stanch the flow. The man must give himself of his own will; and the lake must take his life as it filled. Otherwise the offering would be of no avail. If the nation could not provide one hero, it was time it should perish.*

XIII. HERE I AM

THE LIGHT PRINCESS

THIS was a very disheartening revelation to the king—not that he was unwilling to sacrifice a subject, but that he was hopeless of finding a man willing to sacrifice himself. No time was to be lost, however, for the princess was lying motionless on her bed, and taking no nourishment but lake-water, which was now none of the best. Therefore the king caused the contents of the wonderful plate of gold to be published throughout the country.

No one, however, came forward.

The prince, having gone several days' journey into the forest to consult a hermit whom he had met there on his way to Lagobel, knew nothing of the oracle till his return.

When he had acquainted himself with all the particulars, he sat down and thought: "She will die if I don't do it, and life would be nothing to me without her; so I shall lose nothing by doing it. And life will be as pleasant to her as ever, for she will soon forget me. And there will be so much more beauty and happiness in the world! To be sure, I shall not see it." (Here the poor prince gave a sigh.) "How lovely the lake will be in the moonlight with that glorious creature sporting in it like a wild goddess! It is rather hard to be drowned by inches, though. Let me see—that will be seventy inches of me to drown." (Here he tried to laugh, but could not.) "The longer the better, however," he resumed; "for can I not bargain that the princess shall be beside me all the time? So I shall see her once more, kiss her perhaps, who knows? And the looking in her eyes. It will be no death. At least I shall not feel it. And to see the lake filling for the beauty again! All right! I am ready."

He kissed the princess's boot, laid it down, and hurried to the king's apartment. But feeling, as he went, that anything sentimental would be disagreeable, he resolved to carry off the whole affair with nonchalance. So he knocked at the door of the king's counting house, where it was all but a capital crime to disturb him.

When the king heard the knock he started up, and opened the door in a rage. Seeing only the shoeblack, he drew his sword. This, I am sorry to say, was his usual mode of asserting his regality when he thought his dignity was in danger. But the prince was not in the least alarmed.

"Please your majesty, I'm your butler," said he.

"My butler! You lying rascal! What do you mean?"

"I mean, I will cork your big bottle."

"Is the fellow mad?" bawled the king, raising the point of his sword.

"I will put a stopper—plug—what you call it, in your leaky lake, grand monarch," said the prince.

The king was in such a rage that before he could speak he had time to cool, and to reflect that it would be great waste to kill the only man who was willing to be useful in the present emergency, seeing that in the end the insolent fellow would be as dead as if he had died by his majesty's own hand.

"Oh!" said he at last, putting up his sword with difficulty, it was so long; "I am obliged to you, you young fool! Take a glass of wine?"

"No, thank you," replied the prince.

"Very well," said the king. "Would you like to run and see your parents before you make your experiment?"

"No, thank you," said the prince.

"Then we will go and look for the hole at once," said his majesty, and proceeded to call some attendants.

"Stop, please your majesty; I have a condition to make," interposed the prince.

"What!" exclaimed the king, "A condition! And with me! How dare you?"

"As you please," returned the prince, coolly. "I wish your majesty a good morning."

"You wretch! I will have you put in a sack, and stuck in the hole."

"Very well, your majesty," replied the prince, becoming a little more respectful, lest the wrath of the king should deprive him of the pleasure of dying for the princess. "But what good will that do your majesty? Please to remember that the oracle says the victim must offer himself."

"Well, you *have* offered yourself," retorted the king.

"Yes, upon one condition."

"Condition again!" roared the king, once more drawing his sword. "Begone! Somebody else will be glad enough to take the honour off your shoulders."

"Your majesty knows it will not be easy to get another to take my place."

"Well, what is your condition?" growled the king, feeling that the prince was right.

"Only this," replied the prince: "that, as I must on no account die before I am fairly drowned, and the waiting will be rather wearisome, the princess, your daughter, shall go with me, feed me with her own hands, and look at me now and then to comfort me; for you must confess it *is* rather hard. As soon as the water is up to my eyes, she may go and be happy, and forget her poor shoeblack."

Here the prince's voice faltered, and he very nearly grew sentimental, in spite of his resolution.

"Why didn't you tell me before what your condition was? Such a fuss about nothing!" exclaimed the king.

"Do you grant it?" persisted the prince.

"Of course I do," replied the king.

"Very well. I am ready."

"Go and have some dinner, then, while I set my people to find the place."

The king ordered out his guards, and gave directions to the officers to find the hole in the lake at once. So the bed of the lake was marked out in divisions and thoroughly examined, and in an hour or so the hole was discovered. It was in the middle of a stone, near the centre of the lake, in the very pool where the golden plate had been found. It was a three-cornered hole of no great size. There was water all round the stone, but very little was flowing through the hole.

XIV. THIS IS VERY KIND OF YOU

THE prince went to dress for the occasion, for he was resolved to die like a prince.

When the princess heard that a man had offered to die for her, she was so transported that she jumped off the bed, feeble as she was, and danced about the room for joy. She did not care who the man was; that was nothing to her. The hole wanted stopping; and if only a man would do, why, take one. In an hour or two more everything was ready. Her maid dressed her in haste, and they carried her to the side of the lake. When she saw it she shrieked, and covered her face with her hands. They bore her across to the stone, where they had already placed a little boat for her. The water was not deep enough to float it, but they hoped it would be, before long. They laid her on cushions, placed in the boat wines and fruits and other nice things, and stretched a canopy over all.

In a few minutes the prince appeared. The princess recognized him at once, but did not think it worthwhile to acknowledge him.

"Here I am," said the prince. "Put me in."

"They told me it was a shoeblack," said the princess.

"So I am," said the prince. "I black your little boots three times a day, because they were all I could get of you. Put me in."

The courtiers did not resent his bluntness, except by saying to each other that he was taking it out in impudence.

But how was he to be put in? The golden plate contained no instructions on this point. The prince looked at the hole, and saw but one way. He put both legs into it sitting on the stone, and, stooping forward, covered the corner that remained open with his two hands. In this uncomfortable position he resolved to abide his fate, and turning to the people, said: "Now you can go."

The king had already gone home to dinner.

"Now you can go," repeated the princess after him, like a parrot.

The people obeyed her and went.

Presently a little wave flowed over the stone, and wetted one of the prince's knees. But he did not mind it much. He began to sing, and the song he sang was this:

"As a world that has no well,
Darkly bright in forest dell,
As a world without the gleam
Of the downward-going stream,
As a world without the glance
Of the ocean's fair expanse,
As a world where never rain
Glittered on the sunny plain,
Such, my heart, thy world would be,
If no love did flow in thee.

"As a world without the sound
Of the rivulets underground,
Or the bubbling of the spring
Out of darkness wandering,
Or the mighty rush and flowing

Of the river's downward going,
Or the music-showers that drop
On the outspread beech's top,
Or the ocean's mighty voice,
When his lifted waves rejoice,
Such, my soul, thy world would be,
If no love did sing in thee.

"Lady, keep thy world's delight,
Keep the waters in thy sight.
Love hath made me strong to go,
For thy sake, to realms below,
Where the water's shine and hum
Through the darkness never come:
Let, I pray, one thought of me
Spring, a little well, in thee,
Lest thy loveless soul be found
Like a dry and thirsty ground."

"Sing again, prince. It makes it less tedious," said the princess.

But the prince was too much overcome to sing anymore, and a long pause followed.

"This is very kind of you, prince," said the princess at last, quite coolly, as she lay in the boat with her eyes shut.

"I am sorry I can't return the compliment" thought the prince; "but you are worth dying for, after all."

Again a wavelet and another, and another flowed over the stone, and wetted both the prince's knees; but he did not speak or move. Two—three—four hours passed in this way, the princess apparently asleep, and the prince very patient. But he was much disappointed in his position, for he had none of the consolation he had hoped for.

At last he could bear it no longer.

"Princess!" said he.

But at the moment up started the princess, crying, "I'm afloat! I'm afloat!"

And the little boat bumped against the stone.

"Princess!" repeated the prince, encouraged by seeing her wide awake and looking eagerly at the water.

"Well?" said she, without looking round.

"Your papa promised that you should look at me, and you haven't looked at me once."

"Did he? Then I suppose I must. But I am so sleepy!"

"Sleep then, darling, and don't mind me," said the poor prince.

"Really, you are very good," replied the princess. "I think I will go to sleep again."

"Just give me a glass of wine and a biscuit first," said the prince, very humbly.

"With all my heart," said the princess, and gaped as she said it.

She got the wine and the biscuit however, and leaning over the side of the boat towards him, was compelled to look at him.

"Why, prince," she said, "you don't look well! Are you sure you don't mind it?"

"Not a bit," answered he, feeling very faint indeed. "Only I shall die before it is of any use to you, unless I have something to eat."

"There, then," said she, holding out the wine to him.

"Ah! you must feed me. I dare not move my hands. The water would run away directly."

"Good gracious!" said the princess; and she began at once to feed him with bits of biscuit and sips of wine.

As she fed him, he contrived to kiss the tips of her fingers now and then. She did not seem to mind it one way or the other. But the prince felt better.

"Now, for your own sake, princess," said he, "I cannot let you go to sleep. You must sit and look at me, else I shall not be able to keep up."

"Well, I will do anything I can to oblige you," answered she, with condescension; and, sitting down, she did look at him, and kept looking at him with wonderful steadiness, considering all things.

The sun went down, and the moon rose, and, gush after gush, the waters were rising up the prince's body. They were up to his waist now.

"Why can't we go and have a swim?" said the princess. "There seems to be water enough just about here."

"I shall never swim more," said the prince.

"Oh, I forgot," said the princess, and was silent.

So the water grew and grew, and rose up and up on the prince. And the princess sat and looked at him. She fed him now and then. The night wore on. The waters rose and rose. The moon rose likewise higher and higher, and shone full on the face of the dying prince. The water was up to his neck.

"Will you kiss me, princess?" said he, feebly. The nonchalance was all gone now.

"Yes, I will," answered the princess, and kissed him with a long, sweet cold kiss.

"Now," said he, with a sigh of content, "I die happy."

He did not speak again. The princess gave him some wine for the last time: he was past eating. Then she sat down again, and looked at him. The water rose and rose. It touched his chin. It touched his lower lip. It touched between his lips. He shut them hard to keep it out. The princess began to feel strange. It touched his upper lip. He breathed through his nostrils. The princess looked wild. It covered his nostrils. Her eyes looked scared, and shone strange in the moonlight. His head fell back; the water closed over it and the bubbles of his last breath bubbled up through the water. The princess gave a shriek, and sprang into the lake.

She laid hold first of one leg, and then of the other, and pulled and tugged, but she could not move either. She stopped to take breath, and that made her think that he could not get any breath. She was frantic. She got hold of him, and held his head above the water, which was possible now his hands were no longer on the hole. But it was of no use, for he was past breathing.

Love and water brought back all her strength. She got under the water, and pulled and pulled with her whole might, till at last she got one leg out. The other easily followed. How she got him into the boat she never could tell; but when she did, she fainted away. Coming to herself, she seized the oars, kept herself steady as best she could, and rowed and rowed, though she had never rowed before. Round rocks, and over shallows, and through mud she rowed, till she got to the landing-stairs of the palace. By this time her people were on the shore, for they had heard her shriek. She made them carry the prince to her own room, and lay him in her bed, and light a fire, and send for the doctors.

"But the lake, your highness!" said the chamberlain, who, roused by the noise, came in, in his nightcap.

"Go and drown yourself in it!" she said.

This was the last rudeness of which the princess was ever guilty; and one must allow that she had good cause to feel provoked with the lord chamberlain.

Had it been the king himself, he would have fared no better. But both he and the queen were fast asleep. And the chamberlain went back to his bed. Somehow, the doctors never came. So the princess and her old nurse were left with the prince. But the old nurse was a wise woman, and knew what to do.

They tried everything for a long time without success. The

princess was nearly distracted between hope and fear, but she tried on and on, one thing after another, and everything over and over again.

At last, when they had all but given it up, just as the sun rose, the prince opened his eyes.

XV. LOOK AT THE RAIN!

THE princess burst into a passion of tears, and fell on the floor. There she lay for an hour, and her tears never ceased. All the pent-up crying of her life was spent now. And a rain came on, such as had never been seen in that country. The sun shone all the time, and the great drops, which fell straight to the earth, shone likewise. The palace was in the heart of a rainbow. It was a rain of rubies, and sapphires, and emeralds, and topazes. The torrents poured from the mountains like molten gold; and if it had not been for its subterraneous outlet, the lake would have overflowed and inundated the country. It was full from shore to shore.

But the princess did not heed the lake. She lay on the floor and wept. And this rain within doors was far more wonderful than the rain out of doors. For when it abated a little, and she proceeded to rise, she found, to her astonishment that she could not. At length, after many efforts, she succeeded in getting upon her feet. But she tumbled down again directly. Hearing her fall, her old nurse uttered a yell of delight and ran to her, screaming, "My darling child! She's found her gravity!"

"Oh, that's it! Is it?" said the princess, rubbing her shoulder and her knee alternately. "I consider it very unpleasant. I feel as if I should be crushed to pieces."

"Hurrah!" cried the prince from the bed. "If you've come round, princess, so have I. How's the lake?"

"Brimful," answered the nurse.

"Then we're all happy."

"That we are indeed!" answered the princess, sobbing.

And there was rejoicing all over the country that rainy day. Even the babies forgot their past troubles, and danced and crowed amazingly. And the king told stories, and the queen listened to them. And he divided the money in his box, and she the honey in her pot, among all the children. And there was such jubilation as was never heard of before.

Of course the prince and princess were betrothed at once. But the princess had to learn to walk, before they could be married with any propriety. And this was not so easy at her time of life, for she could walk no more than a baby. She was always falling down and hurting herself.

"Is this the gravity you used to make so much of?" said she one day to the prince, as he raised her from the floor. "For my part, I was a great deal more comfortable without it."

"No, no, that's not it. This is it," replied the prince, as he took her up, and carried her about like a baby, kissing her all the time. "This is gravity."

"That's better," said she. "I don't mind that so much."

And she smiled the sweetest, loveliest smile in the prince's face. And she gave him one little kiss in return for all his; and he thought them overpaid, for he was beside himself with delight. I fear she complained of gravity more than once after this, notwithstanding.

It was a long time before she got reconciled to walking. But the pain of learning it was quite counterbalanced by two things, either of which would have been sufficient consolation. The first was that the prince himself was her teacher; and the second, that she could tumble into the lake as often as she pleased. Still, she preferred to have the prince jump in with her; and the splash they made before was nothing to the splash they made now.

The lake never sank again. In process of time, it wore the roof of the cavern quite through, and was twice as deep as before.

The only revenge the princess took upon her aunt was to tread pretty hard on her gouty toe the next time she saw her. But she was sorry for it the very next day, when she heard that the water had undermined her house, and that it had fallen in the night, burying her in its ruins; whence no one ever ventured to dig up her body. There she lies to this day.

So the prince and princess lived and were happy; and had crowns of gold, and clothes of cloth, and shoes of leather, and children of boys and girls, not one of whom was ever known, on the most critical occasion, to lose the smallest atom of his or her due proportion of gravity.

CLUNY MEDIA

Designed by Fiona Cecile Clarke, the CLUNY MEDIA *logo depicts a monk at work in the scriptorium, with a cat sitting at his feet.*

The monk represents our mission to emulate the invaluable contributions of the monks of Cluny in preserving the libraries of the West, our strivings to know and love the truth.

The cat at the monk's feet is Pangur Bán, from the eponymous Irish poem of the 9th century. The anonymous poet compares his scholarly pursuit of truth with the cat's happy hunting of mice. The depiction of Pangur Bán is an homage to the work of the monks of Irish monasteries and a sign of the joy we at Cluny take in our trade.

"Messe ocus Pangur Bán,
cechtar nathar fria saindan:
bíth a menmasam fri seilgg,
mu memna céin im saincheirdd."

Made in the USA
Middletown, DE
23 September 2024